Substitute Soloist

An Andy Veracruz Mystery Book 4

by

D. R. Ransdell

Substitute Soloist

aakenbaakeneditor@gmail.com

This is a work of fiction. Names, characters, places and incidents are either the product of the author's imagination or are used fictitiously. Any resemblance of the fictional characters to actual persons living or dead is entirely coincidental.

ISBN: 978-1-938436-77-2

Cover Art by Peter O'Connor at Bespoke Book Covers

Dedication

To Linus Lerner,
Friend, maestro, mentor

Chapter One

"Twenty-two. Yours?"

"Sixteen. But Zoran gave me a deal."

I was waiting for the start of my first rehearsal with Tucson's professional orchestra, but I already felt more displaced than an opera singer with permanent laryngitis. The two violinists sitting behind me were discussing how expensive their instruments were. The young men weren't talking in hundreds. They were talking in thousands.

I tried to slump down, which is hard to do for a guy who is six-feet tall. I knew before entering the rehearsal room that I was in for a challenge, but I needed the job. I'd aced the audition because I happened to know the music of the conductor's favorite composer, but by now I wasn't sure whether to thank my luck or send it back.

I continued eavesdropping.

"Zoran made Liza's violin too, but they say hers is magical. I've heard the conductor bought it for her, but Zoran won't say. Have you ever played it?"

"Are you kidding? The other day I straightened her violin so that it wouldn't fall off the chair, and she almost broke my hand."

"Was that the day she broke the conductor's baton?"

"No. That was the week before."

"I'm surprised Moraes didn't kill her."

"From the way Liza shouted back, I'm more surprised she didn't kill him!"

Domingos Rezende Moraes was the conductor, a Brazilian the orchestra had imported from Europe. He was equally at home with Latin or classical rhythms and probably played a dozen instruments. When I auditioned, he noticed that I sight-read in the wrong key. Being able to recognize such a difference made him the keenest musician I'd worked with in over twenty years of musical performance. He was as brilliant as he was confident and self-assured. I couldn't imagine a mere violinist having the nerve to snap at him. In the classical world, conductors were gods. Musicians who wanted to keep working recognized that fact and honored it.

They also honored the rehearsal schedule. The hall filled quickly as the remaining musicians slid into their seats and assembled their instruments. Then they adjusted their music stands, a quarter of an inch this way, a third of an inch that way, as if the height of the stand would make a difference in performance. Then they adjusted their chairs, shifting noisily to the left and right and back again, a sure sign that, no matter how much their instruments cost, their real concern was appeasing Moraes.

I attached my shoulder rest to my violin. I didn't get it on quite right, but I didn't want to join my fellow neurotics, so I left it as it was, slightly crooked, slightly awkward. That was exactly the way I felt.

I tried to blame my feelings on the room, but the rehearsal hall was perfectly normal. It was wide enough to give some seventy musicians enough room to play without banging into one another. As usual, the first violins occupied a column to the left of the podium, two musicians to a stand, six stands altogether. The second violins had the next column and a similar number. The winds sat in the middle with the brass completing the ring behind them and the timpani and other percussion behind them. To the right of the podium were the cellos and then the violas. The basses sat behind the cellos on special high stools. For a moment I felt as if I were back in college, which was the last time I'd played classical music. In the meantime two decades of mariachi playing had sped right by me. Evidently I hadn't even noticed.

The musicians filled the room with a cacophony of scales and tricky passages. I did no such thing. I didn't want people to hear me until it was imperative for them to do so. I had won the fourth chair of the first violin section. That meant I was on the left-hand side of the second music stand, which put me so close to the conductor that he would be able to identify every wrong

8

note I played.

I plucked each of my four strings to check the intonation. The sounds were dull but perfectly in tune. This was the best I could hope for. I might have bought more expensive strings, but the eighty-dollar investment wouldn't have made a noticeable improvement. Instead of playing, I sat back and patted my Roth like a father consoling a child who placed last in a competition. Three decades earlier my parents had paid nearly a thousand dollars for it. The violin was fine for mariachi gigs. By now it was a best friend, an extension of myself. I knew it so well that I could identify most of the scratches. I'd scraped a cufflink on the front one time when my brother Joey and I were goofing around during the intermission of a concert. Another time I'd tossed Joey a set of keys, and he'd used the violin as a shield. Though I was the slightly older brother, back then we shared one instrument. Up until now, the Roth had served me just fine.

I listened for more snatches of symphony lore, but by now the violinists were sawing away as if they needed to punish their bows to make sure they behaved. By this time of the evening, such a frantic warm-up was expected. The long list of rules I'd received along with my contract stated that rehearsals started ON TIME and that I was required to arrive ten minutes beforehand. Indeed, Moraes was at the podium leafing through the score, but the concertmaster, who was the lead violinist and the most important player in the orchestra, hadn't yet arrived.

For the moment the maestro was standing on the podium, a four-by-four wooden square. He was pretending to review *The William Tell Overture*, but he was killing time. He would have already mastered the score, but his focus was so strong that he could ignore all the other noise and concentrate on the music in his head. A few years older than I, he was a charismatic charmer with pale green eyes and large ears. He had unruly black hair that threatened to explode off his head, but he took no notice. He was only about five-eight, but he carried himself as if he were a giant. Maybe he thought he was.

A burly fellow sat down in the chair to my right, thus identifying himself as my stand partner. His wild red beard stretched below his neck, and it was so thick he might have carried his rosin in it.

The man winked. "So you're the new guy."

"Until Moraes figures out I'm an imposter and zaps me with his lightsaber. I'm Andy."

"Kenny." He extended his right hand while holding his violin and bow in the other. "Pleased to meet you. Welcome to boot camp. But you can't be that bad or Moraes would have zapped you at the audition."

"I wowed him by sight-reading Villa-Lobos."

"Who doesn't?"

Kenny assumed I was joking, but I wasn't.

"Who's Zoran?" I asked.

My partner stretched high enough to scan the players in the cello section. "I think he's at a luthier competition, so he might be skipping this concert."

I indicated the empty chair in front of Kenny. "Where's the concertmaster?"

"You mean concertmistress," said Kenny. "Or maybe that word isn't PC."

The thin thirty-something man sitting directly before me stopped practicing long enough to spin around. "You mean concert bitch. She'll be here."

Given the normally fake-polite gentility of the classical world, his use of language surprised me. However, my fellow mariachi players usually inserted the f-word two or three times per sentence, so for a moment I felt at home.

The man extended his hand. "I'm Philip, by the way."

"Andy. Pleased to meet you. And she's a bitch because...?"

"Oh, you'll see," Kenny said. He checked his watch. "It's six-fifty-nine. She'll be here in 3-2-1."

On cue a woman blasted into the room as if she owned it. Blond hair was piled on top of her head, and her slender green

10

eyes matched the green in her sweater. She was about five-feet high, but her ridiculous high heels added another few inches. I was surprised she could walk. Actually, the woman did more of a march, cutting through the space in seconds despite a tight black skirt that didn't allow much movement. Instead of politely placing her violin case off to the side where it wouldn't be in the way, she plunked it down beside her chair. In fluid movements she pulled a red-tinted violin from her case, slapped on a shoulder rest, extracted and tightened her bow, and indicated that she was ready to start. Between her clothing, her stride, and her defiant manner, she reminded me of the strong Hispanic women on my mother's side of the family. She had something to prove. She would no doubt bowl over anyone who dared stand in her way of doing so.

Moraes called her to the podium. In Spanish they quickly and softly conversed about the score as if they were having a private conversation. I caught every word: the tempo here, the crescendo there. Nothing noteworthy.

"What's up with that?" I asked Kenny.

"The podium? It was specially made for Moraes. He hip-hops when he conducts. He's pounded through two regular models already. This one is industrial. Oak, I think."

"No, I mean, is she with Moraes?" Usually I enjoyed being distracted by women. I sensed this one was an exception.

"Liza? Some say so. For his sake I hope not. They come to the concerts together, though. Otherwise we'd never start on time."

The rehearsal started four minutes late, and I was thankful for each of them. Moraes bullied his way through the overture before forcing us through the Mozart clarinet concerto. He knew the entrance for every instrument even though he only had enough hands to cue two sections at once. In contrast to the less skilled conductors I'd experienced in college, Moraes identified every note. Without calling us to a halt, he would yell for the trombone to play a B instead of a B-flat or for the flutes to stop playing sharp. When we came upon a particularly

11

grueling measure, Moraes would have us play it five or six times. He was neither grim nor cheerful. Instead he was straightforward. "Winds, you missed the cue at Measure 40. Oboes, you can bring the volume down at Measure 94. You're covering the bassoon."

My goal was to evade Moraes' attention. I was used to being the boss, not having one. I'd headed a mariachi in Southern California until the restaurant folded. Then I'd followed a fellow player to Tucson, where the only decent group didn't need another violinist. I'd turned to the orchestra because I preferred a music job to anything else, but technically I was on trial. Moraes could terminate me at any time. He wouldn't hesitate if he felt any reason to do so.

Suddenly I envied the second violinists. They didn't carry the melody as often as the firsts, and they didn't have as many high notes that called for delicate fingering. The firsts spent half their time on the E-string. Not only were the sounds shrill, but sometimes the string was so taut that it snapped mid-performance. You had to pay attention so that a wayward piece of steel didn't sting your nose.

I struggled to concentrate on the written music, but I had to fight with myself. For twenty years I'd played by ear, so the discipline of reading each note was taxing. So was the entire rehearsal. I even had trouble with the overture, which should have been the easiest of the selections, because I'd been practicing way under tempo. I did better with the concerto. I'd been listening to it on the Internet for the last few days, and I loved the lyrical melodies. I even remembered most of them.

The concertmaster, however, didn't play the concerto according to the score. She took liberties with rhythms. She held notes unexpectedly, which confused the rest of us, including the clarinetist who was the soloist. Liza wouldn't have noticed that we were scrambling to follow her, however. She was playing in her own bubble, her own little world.

I was surprised that Moraes granted her such leeway, but I couldn't deny that she played well. She shifted gracefully,

12

hitting each note squarely on the top instead of adjusting to improve intonation. She played deliberately and commandingly as if she were the only artist in the room. Moraes often frowned as he turned to her, but he followed her erratic interpretations rather than stopping the orchestra. This wasn't out of concern for our well-being. We only had two rehearsals before the concert, so Moraes couldn't stop for every detail. Instead he worked us as hard as possible. By the time we completed our two-and-a-half hours, I was drained. Worse yet, I'd made a long list of passages I needed to review at home before I braved another rehearsal.

I packed up my violin and exchanged cursory "good nights" with Kenny and Philip. Kenny assured me I'd done a good job, but I was aware that he had outplayed me. Twice he'd even shown me where we were. For the thousandth time, I wished I were back with my mariachi.

By the time I unlocked Rachel's Prizm and stored my Roth in the trunk, I felt defeated. I didn't have a car of my own, and I'd left my scooter back in California. Hence I didn't have my own wheels; I was living on charity. I was so distracted that I missed a turn and found myself on Broadway, which was a mile too far south.

I did a U-turn, legal at most Tucson intersections, and headed towards the university area. The time of my arrival didn't make any difference. Rachel wouldn't be home for another hour or so. She would still be at her mariachi restaurant having a whole lot more fun than I had. I kept praying she could convince her boss to include another violinist in the group, but so far Heriberto claimed he didn't have enough diners to justify more sound.

The scenario was familiar. Back at Noche Azul Restaurant, we'd been on an even tighter shoestring budget. I'd been the sole violin accompanied by the other mandatory elements: a trumpet to help with melody lines, a *vihuela* for upbeats, a *guitarrón* for downbeats.

Once I reached Rachel's duplex, I shuffled up the creaky

steps to the front porch. Before entering I paused for a few moments on the porch swing. The January night was chilly, but I was still hot from all the bowing. I'd worked harder reading music than I would have in a week performing mariachi gigs.

When I finally headed inside, a streak of white fur scooted out. Treetop had her own cat door, but she preferred to squeeze past me as if to emphasize my status as a lowly visitor. Despite the ungrateful feline, I appreciated the homey living room. Rachel didn't have a high-end apartment. She had a space that she'd made her own. A mishmash of artwork colored the walls, including pieces she'd collected in Mexico and Thailand. Bean bag chairs served as couches, not because she couldn't afford better furniture but because she liked sitting on the floor.

I would have sprawled out across the vinyl, but I knew what was best for me. I took out my violin and spent the next ninety minutes reviewing passages.

~

"Rough rehearsal with the TucAz?" Rachel asked as she entered her living room.

Technically I had a job with the Tucson Arizona Symphony Orchestra, but almost everyone called the organization by its abbreviation, which was pronounced Too-KAZ.

I picked up my cell phone, which was on the floor near the legs of the music stand. "I remembered to turn on the ringer. I was expecting you to call when you were finished."

"I got a ride," she said nonchalantly.

I resisted asking from whom.

"Tell me about your first rehearsal," she said as she took off her black leather mariachi boots.

"There were multiple passages I faked my way through. We only have one more rehearsal before the concert."

"You can't expect to learn everything at once."

"I'll have to step up my practicing or risk being eaten alive. Tonight I tried to be invisible. You should have seen Moraes' look when I loudly played a rest."

14

"Were you in tune?"

"Yes."

"Then it could have been worse!"

"How did I sound just now?"

Rachel pointed to my violin case and indicated where I should shove my instrument. "Andy, you sound pretty good. You're just a little coarse. You're used to a harsher style. That's natural. It will take you some time to develop finesse."

I took the hint that she wanted to talk and started loosening my bow. "The other violinists? Their instruments cost more money than I made last year."

"You had a difficult year."

"That's looking on the bright side."

"You'd rather I look a different way?" She went to the bedroom, and I followed her. "Besides, if you were rich, you wouldn't have the excuse to stay with me."

She took off her black mariachi jacket and carefully hung it up. She did the same with her white blouse. Then she slipped out of her mariachi skirt, a traditional A-line with metal jingles down the sides. While the outfits were smart, they weren't comfortable.

"I'm glad to be staying with you. But I don't want to impose."

She pulled on a T-shirt and sat next to me on the bed. "Don't worry, Andy. I know you're not in love with me."

Just what I needed. A woman who could read my mind. How was I supposed to answer that? The worst part was that she was right. I wasn't in that crazy, can't-get-enough-of-you mindset. I didn't spend every spare moment thinking about her. I didn't have grand illusions of the perfect life we could create together. I was living day-to-day.

"Rachel, I do love you though."

"Yeah, yeah," she said. "That's a little different, isn't it?"

I felt like someone had ripped off my clothes while I was in the middle of a crowded intersection in L.A., and none of the drivers enjoyed what they were forced to see. "I don't know what to say."

"Andy, I'm not in love with you either. I could be, I think. Emotionally I've been holding back. I won't let myself fall in love with you until I know I can trust you."

I might have said something comforting. I might have admitted that I had purposefully kept myself from love in an eerily similar fashion. True love meant commitment. Sacrifice. Quiet nights at home. Years with the same person. I'd never seriously entertained the possibility.

"You make it sound as if loving me would be a long shot."

She pulled me down beside her and stroked my forehead as we lay side by side. "I know you've had a hard time. You don't have to remind me about your past."

If she'd wanted me to hold her or if she'd sent me to sleep on the couch, I wouldn't have blamed her either way. But that's not what happened. Instead she let me make love to her as best I could, even without my being totally emotionally engaged, even knowing I had a lot of faults. Not being a proficient or lucrative violinist were minor ones.

But I did know how to please her, or at least she pretended I did. She fell asleep in my arms while I lay awake knowing I was on borrowed time. I needed to make some real money. How could I possibly afford a professional violin, a house, and a car? Up to this point I'd been lackadaisical. Back in Southern California I'd had a relatively low-rent apartment in a quaint but mediocre neighborhood close to the restaurant where I worked. I didn't have an insurance plan or a 401k. Yet here I was holding a woman who knew I wasn't in love with her, recuperating from a toxic rehearsal, and realizing I'd made lots of mistakes and would probably make a lot more.

All I knew for sure was that it was January 17th. I only paid attention to the date because in exactly six months, I'd be turning forty. I wanted to have something to show for it, but that too seemed like a long shot. I'd never been married, I didn't have any kids, and the only violin I owned was factory-made.

16

Chapter Two

I practiced all afternoon, forgot to watch the clock, and cut it too close to make it to the rehearsal on time. I ran into the building worried that Moraes would notice not only that I was late but that I hadn't mastered the passages I'd butchered the day before.

No one noticed my arrival, however. Everyone in the room was focused on Liza. She was standing near her chair clutching her red violin as a child clutches a favorite teddy bear. Her hair spilled off the top of her head, giving her a purposefully disheveled look. Her heels were so high that they made my feet tingle, but what stood out was the clingy, canary yellow sweater that stretched down over the top of her short black skirt. She was a human danger sign.

But it wasn't her dress or her shoes or her violin or her stance that demanded my companions' attention. The musicians were staring at her because she was yelling at Moraes at the top of her lungs.

"You will not tell me what to wear!" She pronounced "you" with a bit of a "j" sound, which was common for people whose first language was Spanish.

"It has nothing to do with me, Liza," Moraes said. "These decisions are made by the symphony board. You know that."

"You want to control me, but I am the concertmistress! I do as I like! Of course people look at me! Why not?"

I slid into my seat beside Kenny, who was grinning. He was thoroughly enjoying the show. So were most of the others. Liza was one step away from a temper tantrum, which meant that Moraes was in the difficult position of either figuratively slapping her or letting everyone know that she was the boss.

Liza was right about one thing. People were supposed to look at her. It was up to the concertmaster to make a grand entrance right before the beginning of the concert, to ask the oboist to sound an A so that we could tune to the same pitch, and then to signal for the orchestra to stand when the conductor came on stage. It was her job to lead the orchestra as dictated by the conductor. She was expected to emphasize the dynamics so that the lesser players, meaning the rest of us, would attempt to match her nuances. It was also her job to decide on the bowings for the first violins, bowings that would then get translated to the second violins, the violas, the cellos, and sometimes the basses. The concertmaster was supposed to be the most competent, most sensitive, and most important player in the room. Liza was paid a lot extra so that people would pay attention to her.

"Liza, there is no reason for you to be upset," Moraes said.

"What's the catastrophe?" I whispered to Kenny.

"For performances the men wear tuxes, but the women are supposed to wear plain black. Nothing showy."

"Why not?"

"So that the musicians blend. So that the women, in particular, don't call attention to themselves. You can imagine the problem."

"Liza is crazy about attention."

"She's like a three-year-old jealous of an infant. At the last concert, she wore a black dress with big red sequins."

I could imagine the scene. The orchestra was about forty percent women. The others would have followed the rules and worn boringly nondescript combinations of black. Liza would have paraded onto the stage in a sequined dress that was too tight to let her breathe normally. I suspected her curves had sneaked up on her, so she ignored them by squeezing into clothes that would have fit more appropriately twenty pounds ago. I'd seen the same call for attention in mariachi groups— women who tried to stand out by painting their faces with bright rouge or spraying their heads with cans of hairspray. The results were ludicrous because the women turned out looking more like manikins than people. That was another detail I appreciated about Rachel; she didn't give in to all that nonsense. I'd seen some makeup in her bathroom, but so far I hadn't seen her use any.

18

Liza gesticulated as if Moraes couldn't hear her without visuals. I'd seen twenty-somethings throw tantrums, usually when they were drunk, but I guessed that Liza was right around my age. That also made her about the same the age as Moraes. And much too old to throw a tantrum.

By now Liza had set down her instrument and was clutching her sweater. "What I wear is sign of my personality!" Liza spoke English pretty well, but she tended to leave out articles. She probably didn't want to take time for them. Anyway, her message was perfectly clear.

"I dress how I feel!" Liza said, putting her hands under her breasts and lifting. "I am musician! I need to breathe! I need the passion! I need the life!"

"Liza," Moraes said patiently, "all you have to do is wear plain black. It's not too much to ask."

She stamped her feet so vigorously I thought she was might fall off her heels. "The board cannot understand music! The board cannot understand how I should feel!" Moraes visibly pulled his phone from his pants pocket and checked the time. I had a feeling he'd done that once or twice already. "I have to start the rehearsal. Concert dress is black for women, no bling. You can wear a small necklace. Or earrings. Or an ankle bracelet. Please sit down."

"If I do not feel right, I do not play my best!"

Moraes indicated the oboe player. "An A, please?" This was out of character; this was the job of the concertmaster.

Liza picked up her violin and offered it to the conductor. "Oh, so now you want my job? I give to you! You play the violin! Let's see if you can play and conduct at the same time, you are so smart!"

For a moment their eyes locked. "Sit down, Liza," Moraes said. He didn't spit the words, but he said each one slowly. "Sit."

When she did, the rest of us started snickering. It was pretty hard not to.

Moraes pretended not to notice. "The overture," he said.

19

And finally we started rehearsing.

But Moraes didn't have the same concentration he'd demonstrated the day before. He paused to take sips from an energy drink. He still pointed out a wrong note here, an overly loud phrase there, a lack of staccato in the back of the section, but his heart wasn't in it. Liza had sucked away his strength. Since this was the first time I'd seen a hint of weakness in the man, I was surprised. I couldn't decipher the dynamic between them. Liza acted as a privileged lover, a relationship that should give members of any symphony board a round of heart attacks, yet I detected no affection between them. Or perhaps they'd been lovers forever, or they were married, and any affection had seeped out of the relationship a long time earlier. Happened all the time.

I tried to concentrate, but over and over my eyes drifted off the page. This happened most often during the clarinet concerto. When the violins had long passages of rests, I couldn't be bothered with counting them. I merely listened for what sounded like the right time to come in and watched for when my stand partner raised his instrument. That was a lazy way of rehearsing, but I was giving myself another hour or two to adapt to playing classical music. That was all I could afford.

Moraes himself distracted me. Perhaps he was drawn to Liza and didn't know why. Perhaps she was fascinating when she wasn't angry or complaining, or perhaps her mood swings were the source of fascination. Her attitude was as ridiculous as that of the board. What did the audience care about what we wore? Most concert halls had a wide gulf between the stage and the first row of seats, so the audience could barely see us anyway. They came to listen, not to judge a fashion show.

As we continued with the concerto, I wondered how many times Moraes and the board had argued about Liza. Tonight she rehearsed without passion or feeling, but maybe this was her normal post-argument demeanor. She too had lost concentration. Near the beginning of the fast, third movement, she missed an entrance. I came in accidentally; I hadn't

20

realized I was coming in without her. Normally a section might have waited—to be in unity. But dumb me played straight through three measures without realizing I was alone.

"Stop." Moraes held up his hand, signaling for the orchestra to crunch to a halt. He pointed to the first violin section. "Who came in?"

I was sure he already knew. I raised my bow half-staff as a flag on a day of mourning.

"Yes, Andy. You were the one. And why did he do that?" Moraes asked the others.

I hadn't been counting. Mariachi-style, I had only been listening. "I thought I had counted correctly," I lied, "but I guess—"

"But I guess Andy, the new guy, is the only one who could hear the right place to play," Moraes snapped.

"The horns were wrong," Liza snapped back. "How do I come in right when they make mistakes?"

"I don't know, Liza. That is too big a question for me. Horns! What were you thinking? Everyone, take it back at Letter A. 'A' for Andy."

Everyone in the orchestra now knew my name. In the land of competitive orchestra playing, that was surely a bad thing. I hadn't been trying to save the day. I'd done what had come naturally, which meant playing by intuition. In contrast Liza had either made a mistake herself and tried to cover by lying about it, or she had let the horns take the fall on purpose. I wasn't sure.

I was relieved when we started rehearsing *Scheherazade*, the Rimsky-Korsakov piece based on the framing device from *The Arabian Nights*. According to legend, the Persian king Shahryār was going to put his bride Scheherazade to death in the morning so that she wouldn't have the chance to cheat on him. To thwart her husband's intentions, the clever woman began telling such an engaging story that the king granted her another day to live so that he could hear the end of it. The next night she finished one story and started another, and so on and so forth.

The symphonic piece wasn't a violin solo per se, but it included several solos the concertmaster traditionally performed from his or her seat. I knew the piece backwards and forwards from college orchestra days. As the two top players, my brother and I had alternated playing the solos. The same passages had been part of my audition for the TucAz, so the melodies were in my head as well as in my fingertips. When Liza dived into the first solo, I was momentarily jealous. Given my work with the mariachi, I relished being the center of attention. But Liza played the first solo more beautifully than I'd heard it on any recording and more passionately than I'd ever imagined it. All at once the passage was tender, vigorous, commanding. As Liza varied the tempos, she wrenched emotion from every note. She closed her eyes, blocking out her surroundings to concentrate on pure sound.

Part of her wizardry would have been the violin itself; I couldn't imagine the price of an instrument that could sing as much as hers. The red seemed overboard, but the color couldn't override the sound. The instrument had the right timbre, the right projection, the right sweetness. Zoran had obviously given over every part of himself in the instrument's creation. But no matter how wonderful an instrument, it had to be in the right hands. This one was.

Finally I understood why Moraes put up with such a canary. Any conductor would have done the same. I hadn't detected genius when Liza played the other music; she wasn't invested in a Rossini overture or a Mozart clarinet concerto. But the magical *Scheherazade* was a piece that she believed in. It was a piece she embodied, living through the story each time she played it. She would make every last listener believe in the magical storyteller as well. If some of the audience swooned as Liza performed, I wouldn't be surprised.

~

When we finally took a break, I wiped down my violin with a rag. Given her fine instrument, I expected Liza to do the same. Instead she stood, reached her hand into Moraes' bulky briefcase, took out his energy drink, and downed a third of it.

Strange. In Mexico there's a saying that if you drink from someone's glass, you know all their secrets. I wondered what lay behind both Liza's passion and her anger. I was too busy wondering about her to notice that she was heading straight for me, and by then it was too late to avoid her.

"You are new. This is your first day?" she asked.

"Second."

She would have been blind not to notice me the day before, but what better way to put someone in place than by pretending you hadn't? Liza eyed me as if the faults in my playing were evident from my facial features, but maybe she was focusing on my black hair and deep tan.

"You are from where?" Liza asked.

"California."

"You look Mexican."

"*Lo soy. Pero nací aquí.*" I am, but I was born here.

It was a test. I looked as if I spoke Spanish, so I ought to. As a matter of fact, I spoke it almost as well as I spoke English. Some days, even better.

"*¿Y tú, de dónde vienes?*" And where are you from?

For a moment she hesitated. I'd used the informal "*tú*" form with her instead of the formal "*Usted.*" My choice had been deliberate. She may have been the concertmaster, but in Spanish, we were equals.

"*La ciudad de México,*" she replied.

The difference was subtle, but saying she was from "the city of Mexico" was a more sophisticated way of saying she was from "*el De-Efe,*" D.F., meaning the Federal District, which was the way everybody else said it.

"Tired of living in the capital?" I asked.

"Ha! More or less."

"*Starting at ten a.m. you can't find a place to park,*" I said, quoting the first line of "*Sábado, Distrito Federal,*" a well-known Chava Flores tune. With spot-on clarity, the

23

famous singer-songwriter had targeted the gamut of Mexican social ills. His lyrics about the chaos of a normal Saturday in Mexico City were typical.

Liza frowned. Evidently she rejected any criticism of her hometown.

"Do you like living in Tucson?" The lame question was the only one I could think of.

"Eh. Not yes, not no. But you? Why have you come here from California?"

"My mariachi broke up."

"Mariachi?"

"The restaurant closed. The band members scattered."

"Mariachi!"

"We played five nights a week. Sometimes six."

"You wasted your time on mariachi!" She turned and marched off.

I wasn't the least surprised. A lot of people took mariachi music to be the lowest possible art form, although such people were hardly ever Mexican. So I had been dismissed by the great Liza for not being a serious violinist. Good. I didn't want her to focus on me at all. And I certainly didn't want to show her up by playing when she'd failed to do so herself.

Before Liza could insult me again, I scooted outside. The day had been warmer than usual for January, but as soon as the sun had set, a chill had bullied its way right in. The chill might have been nicknamed Liza.

I sped-dialed my brother. "Joey? Sorry to call now. I know it's early in the UK."

"I just woke up. How's it going?"

"The rehearsal is killing me. I'm in over my head."

"You knew that ahead of time. Ready for an architecture job yet?"

"Not yet." We'd completed the same degrees. I'd often worked with Joey, but he was the better architect, and I was the better musician. "We perform the concert twice. I might have it right the second time around. For the moment I'm exhausted."

"Maybe the conductor will get tired and let you go home early."

"The guy is an Energizer bunny. He doesn't *get* tired."

"Here's a great solution. I'll learn half the music for your concert. Then you can play the first half, and then we switch places and I play the second half. Nobody would know the difference. Sound fun?"

"If you hadn't taken a contract in London, it would be perfect."

"Details. Only details."

Although thirteen months apart, we were lookalikes. In our youth we'd often switched places. For a while there was a height issue, but by my senior year in high school, when my brother was a junior, we could switch easily, and we often did. Sometimes we covered classes or rehearsals for one another. At boring family parties, we switched for sport. We'd done so less frequently as adults. By now his hair had gone a little gray and he'd put on a few extra pounds. But in a pinch, and in bad lighting, we could still fool people.

"You're just glad you're not me," I said.

"As always! But why complain to me instead of pouring your heart out to Rachel?"

"She's at the restaurant. Are you too busy to talk?"

"Even if I were."

He didn't have to finish the sentence. Joey always made time for me. Our whole adult lives, he'd watched out for me instead of the other way around. Sometimes he became too zealous in his assistance. That's why he'd taken his wife and kids abroad. He wanted to make sure to steer clear of my enemies.

"Why not ask the concertmaster to let you play one of the *Scheherazade* solos?" Joey continued. "You play them at least as well as I do."

"She's a woman. And she wouldn't let me have one of her solos if I paid her for the privilege."

"You'd only get to perform them over her dead body?"

25

"Right. That would be the only way."

Chapter Three

By the time I reached the theatre, all the other musicians were on stage warming up. I ran through the building, taking two wrong turns in the cold gray basement tunnels under the stage and rushing up the stairs three at a time. Late for the first concert! I'd be fired by the end of the night if not sooner. How was I supposed to know that parking in campus on a Saturday night was nearly impossible?

At the top of the stairwell I came across the stage manager, who was watching a University of Arizona basketball game on old-style miniature TV. He saw me running and grinned. "Relax, pal. There might not be a concert anyway." He pointed me in the direction of the wings, where Liza and Moraes were standing with an older gentleman who wore a leisure suit. His floppy moustache was the kind that might collect cookie crumbs for years at a time.

Cautiously, I approached. Moraes, in a sparkling tux and black dress shoes, was so concentrated on the conversation that he didn't see me. Liza was facing the gentleman, violin and bow in one hand. She was using the other hand to gesture as she shouted in whispers.

"This is only dress I have. You want I take it off? That is what you want?"

"The requirements were clear. We have our values!"

"I show the fine things in life! Fine jewelry, fine music! Why can't you understand?"

"Your fellow musicians can't afford such things. There's no reason you should stand out because you're the concertmaster!"

"I am concertmistress! Or you can't see I'm a woman?"

I was thrilled to make it to the concert before it started. I was more thrilled Moraes hadn't noticed my arrival. But I couldn't contain my curiosity. Instead of quickly slipping on stage, I ventured close enough to take a good look at Liza's outfit. Her short black dress barely covered her hips, and its low V revealed the edges of her breasts. However, the man was pointing to Liza's waist, where the strips of material were joined together with what glimmered as a diamond except that no one would have been insane enough to wear a rock that large.

"We said no jewelry!" the man shouted.

Liza clutched the fake stone. "This is not jewelry! This is clothing!"

At that point Moraes noticed me. He might have glared, or he might have already been glaring. He straightened his white bowtie and turned back towards Liza.

Weaving around the other players like a cat in a minefield, I slipped on stage and gingerly took my seat.

As I sat beside him, Kenny stopped practicing and grinned. "We weren't sure whether or not you were coming," he said. "Then again, we're not sure whether or not we're having a concert."

"Who is Liza yelling at?"

"F.J. Gómez. He's the new head of the symphony board."

"He's a big deal?"

"They say he's an industrialist who owns half the town, but what would I know?"

I indicated the trio in the wings. All three were still whisper-shouting. "Have they been at it a long time?"

"When Liza came out to adjust her music stand, I saw F.J. leave his seat to go backstage. I knew he was going to chew her out. The rules are stupid, but the other women are too intimidated to break them."

"Asking the women to refrain from using jewelry is like asking the men not to wear cufflinks."

"Right!" He nodded towards the audience. "They wouldn't notice either way. They will, however, eventually expect some music."

The main floor held a large seating area that was about three-fourths full. The same was true of the balcony. So far the patrons were happily chatting; they didn't realize there was more action behind the curtain than we would offer on stage.

"The Saturday night crowd is always lively," Kenny told me. "Tomorrow the audience will be more subdued. That is, if we're still in business."

I gestured at the wings. "Is this a long-standing argument?"

"Sure. It started in September, which is when Liza suddenly started playing with us."

I cocked my head. "Suddenly?"

"She never auditioned."

For a professional orchestra, the situation was practically unheard of. "Did the former concertmaster drop dead?"

Philip twirled around from his position in front of me. "He did not die. He scooted over."

"Philip was the concertmaster last season," Kenny said. "When we came to the first rehearsal, Liza was in his place."

"She's either sleeping with Moraes, or she's the girlfriend of a mobster," said Philip. "Or both."

It was too much to digest. Concertmasters came into their jobs by winning auditions, as it was called, not by waltzing in and shoving everyone else down a notch.

"She's good, but she's hardly perfect," I said.

"I've been studying the solos for *Scheherazade* for a year," said Philip. "A whole year!" He turned and attacked the Rossini.

Kenny laughed as he tightened his bow. "Fasten your seat belt. Here comes Liza."

The woman marched on stage and signaled for the oboe player to sound an A, but by now none of us bothered with extra tuning. Seconds later Moraes came out himself. Traditionally Liza would have stood in respect to the conductor, and the orchestra would have done the same. Instead Liza sat steadfastly. So did the rest of us.

I turned to Kenny; he was as astonished as I was. This was completely against protocol. It was a slap in Moraes' face. I'd never seen it happen before. From the way the musicians squirmed, they felt as awkward as I did.

Moraes pretended not to notice. He bowed to the audience, offered us a fake smile, raised his arms, and began the overture. He gave the right cues, but he wouldn't have cared if we'd played every note wrong because he wasn't listening. He was somewhere else, somewhere far away. I hoped it was a nice place where he didn't have to worry about difficult women like Liza or board members who made up outdated rules. Moraes didn't deserve such problems because he would have never caused them himself. All he cared about was the music. Anything else was an obstacle.

The overture was a quick dozen minutes, but I prayed it would be long enough for Moraes to get ahold of himself. Instead, when we ploughed into the concerto, he was even less engaged. He didn't know how to tame Liza, so he'd given up. Rather than helping the clarinetist negotiate with the concertmaster, Moraes let them fight it out. The results were breathtakingly erratic tempos. More than once, one section of instruments was on the brink of colliding with another, but Domingos ignored the problems. He simply went forward. Liza ignored him altogether and eventually the clarinetist ignored both of them. We were fortunate to end the concerto at nearly the same time.

As intermission started, Liza beat the rest of us off stage. I watched as she marched into the wings and headed down one of the corridors. Maybe she had a premonition that she should distance herself. That way the rest of us could enjoy gossiping about her. As I milled around, occasionally introducing myself to other musicians, the conversations were along the same lines: Moraes has to get rid of her; she's going to cost us our funding; who told her that she's the queen of the music world? There were comments about Moraes as well: "How many times a night does he screw the bitch?" was the most frequent.

In a sudden feeling of camaraderie, I headed to Moraes' dressing room. I wanted to offer him a kind word. He was a decent guy, but he had a wildcat on his hands, a group of terrified musicians on his stage, and another half a concert to get through. I was about to knock on the door when I heard Liza scream *"¡Pendejo!"* I'd been wrong during rehearsal; she had a much louder voice than I thought. And she didn't hold back. In Mexican Spanish, a *pendejo* was an "asshole."

I immediately turned away and joined the others. The conductor was on his own. Since I didn't own a tranquilizer gun, there was nothing I could do to help him. As long as his dressing room was a lion's cage, I was staying out of it.

~

"Enjoying your first concert?" Kenny asked when I returned to my seat.

We broke into laughter. "Silly me. I thought playing classical music would be dull."

Kenny arranged the Rimsky-Korsakov piece on the stand. "Liza's a regular Scheherazade."

"How was the last concert, or dare I ask?"

"More of the same," Kenny grinned. "F.J. came backstage at intermission and made a fuss, and Liza yelled at him."

"Red sequins, eh?"

"About as big as my hand."

Liza marched on stage, stood before the orchestra, and signaled for the oboe to play an A. I couldn't help laughing out loud. I wasn't the only one. Liza's dress now had a half-foot circular hole in place of the fake diamond. She reminded me of a belly dancer, but I didn't have time to share my mirth with Kenny. Liza's piercing eyes shamed us into silence. No one bothered to tune. When Moraes came out, however, Liza didn't hesitate to stand.

As soon as we started playing, I lost concentration. Normally I might have watched Liza to make sure my bow was going in the right direction, but I was too distracted by her demeanor, which seemed to fall halfway between disdain and disgust. I was ready to pay good money to know what she was thinking and what she'd told Moraes. She showed no qualms at displaying her stomach. Between the short skirt and the

31

plunging neckline, she was as exposed as any showgirl. She didn't seem to mind.

Strangely enough, Moraes had calmed down. When he smiled at the brass players, he seemed sincere. Ditto with the woodwinds. I held my breath as we approached the first violin solo, but when Moraes cued Liza, they put their differences aside long enough to create a vivid moment together.

And it was beautiful. The solo was the kind of piercing, haunting melody that lingered in your mind, that made you think of the Middle East, and, rightly or wrongly, made you imagine harems and hidden lovers behind closed doors. No wonder audiences loved the piece. They appreciated Rimsky-Korsakov's composition, but they absolutely adored the drama that governed it. They rallied around the thrill, the hint of death. The experience was exhilarating.

I might have simply continued to revel in the music, but during a particularly loud passage, I heard an audible gasp. I naturally turned to Kenny, but he gestured at Liza. The E-string had sprung loose from the neck of her instrument. She kept playing, shifting around awkwardly to reach the notes that normally would be played on the highest string. When we reached a section where the violins had a long rest, she stood.

"Here!" I said, extending her my instrument.

She glared as if I'd offered her a dead mouse and marched off stage.

Moraes morphed into a cartoon character who was sailing over a cliff. His mouth opened wide enough to swallow a pineapple while his eyes remained glued to the steadily receding figure. The conductor couldn't believe what he was seeing. Neither could the rest of us.

I'd once witnessed a similar technical difficulty. In the middle of a Bartók concerto, the first violinist from the Kronos Quartet had broken a string himself. The other three musicians instantly stopped playing. The violinist bowed and left the stage. A couple of minutes later he came back with a full set of strings. He smiled at the audience and nodded to his companions. They backed up a few measures and continued playing as if nothing had happened. A possible disaster was averted by a simple solution.

This situation was different. We were in a much larger space, and there were lots of us. The brass players, who were sitting in the back, might not have noticed Liza's absence. As we violinists reached the end of our measures of rest, a trembling Philip led us through the next passage. By now several minutes had passed. Liza should have had plenty of time to reach her violin case, change her string, and return to the stage. Instead we were approaching the next violin solo without a single sign of the soloist. Moraes might have stopped the whole orchestra, but instead he kept conducting, staring at Liza's seat as if he could produce her holographically if he tried hard enough.

We reached the violin solo. For a split second, silence reigned. I suppose we'd all assumed the same thing, that Liza would appear from the wings and start playing. She didn't. Moraes looked sharply at Philip, who had become a concrete statue. Kenny played it even safer by studying his shoes.

A sixty-seven-piece orchestra was waiting on a violin solo, a luscious passage that should have soothed everyone's heart and carried us off on a magic carpet. Philip and Kenny were useless. Since the whole audience was waiting, I took the only action that was possible for me. I put my violin to my shoulder and began to play.

Chapter Four

I had no time for nerves. I had to rush through the first notes because I'd hesitated, but then I caught up to the beat. I wavered on a couple of eighth notes. One was out of tune. Nevertheless, I kept the orchestra going. The look of alarm on Moraes' face relaxed into half-alarm. After the solo ended, we had a page and a half to go before another solo came up. Liza would be back by then. I listened for her impatient heels on the wooden stage.

While the measures slipped by, however, there was no hint of the concertmaster. The situation was unprecedented. If Liza hadn't found an extra string, she might have asked any of us to loan her an instrument. Even my Roth was better than nothing.

The next passage involved an especially tricky shift, one that I would only be able to accomplish with a gypsy-style glide. I could get away with such schmaltz for a mariachi song, but in the classical world such positioning would be considered sloppy and uncouth. They audience didn't expect gypsy. They expected clean.

Hence I listened earnestly for Liza's heels.

Nothing.

"Philip!" I whispered.

The de facto concertmaster refused to turn around. Coward.

"Kenny!" I whispered a bit louder.

My stand partner shook his head. "All yours."

We were down to ten measures before the solo entrance. Five. Two. No Liza.

Then Moraes turned to me. As our eyes locked, he cued me in. He left me without a choice. Once again I took a leap of faith. I plunged in, played the first notes with as much vibrato and passion as I could, closed my eyes, and jumped to the high note. I even made it.

As I played the next notes, I started enjoying myself.

Because I knew the piece well, I performed it better under pressure. As the winds took over for the next measures, I stopped willing Liza to appear. I was having too much fun.

When we reached the final solo, Moraes beckoned me to stand. As if I were a cobra entranced by a snake charmer, that's exactly what I did. From my otherwise safe zone on the inside of the second stand, I faced the audience and played with every inch of myself. In that final, jeweled passage, I vibrated vigorously, playing from memory as I caressed the sounds. I felt the power of Rimsky-Korsakov and the genius that allowed him to compose such a piece. I imaged a beautiful woman, Scheherazade herself, lying on the soft blankets of a king's bed, surrounded by luxury and wealth as she reached out with her soul. I tried to reach out as well, to the patrons in the front as well as those in the balcony's uppermost rows. As my solo permeated the hall, I imagined my teachers, including the patient old man I'd studied with in high school and the hip but strict instructor I'd had in college. I imagined my parents, music lovers who were both long gone. I imagined Rachel, who would have applauded my success. Lastly I imagined my brother, who would have been prouder of me at that moment than at any moment in our whole lives. He would have been ecstatic.

The thunderous applause startled me. The last ten minutes had included some of the most alarming and yet exhilarating moments of my life. It was as if all my years of studying, all the seasons of performing, and all the hours of rehearsing had come together in undeniable perfection. I hadn't done my best; I'd done better than my best. I'd outperformed myself. The adrenalin had worked for me, not against me. I hadn't used sophisticated bowing or shifting, but neither mattered. One way or another, I had gotten through. In an emergency situation, that was more than enough.

As Moraes singled me out for a solo bow, I heard sirens. That's what we got for playing on a college campus. There was always a crisis. Campus police were always coming around.

Here a suicide, there a fight, and in the distance a gang out to steal rich kids' bicycles. Maybe the orchestra needed a new venue. What if the sirens had started while I was playing the softest, gentlest notes? Such an ugly, piercing sound would have been enough to throw me off. My attention would have wandered enough to make me lose my place. As it was, I couldn't have been more pleased with myself. I'd held my own and triumphed. I might have been late to the concert, but at least this one time, I was worth waiting for.

Moraes went off stage while the applause steadily increased. Someone near the middle of the audience shouted "Bravo!" When the conductor came back out, instead of shaking Philip's hand, he shook mine. He dragged me out in front of the other players so that the two of us might bow together.

When Moraes left the stage for good and the applause finally slowed, I sat. Though I rarely sweat, there were beads on my brow.

"You nailed it, partner." Kenny slapped me on the back so hard I nearly let my instrument fly. "Thanks for saving our butts."

Philip turned around. "I should have come in. I don't know why I didn't."

"I didn't mean to steal your solos," I said.

"Believe me, they weren't mine," said Philip. "The next time Liza gets a wild hair up her ass during a concert, feel free to take over."

The situation wouldn't repeat itself. The Rimsky-Korsakov solos were among the few classical passages I knew by heart, ones I'd learned when I was still a teenager. They were lodged in the back of my brain alongside all the mariachi stuff. I'd been lucky to receive my allotted minutes of fame. Enough!

As the musicians moved towards the wings, several complimented me for saving the day. I thanked them but shuffled towards the huddle of musicians and stage hands. I wiggled through in search of the maestro. I wanted to congratulate Moraes in person. I'd played the notes, but he'd conducted them. We'd both kept our cool, just barely, and now what we needed was to go out and celebrate. Preferably with alcohol.

I pierced the huddle, but I didn't find Moraes right away. Instead I had to make my way to the stairs leading down to the basement. The conductor stood halfway down the staircase, but he wasn't thanking congratulatory patrons. He was being restrained by three police officers who were stationed below the first landing. Being tall, I managed to stick my neck over the growing crowd long enough to peer into the stairwell.

An elderly gentleman was sprawled over the stairs, his feet higher than his head. Blood dripped from his mouth, but the policemen weren't doing a single thing about it. They didn't need to. F.J. Gómez, the great curmudgeon and board member, had made his final complaint. A knife protruded from his chest.

Liza was nowhere to be found.

~

By the time I turned the key in the lock, it was after two a.m.

"Andy?" Rachel whispered.

"Yes. It's me. I'm sorry."

Rachel opened the door. She was wide awake; she'd been watching TV. Treetop was fast asleep on a cushion.

"It's late," I said.

"That's all right. I've only been here an hour anyway. I assumed you went out with some of the musicians to celebrate the concert."

I set down my violin case and my music folder and sank into her bean bag chairs, sprawling over two at once.

"Andy?"

"I didn't think to call."

"What happened? It's okay if you got fired. It doesn't matter to me."

"I didn't get fired."

"You're white."

Given my healthy tan, this was indeed an accomplishment. "Talk to me."

"Rachel, you'll never believe what happened."

She turned off the TV. Then she sank beside me and stroked my arm. "When it comes to you, I'll believe anything. Try me."

"Liza dashed off stage mid-concert, killed a board member, and fled."

Rachel put her hand on my forehead. "Well, maybe not everything."

"I'm late because I was talking to the police. They tried to sequester the whole building, but half the audience left before the squad cars arrived."

Rachel regarded me earnestly. She'd only known me for six months, and in that time I'd managed to tell her more crazy things than one woman should have to hear in a lifetime. I was surprised we were on speaking terms.

"Do you want to start at the beginning?" she asked.

"Sure. But it won't help."

I proceeded to tell her as much as I could remember. She listened intently, stopping me several times so that I could back up and fill in details, but they weren't helpful. Liza, F.J., Moraes. They were all swirling in my head. The high I'd gotten from soloing respectably well had faded as soon as I'd seen F.J.'s body in the stairwell.

"Andy, I don't know what to say. Brandy? Coffee? Both?"

"I played better than I could have hoped to. At the time I thought I was saving the concert. Instead I might have been securing Gómez a death sentence."

"Maybe she would have killed him anyway."

"I gave her the perfect opportunity."

When someone banged on the door, Rachel and I jumped while Treetop scampered to the bedroom. Even in a student area near the university, we hardly expected company in the middle of the night.

"Go to the kitchen!" Rachel whispered, pushing me away from her. "Call the police! Find a weapon!"

"Don't answer the door," I whispered as Rachel hurried towards it.

"¿Quién es?" Rachel shouted as if annoyed. Then she translated herself. "Who is it?"

"Eu sou Domingos," he began. *Je suis Domingos. ¡Soy Domingos!* I mean, I'm Domingos, goddamn it!"

The conductor wasn't swearing at Rachel but at himself. He was more messed up than I was. He'd introduced himself in Portuguese and French before he'd wound his way through Spanish and English. No doubt he spoke all four languages with equal ease, though not usually simultaneously.

Rachel threw open the door. "Come in."

Domingos Moraes was still wearing his tux, but he was disheveled. His bowtie, no longer a sparkling white, lay limp alongside his neck. As he stepped inside, he scanned the room as if checking for toddlers.

"Maestro," I said.

"Call me Domingos. You too, Miss—"

"I'm Rachel."

"Miss Rachel. I'm sorry to intrude. Really. But I need to talk to Andy."

"I think we need coffee," Rachel said.

She ushered us into her small kitchen that barely had room for a table for two. She invited us to sit before returning with an extra chair. As soon as she came back, she addressed Moraes. "Would you prefer a stiff drink?"

"Water for me," Moraes said. "Forgive me for barging in. Andy, I found your contact information through one of the board members—one that's still living."

"What did you find out from the police?"

"Three things are missing. Liza, her violin, and her case."

"Did anyone hear screams when it happened?"

"Over all that brass? No."

"So you know nothing," said Rachel.

Moraes sighed slowly, from the depths of his belly. "I know Liza did not kill that man."

"But Maestro—Domingos—isn't it obvious that she did?" I asked.

"Liza wouldn't have killed him."

"Who, then? The stage manager? He was watching TV."

"I don't know who killed him. I have no idea."

Rachel handed Moraes a glass of water, which he drained. She started to serve him another, but he raised his hand. "Thanks. I'm fine. Well, I'm far from fine. I'm less fine than I've ever been in my entire life. Given my upbringing, that's saying a lot."

"How can we help you?" Rachel asked as she sat beside him.

"Did Andy tell you about his performance?"

"He explained about the solos."

"Philip and Kenny, those two pieces of brick, just sat there. Philip nearly shit his pants. Or maybe he did. Kenny pretended he was invisible. Imagine! That lardo must weigh two hundred pounds."

Rachel turned to me and raised her eyebrows. I could guess why. On the symphony website, Domingos Moraes was dressed to kill in a fitted tux and shiny cufflinks. Even the soft, fluid movements of his hands sang sophistication. Off the podium, however, the conductor was a barrio boy who might have slipped right back into the toughest neighborhood. Or maybe he didn't know English well enough to understand the nuances of his choicest words.

"None of us were prepared to fill in for the concertmaster," I said.

"No, of course not. Yet you pulled it off. Bravo. Excellent work. Andy, I thank you for your quick thinking and all that. But right now it's late and I'm pressed for time. I want to go home and attempt to relax. But first I wanted to speak to you in person."

41

"What about?"

"I need you to be the concertmaster for tomorrow's concert."

"What?"

"Who else? Philip was so petrified that the emergency team offered to carry him out in a stretcher. Kenny pasted himself to third chair with five tubes of Super Glue. Please tell me you'll do it."

"But Philip used to be concertmaster, right?

"That was before Liza told him he played like a bluegrass dropout. Now he plays like a shadow. No, Andy. Saving this concert is up to you."

Concertmaster! Lucking out for the audition was one thing, but skipping to the front of the line was another. I took my *koboloy* out of my pocket. The worry beads were strung on a small, sturdy chain. I used my three-euro souvenir every time I needed to keep my hands occupied. In the six months since I'd traveled to Greece, I'd practically worn the thing out.

"Philip has better intonation," I said as I flipped the beads over my hand, Greek style. "Kenny has better timing."

"Maybe so, Andy, but they can't handle being concertmaster. Not on short notice. For the next concert, maybe. For tomorrow, I need you."

"I was unsure of the Mozart. I lost count several times."

"I'll cue you in. The piece is easy, and the clarinetist is quite talented. If need be, she'll follow us."

"Philip and Kenny will resent my scooting in front of them."

"Wrong! They would pay you to do so. I'm surprised they didn't already offer."

"My hand positioning on the overture—"

"Stop, Andy. Yes, you need to learn to make more use of second position. Yes, your playing is rough. Tonight your bow hand was wild and your intonation was a guestimate. But Rimsky-Korsakov is smiling down on you. He's thinking, there's one gutsy person in that orchestra. Well, two of us."

42

"And Liza?"
"Oh, yes, Liza. She's gutsy too."

Chapter Five

I'd planned to sleep in, but I woke early and couldn't get back to sleep. I left Rachel in bed and went to the living room to study the music. Even without getting out my violin, I could review the passages in my mind. No matter how much technique I'd learned, playing well was a mental game. If I could imagine it, I could play it. I'd used the method extensively. Usually it worked.

I went through the fast parts of the Mozart slowly, trying to gain control. I'd tripped up the day before during a four-measure stretch when I couldn't read the music fast enough to tell my hands what to do. At that point we were playing *piano*, "softly," anyway, but I wanted to perform the passage correctly. I would gain an immense satisfaction from doing so. The audience would never know the difference. I would.

It wasn't practice I needed. It was self-confidence. I needed the assurance that from somewhere deep inside, the right notes would come at the right moments. I'd managed the night before on the strength of all the times I'd performed under pressure. In mariachi playing, I'd most often felt under the gun when I couldn't remember a song or barely knew it, or I was playing for someone famous I needed to impress, or I was entertaining an especially large crowd. In such instances I buckled down, tuning out everything except for the phrases themselves so that I could use every ounce of energy to pull all my strengths together at once.

"Wow," Rachel said. "I don't believe this." She stood at the doorway, sleepy but sexy in a short nightshirt with spaghetti straps and pink panties "You can stop rehearsing. You made it through the concert last night. You'll do the same today."

"Last night I wasn't concertmaster."

"Moraes will help you. He knows what he's asking of you."

"Remember, I'm on probation."

45

"You saved his neck last night. And Liza's."

I shrugged. "Who knows if anyone will remember?"

"Relax. I thought Moraes wasn't conducting the next concerts. He can't fire you until after that."

Rachel was correct. While Moraes went to conduct in Timbuktu or wherever it was, we would have a guest conductor for a couple of weeks. Nevertheless, I popped open my violin case. "To be on the safe side, I'll rehearse the toughest spots a few extra times."

"Andy, no one will be thinking about the music anyway."

"What do you mean?"

"After a murder last night? Sorry, but that's much more exciting than Mozart."

My mind jumped to the image of F.J. lying over several steps, the same steps I'd run up shortly before the concert had started.

"Why do you think Liza killed the guy?" Rachel asked.

"Domingos says it wasn't her."

"I heard him. You don't actually believe him, do you?"

Of course not. Briefly I imagined Madame Concertmaster throwing F.J. Gómez down the stairwell, the stage manager off the stage, Philip out of his chair. Undoubtedly, she found great joy in throwing things. That was a sure way for high-strung people to let off steam. "She's a rather small woman. I'm not sure she's strong enough to throw someone down the stairs."

"No, she would have tripped him instead. Come on. Why do you think she did it?"

"It's an unfair question. I don't know much about her." And yet in a way, I did. Two short rehearsals had shown me that she adored drama and that she craved control. That she insisted on being the center of attention. That Domingos was used to dealing with their power struggles. That he was even used to losing them. "Liza is nothing more than a spoiled child."

"Andy, the naughtiest children don't murder someone over clothing."

46

"Liza might have."

Rachel shook her head. "No. There's more to it than that."

"She likes to throw temper tantrums. Kenny told me about one. The conductor played some kind of joke on the whole orchestra, and she got so mad that—"

"Does Kenny think they're lovers?"

"He says no, but Philip says yes. They keep debating."

"One thing is certain."

"What's that?"

"Domingos is on the losing side."

~

Kenny had promised that the Sunday matinee crowd would be more subdued than the crowd we had for Saturday night, but this time he was wrong. The patrons might have been a sea of white-haired elders, but they were louder than a forest full of cicadas. They weren't discussing the music or the weather. They were gossiping about F.J. Gómez, and not a single one was in tears.

The musicians, however, were zombies. At first I assumed they were sleep-deprived, but when I said hello to a few of them, they whispered back in such low tones that I could tell they were all as unnerved as Philip had been the night before. They were too stunned to discuss what had happened. They were classical musicians. For them danger meant sixty-fourth notes in a *vivace* passage, not a dead board member in a stairwell.

A few minutes before the concert was scheduled to start, I joined Domingos in the wings. He greeted me cheerfully and shook my hand as if I wouldn't be needing it anymore. How could he be so upbeat? If I hadn't known better, I would have assumed he hadn't been near the theatre the night before. I was defenseless against such raw optimism, so I went straight for practicalities. "You might have to cue me in the Mozart. Whenever there's a tempo change—"

"Andy, I'll take care of you." Moraes took my hands again. His were only medium-sized, but they were as warm to

47

the touch as if he carried a perpetual inner fire. Maybe he did. "All we have to do is sail through the concert. You have no reason to be nervous."

"Of course not, Maestro."

"Call me Domingos." He pointed to the stage as if afraid I'd start running the other direction. Momentarily I considered it. Then I walked across the wood with fake confidence, acknowledging the audience's unearned applause. Then I accidentally pointed to the clarinet player instead of the oboe player to ask for an A.

~

At intermission Rachel rushed the stage with her younger sister. Gina was an easygoing young woman, fairer than Rachel, who acted as if she'd spent her whole life hoping to come to an orchestra concert. I'd never been happier to have such a cheerleading squad.

"The orchestra sounds great, Andy," Rachel said. "I haven't heard the TucAz for years."

"And I don't remember hearing it ever!" said Gina.

So far we'd been lucky. The overture was such a standard that it had practically played itself. On the concerto Philip had saved my neck one time by accurately managing long measures of rest, and twice Domingos had cued me in when I got confused. On balance, however, the piece had gone well. "Domingos has a good sense of music. He—"

"He's charming and charismatic," said Rachel. "Last night I couldn't be sure, but today he's on top of things. No wonder ticket sales are going well."

"When he conducts he's so dramatic," Gina said. "He's like a tango dancer."

"More like a prancing bear," I said. "He exaggerates more than he needs to."

Rachel shook her head. "That's part of the show. He keeps the audience from falling asleep."

"I thought the concert would be boring," Gina said, "but Moraes makes it exciting. From the expressions on his face, you can tell he loves his job."

"Mostly you saw his backside," I protested.

"Wonderful view," Rachel said. "He's a couple of years older than you, right Andy? He seems younger."

"When he gets too excited, it's hard to follow his arm movements," I said.

"Nonsense," said Rachel. "He conducted perfectly. He even knew when to cue you in, Andy."

"Forget about the conductor," I said. "How did I sound? How did I look?"

Between the two of them, they filled me with reassurances. No, I didn't look nervous. Yes, I sounded fine. No, they hadn't noticed when I'd played a rest at the beginning of the third movement. About the latter I was sure they were lying, but silently I thanked them for trying to boost my ego. I'd missed some other details too; I'd crunched into a loud passage that was supposed to be soft, I'd forgotten to slow down for a *ritardando*, I'd rushed a slew of thirty-second notes. Such details frustrated me, but few listeners would have noticed. And Rachel was right; on the day after a murder, none of the musicians were paying any attention to the music. They were formulating exit plans in case they needed to escape from the theatre.

~

Before the second half of the concert began, Domingos took the microphone. The honorable board member, F.J. Gómez, had passed on the night before, but further details were unavailable. F.J. had served briefly, but his contributions were innumerable. His spirit would continue protecting the orchestra because he'd left a spiritual legacy. All we had to do was claim it. The audience nodded approvingly.

"I will mention something else about today's performance. Our concertmaster has taken ill, so Anthony Cruz has agreed to lead us today."

The audience applauded for someone who didn't quite exist: my last name was Veracruz, not simply Cruz, and my formal name was Andrew, not Anthony. Close enough, especially if I messed everything up.

"And without any further." Moraes didn't finish the phrase. He turned around, snatched up the baton, and led us into *Scheherazade*.

I could feel my legs trembling; I'd played more naturally the day before when taken by surprise. Nevertheless, I sallied forth as if leading an army of musicians against a sea of silence. I kept my head glued to the page, ordered myself to concentrate, and then yelled at myself to relax—a contradiction that didn't work at all. I played nervously, riding on the edge. Finally we reached the first solo. For a few seconds I closed my eyes, coaxing the notes from my instrument in the kindest possible way. I thought of soft pillows and the delicate voice of a determined storyteller. I pointed my violin to the audience and exaggerated the vibrato as if my life depended on the passage the same way Scheherazade's life had depended on her words. I opened my eyes again as the solo ended. That's when I noticed the podium. Instead of holding steadfastly as Domingos swung his arms and stamped his feet, the podium danced with him.

This was not right. Not only did the contraption creak, but I wasn't sure it would hold Domingos' weight. He was lean, but as he rocked back and forth, he shook the entire wooden block. My concentration flickered. The podium should have been rock solid. It should have been under warranty.

I had no idea what to do with this observation. I could have shouted something to Domingos, thus breaking his concentration and alarming the audience. I might have shouted in Spanish, which would have been more subtle, but I didn't know how fluent he was. Also, I couldn't think of the word for "podium." I wasn't sure I'd ever heard it before.

During the next solo I kept my eyes on the conductor. This effect backfired; Domingos assumed I wanted his help and thus made greater arm movements, which in turn caused more creaking. I started to feel dizzy, as if we were riding the waves in a runaway motorboat whose driver had jumped ship.

It wasn't until we reached the calmest, slowest section of the piece that I blocked out my worries. I played the middle solos as if I'd been born to do so. I used vibrato with the passion of any lover who adored music, that perfect, irascible master. I granted myself a moment's satisfaction. All those years of study had paid off! All those hours of playing! Had Liza herself heard me, she would have been the tiniest bit worried that someday I might catch up.

As we roller-coasted into the final section, however, my sense of calm evaporated more quickly than a raindrop in the dry season. As the orchestra grew louder and Domingos cued in more instruments, he became more animated. He bounced up and down when signaling the brass. He thrashed about when cueing the timpani. As he clamored for more energy from the first violins, however, the podium gave up its ghost. Its side caved in, sending Domingos flying our way.

At that point I did something none of the other violinists would have done in a million years. It wasn't a conscious decision I could take credit for. Nonetheless, as Domingos crashed towards me, I threw down my violin so that I could use both hands to break his fall.

Chapter Six

"Thank heaven we'd nearly made it to the end of the concert," Domingos quipped from his hospital bed. "Otherwise people would have demanded their money back."

"We only gypped them out of a few measures," I said. "They were willing to grant us that much leeway."

I was trying to sound light-hearted. I hadn't been allowed in the ambulance, but I'd caught up with Domingos at the university hospital. The staff wanted to keep him under observation. Despite my best efforts, the fall had knocked him out. He'd come to, asked where he was, and immediately blacked out again. The doctors had insisted on some tests, but Domingos hadn't broken anything. He had a bump the size of a lime on the left side of his head and two swollen wrists. In every other way he'd bounced back to his normal self.

My Roth, not so much. The violin had split apart down the middle. It would need serious repairs.

Domingos threw back the white sheets, revealing briefs. His tuxedo was on a nearby chair. "It's a good thing you joined this orchestra, Andy. Last night you saved the concert. Today you saved me."

"I broke your fall. By the time I saw you flying towards me, that was the best I could do. Couldn't you feel the podium swaying underneath you?"

"It always does. That's normal."

"You couldn't feel it start to break?"

"During a concert, I only feel the music."

"You almost made it through."

He sighed. "It's just as well I didn't."

I tried to find logic in his sentence, but I couldn't manage it. "Half the musicians thought you were pulling a stunt. They said you like practical jokes."

"Not during a concert! Never mind. Andy, I need you to do me a favor."

"Want some magazines or something? A headset?"

"A chauffeur."

I checked all four walls to make sure I was in a hospital. "You can't leave. You're under observation."

"You can observe me as well as the doctors can. By now they're headed home for the night anyway." He stood, fell back into the bed, and got back up.

"You can barely walk."

"Not true."

Domingos kept his balance long enough to pull on his pants. He was like a small child escaping from nap time. I fought the urge to grab his waistband and hold onto him. Instead I slid my hand down the once-white wall. "It's not so bad here. What's your rush?"

He gestured towards the door. "Don't you see, Andy? I'm in danger."

"Lots of germs circulate in a hospital, but—"

"That podium was built to hold an elephant. The board members ordered it for me because they were afraid I'd go sailing into the audience and cause a lawsuit. They bought the best one on the market."

"They're fond of you. I knew that already. So?"

Domingos thrust an arm into its shirtsleeve. "Andy, podiums like that don't fall apart."

The manufacturer might have used old glue. Despite the price, the model might have been made cheaply overseas. Overpaying for something didn't mean it was quality.

The conductor sat on the bed long enough to wiggle into his socks. "Obviously someone tampered with it."

People tampered with locks. With cars. With sports equipment. No one had ever tampered with a podium. Domingos had hit his head harder than I thought.

"That's crazy. The podium was in plain view during the whole concert."

"Lots of people could have slipped into the theatre beforehand."

I suddenly imagined a lumberjack-sized janitor wielding

an ax. "No."

"I'm certain of it."

"Maybe it was Liza. Compared to shooting someone, how hard is it to rig a podium?"

Domingos clutched his chest. "F.J. was knifed, Andy, and not by Liza. What killed him was probably falling down the stairs head first. Anyway, Liza would have never touched the podium."

"Your reasoning?"

Domingos shook his head. "She wouldn't do that to me."

"That's all you've got?"

"She's clever. She was probably on a plane by the time we finished yesterday's concert."

"Guilt has swift feet."

"Nonsense. Liza ran because she was a target. Thanks to her, I am too.'

"That makes no sense at all."

"We'll have time to theorize later. For now, get me out of here. I've got a plane to catch."

I would have argued with him, but before I could get in another word, the man was halfway down the hall.

~

"Turn right," Domingos ordered as we left the parking lot.

I did as told. I'd already absconded with a patient, so how much worse could it get? "They can find another conductor, Domingos. You shouldn't strain yourself. Wait and fly tomorrow."

"Trust me. I can't afford to buy a last-minute ticket to Bogotá. I must use the one I already have."

"Or else don't go. You've got bigger issues than money." I drove onto Campbell Avenue, feeling halfway between an Uber driver and a fugitive.

"Andy, think about it from my point of view. I promised to guest conduct. The staff in Colombia has made announcements and printed fliers. How can I suddenly call in sick? That's not how it works in my world."

"You could make an excuse."

"I will be more careful. I'll know what to watch out for."

"But in an extreme case—"

He shook his head as he directed me to turn right onto Grant. "Andy, if you were me, what would you do?"

A brotherly side of me wanted to lie to him, but we'd made terrific music together. We'd connected under intense circumstances. If I lied to him now, I'd break the bond rather than strengthening it.

"I'd fly to Colombia."

"Of course you would." He pointed. "Take a left. Turn in at the first opportunity."

I pulled into the driveway of a modest one-story dwelling and turned off the motor.

"Aren't you coming in?" he asked.

"I thought you said your suitcase was ready."

"This isn't my house."

"What?" I scrambled out of the car, but he was already fifteen feet ahead of me.

"Where are we?"

"Liza's."

"And you have her key?"

He pulled a keychain from his pocket. "A couple of weeks ago I watered her plants."

"You need to water her plants now?"

He winked. "You wouldn't want them to die, would you?"

Domingos unlocked the door and flipped on the light. Although Liza had been in Tucson for several months, her walls were still bare. The furniture was serviceable but standard; perhaps she'd rented a furnished home. In Tucson they were popular.

"Shouldn't the police have blocked this place off? She's a murder suspect, for crying out loud."

Domingos shrugged. "I'm the only one who knows about the house."

"You lied to the police?"

"They never asked if I knew where she lived. Why would I know that?"

"When I signed my contract with the orchestra, I had to list a street address."

"Yes, Andy. Which is how I found you last night after the concert. But when Liza first came here, she stayed with a friend. She never listed a permanent address because she didn't have one."

I felt as if I were going down a drain that had been cleansed with Liquid-Plumr. I was swirling so fast that it was too late to reverse directions. "I don't see any plants."

"There might be one in the kitchen."

"What's the real reason we're here?"

"We're looking for something."

"And what would that be?" I asked.

"I don't know. Something wrong."

"That's easy. Everything about Liza is wrong."

"Her playing is not wrong," Domingos said calmly.

"Agreed. But her attitude, her brash mouth, her—" I stopped. I might have been talking to her lover—past, present, or future.

"Yes, yes, I know all that. Better than you do. Help me look around."

So I did. But the dwelling taught us nothing. We found no clues as to her exit strategy. There were no signs of hurried packing or anything else that suggested distress. While Domingos sifted through paperwork that cluttered a dining room table, I wandered aimlessly, here examining a bowl from Oaxaca, there a trinket from Acapulco. Then I started opening kitchen drawers. In a bottom drawer, I came upon a framed picture of a couple on a sailboat. Liza was holding the tiller with the help of a handsome man. They were wearing swimsuits, hats, and shades as the sun bathed them in late-afternoon light.

I held up the photo. "Who's this?"

"Miguel."

The man had dark skin and a robust moustache that drooped over his upper lip. His flat forehead suggested Indian blood, but the long face was Spanish. The combination gave him a certain allure. He reminded me of the actor who was in the hottest current Mexican soap opera, *Encarcelado por amor*, *Jailed by Love*, but the TV actor was a decade or so younger and thirty pounds lighter.

I studied the photo a few more seconds trying to decide whether the shoreline belonged to Puerto Vallarta or Mazatlán. The western beaches had similar features, and I couldn't spot any landmarks. The bright smiles, however, announced pure happiness.

"Did you ever meet him?" I asked.

"Now and again."

"Not a musician?"

"A fan." Domingos walked in circles. "I don't see anything of interest. Do you?"

"No."

He sighed as his eyes scanned the living room one more time. "Everything seems normal."

"So now what?"

He checked the clock on the wall. The big hand was past the saxophone, but the little hand was on the harp. "We swing by my house. Then on to the airport. We have just enough time."

"Need anything else?" I meant it sarcastically.

"As a matter of fact. When you have rehearsal next week, I want you to keep your eyes open."

"For what?"

"I don't know."

~

"You did what?" Rachel asked.

"I know it sounds crazy."

"Try insane."

"He insisted."

"What if he'd had a relapse? Lost consciousness again?

58

Then what?"

"I didn't have time to think things through." How could I admit that Domingos had zapped my free will? I didn't understand it myself.

"You told me you were going to check on him and come straight here. I expected you a couple of hours ago. At least you could have called."

"I didn't think about it." For many reasons I should have. After all, I'd been driving Rachel's car.

Rachel eyed me from across her kitchen table. She was finishing a big plate of pasta she had made for herself, but I was hoping I might raid her refrigerator as soon as she calmed down.

"Domingos survives a potentially life-threatening fall and then turns you into a cab driver. Sweet."

"Everything happened so fast."

Rachel nodded slowly. I hoped that meant she vaguely sympathized with my point of view. "He certainly is a surprising character."

"You and Gina both found him handsome, right?"

"Andy, it's not his physique. It's his determination. The poise. He's sure of himself, yet not in a bad way. He reminds me a little of your brother."

"Of Joey? How's that?"

"Joey always seems to know what he's doing and why."

Rachel didn't have to say it, but that meant he was a perfect contrast to me.

"No matter what Domingos is up to, Andy, one thing is clear. He likes you. He appreciates the fact that your background is in folk music."

That much was true. At some point he must have played such music himself.

"He's taken you under his wing. Someone so high on life is a good role model for you."

On more than one occasion, Rachel had accused me of negative thinking. She herself was more like Domingos. She looked forward, never back.

"Was this conducting job so important to him?" Rachel asked.

"I couldn't tell. He seemed glad to be leaving town."

Rachel lingered over another bite of noodles. "Of course. He wants the air to clear."

"About F.J.?"

"No, Andy, about him. That podium didn't rig itself. Who would want to make him look bad?"

"You think that's what it was? A stunt for him to lose face?"

"No one dies from falling off a podium. At least not right away."

True. There were better ways to kill people. Such as tossing them down the stairs and sticking a knife through their hearts. "He says the podium incident has to do with Liza. That whoever is after her is after him. Kenny says she never auditioned, so I guess it could be a rival."

Rachel checked her watch. "No."

"Why not?"

"Domingos is a fabulous conductor. Other musicians would respect that. Andy, have you always had a knack for getting yourself into problematic situations or just since meeting me?"

I thought it best to ignore her question. "I took Domingos to the airport as he asked. That should be the end of it."

"So now what?"

"Now nothing. I start rehearsing for the next concert."

"Will you be concertmaster?"

"Philip has the honor if he doesn't die of fright first."

Rachel winked, which told me that I was pardoned for being AWOL while chauffeuring a crazy conductor. "Try not to startle Philip. He seems pretty frail."

Chapter Seven

Though I was vigilant at the next rehearsals, I didn't notice anything useful. Domingos' substitute conductor was a recent graduate from the university in Tempe, which was ninety miles up the road. Iliana Sánchez was cheerful and pleasant, but no replacement for someone as vibrant as our Brazilian. Although the musicians were cooperative, no one took the rehearsal seriously. How could we? We were Domingos' disciples. Since he wasn't listening, we couldn't trouble ourselves to work as hard. Or maybe we hadn't recovered from the last concert.

Philip certainly hadn't. He should have taken the concertmaster's spot, but he refused to do so. He told Iliana that the concertmaster would be back for the next rehearsal, and no one contradicted him. News concerning Gómez' death had hit the papers, but none of the articles mentioned Liza.

The orchestra members, however, spoke of little else. While here and there a Pollyanna praised her playing, all the rest had one burning question: How did she manage to kill F.J. and not get caught?

Kenny gossiped with me at every opportunity. Domingos seemed to like me, Kenny said. What had the conductor told me about Liza? Had he loaned her money? Or his car? I liked Kenny; he was friendly and gregarious. But I wasn't sure what he might say to fellow players, so I claimed the conductor had told me nothing.

Yet while we were rehearsing, I was distracted by what I did know. Domingos insisted that Liza wouldn't have killed anyone, but he'd been conducting at the time of the murder. He had no way of knowing what really happened. If Liza were his protégée, he might be too blinded by her talent to recognize a killer instinct.

In the meantime I studied my fellow musicians. While all were topnotch, the TucAz was fulltime work for part-time pay. Most of them taught private lessons to make ends meet. Any truly serious players would use the position as a stepping stone for orchestras in bigger cities with better funding. That was true for the conductor as well. Domingos was extraordinary. He had the necessary qualifications to become a world-famous conductor, so what could explain the fact that he'd given up Europe for Arizona?

"Let's take it again from the top," Iliana said.

Even without studying the score for the Offenbach overture, I knew that the winds had missed an entire section, that the basses had started in the wrong key, and that only half the violists could handle the thirty-second notes. I tried not to blame the substitute conductor. No one could fill Domingos' shoes. Maybe not even Domingos.

~

By the time I reached Rachel's place, Domingos had called and left three messages. I settled into one of Rachel's bean bag chairs before calling back. The rehearsal had drained my energy. Unlike Domingos, I didn't have an unlimited supply.

"Andy! I assumed you'd lost your phone. How was the rehearsal?"

The music had been so-so, but the gossip had been more striking than lightning in a thunderstorm.

"It was all right," I said.

"What were people saying about Liza?"

I hadn't expected such a direct question, so instead of answering I tiptoed around hot coals. Of the dozen players I'd talked to, at least ten were convinced she had cold-bloodedly murdered the board member.

I was thankful the conductor and I weren't Skyping. I always found it harder to lie to someone face to face. "I had to concentrate on the music, Domingos. I didn't pay much attention to anything else."

"And Philip? Did he do a good job leading the violins?"

"Doing a good job" would depend on how Domingos defined spending the whole night in denial. "Philip was a little timid. He insists Liza will be back."

"I see, I see. Well, Andy, I need you to do something for me."

I'd already seen it coming. Fill in as concertmaster. Bypass Philip. The other violinists would either hate me or thank me. Probably both. None would clamor for the position themselves. Ordinarily we might have hired the Phoenix concertmaster, but the Phoenix Symphony had concerts the same nights we did; I'd already checked. Thus I knew there would be only one possible solution.

Still, I played along. "What do you need me to do, Domingos?"

"Fly to Delft. I already made your reservation."

"What?"

"I used to conduct the orchestra there. Liza played with me. Also in Lyon."

"Where's that?"

"The Netherlands, of course. Well, Lyon is in France. Anyway, Liza was the concertmaster in both cities. I think that's where she went."

"Delft?"

"She liked it better than Lyon. Then again, I think it was the French accent she didn't like. Actually she disliked the cities equally. Never mind. I need you to go there for me and nose around. See if Liza has turned up. If she's gone to see any of her old friends."

"You must be kidding."

"I have a list of places for you to check out, cafés and so forth."

"You're asking me to fly to Europe to hunt for Liza."

"Well, yes."

"All expenses paid?"

"Within reason."

"And you want me to be your detective?"

"I don't need photographs or anything, although before I forget, I'll send you one of Liza."

"What am I supposed to do?"

"Scout around. Chat with the musicians."

I imagined myself walking up to perfect strangers and asking if they played in any orchestras. Then I imagined hurrying in the other direction when they thought I was a lunatic. "How am I supposed to track down the musicians?"

"Easily. By playing in their next concert."

I would have asked Domingos to clarify "easily," but we would have been speaking different languages. "I don't speak Dutch."

"The orchestra is international. You'll be fine." He spoke as calmly as if he were asking me to conduct a survey about favorite composers.

"This is one of your practical jokes, right?"

"They're expecting you. The conductor's name is Steven Schroeder. Nicest guy. He'll help you. And the orchestra members are all congenial, especially the Janssen family. You'll be staying with them."

I would be traveling to Europe to ask a few musicians some pesky questions, and to make matters worse, I would be sleeping on their sofa.

No. No, no, no. I couldn't even remember where I'd stashed my passport.

"Any questions?"

"Nice idea, Domingos, but it's completely crazy."

"I have it all worked out. The orchestra frequently has guest musicians. Yes, they're doing me a favor, but they won't mind. They're flexible. Luckily the timing is perfect. Their next concert is at the end of next week. You'll arrive in time to catch your breath and relax."

Somehow I'd missed a crucial sequence of events. Perhaps I'd blinked. I felt like a patient who had been scheduled for an operation before he realized he was sick. "Who said I would go to Delft?"

"I did, Andy. Because I really, really need you to."

It was one thing for Domingos to ask me to play the solos for *Scheherazade*. Another for him to ask me to be concertmaster. By now it was clear the man had gone off the deep end. He'd lost more than pride when he cascaded from the podium. At any rate I wasn't prepared to go jetting off to Europe on a lark.

I glanced around the living room. In the corner Rachel's keyboard was crowded with notes for songs she was writing. She was as good an excuse as any. "Domingos, I'm not sure what Rachel would say if—"

"Take Rachel with you. I wish you would. The flights aren't crowded this time of year. I'm sure I can get a second reservation. Send me your passport numbers. I'll take care of it."

"But Domingos—"

"What's wrong?"

My new boss wanted me to fly halfway around the world to track a woman I never wanted to see again. "Nothing. Everything."

"You're contradicting yourself."

"The logistics, then."

"Who needs logistics?"

I could feel myself wearing down. I realized how Domingos beat his opponents; he out-energized them as he sprinted forward. "How can you be so sure Liza has gone to Europe?"

"I'm not. I'm tracing the possibilities one by one. Music is her life, so she'll return to one of the places where she performed. This I'm sure of."

"You could call the personnel manager."

"No. I must absolutely be more discreet."

What alarmed me was that I could almost follow his line of argument. Lose a violinist? Track her down by retracing her career pattern and interrogating her colleagues. Next I would be hiding behind trees and jumping out to confront her with a Canon.

"Domingos, why go to all this trouble—all this expense— for a woman who murdered someone?"

"Liza did no such thing. It's a long story, Andy, but she saved my life once. So I owe her this much. I have to try."

"So go yourself."

"I have three concert engagements in Brazil within the next week and a half. Then I have to get right back to Tucson."

Of course he did. He maximized his schedule. I was surprised he didn't always fly west so that he could constantly be gaining time.

"Orchestras resist new members. It might be weeks before the musicians would confide in me."

"You're not going as an orchestra member, Andy. You'll be the soloist."

I laughed out loud. Soloists raced around the world from one concert to another performing a repertoire they'd rehearsed extensively and memorized by heart. Booked by agents, their schedules were planned out a year or two in advance.

I had no such repertoire. If I started conversing with any of the musicians, I'd be detected as a fraud straight away. But none of this mattered because I wouldn't do it. I would draw the line. "Domingos, I soloed at the last concert by accident."

"The audience will love you. You're exotic."

Exotic? I was Hispanic. I was a mariachi player. In my own world, at least I was normal. "I might not have mentioned it, but my violin has a long crack down the middle. I had to use one of Rachel's student violins for the rehearsal."

"The cellist is going to lend you a proper violin."

"What?"

"Zoran is a friend of mine. He's also an excellent luthier. He makes two or three violins a year, each one a masterpiece. He's expecting you at his house tomorrow afternoon so that you can pick out an instrument to take with you. I sent you the address via email."

I felt like a lab rat in a mile-long maze. Every time I found a new corridor, a scientist had beaten me to it and closed the door. I couldn't make a decent decision on my own because I was thwarted at every turn. I strained to imagine a packed theatre with me as the soloist, but the scene faded away like the patterns on an Etch A Sketch. The idea was that ludicrous.

"Domingos, I'm no classical soloist. You know that. You know exactly how I play."

"Don't worry. Most soloists are notoriously bad. They have a limited repertoire of a few solos that they play over and over. Trust me, Steven is a friend. He owes me a few favors. You'll be fine."

"The only appropriate orchestra solo that I can play halfway decently is *Scheherazade*."

"Exactly! That is what you'll play."

"The orchestra in Delft happens to have *Scheherazade* on the program for next week?"

"No, but they appreciate spontaneity. Plus I begged. Any questions? A whole orchestra is waiting on me to start rehearsal."

I already felt tired. Very tired. "Just one question, Domingos. When do we leave?"

~

"This is so romantic!" Rachel said as she snuggled up next to me. She spread her own blanket over her legs and mine over her arms. "I've always wanted to go to Holland. I don't mind that we can't spend a long time."

"At this rate the journey itself might take a week."

"I'm enjoying myself already." She closed her eyes and nuzzled me.

I wasn't enjoying the logistics. Our flight from Tucson to Chicago had been delayed for three hours, and we'd run like thieves to make our trans-Atlantic flight. In the morning we would have to switch terminals in London to catch our flight to Amsterdam, and from Schiphol we'd have to make our way to the train station to catch a ride to Delft. This meant that I had to remember to pick up my carry-on and my borrowed violin about twenty times. I wasn't convinced I could reach Delft with both of them.

"I'm so proud of you. Really, I am," Rachel said. "Of

course, you were also lucky. What were the odds?"

Rachel kissed me as if to wish me good night. As far as she knew, the orchestra genuinely needed a last-minute soloist to perform *Scheherazade*. I didn't think "Domingos talked me into something ridiculous" would otherwise be a convincing explanation for why we were suddenly traveling to Europe all expenses paid.

It was a crazy proposition. I'd told Domingos the same via text, via email, and via Skype. Each time he came up with the same explanation: He needed to help Liza by taking action, and this was the most logical step he could think of. I tried to point out that I was the one actually taking the action, but this line of argument went nowhere. After all, Domingos had bought the tickets. He'd done the planning. He'd done the schmoozing. All I had to do was present myself. Surely I could do that much?

I shut my eyes, but not even the most boring of the cheap kids' movies could lull me to sleep. The thought of masquerading as a soloist had wired me more than two dozen coffees. It was healthy to stretch your abilities, but you were supposed to do so step-by-step, not by letting someone push you from a high diving platform. I knew I could get through *Scheherazade*, but that wasn't the point. As soon as the other musicians realized I was unprepared, that I only knew one solo, they'd hate me. They'd think I was presumptuous or delusional or both. Consequently, they wouldn't share any gossip. They would clam up whenever I was in the vicinity because most of the time they would be talking about me. And laughing.

My only secret weapon was the instrument I'd borrowed from the cello player. Zoran had made some thirty violins, but most had been sold to professionals around the world. The best model he had available was one of his earlier creations. On first glance it was nothing special. The wood was an uneven blend of dark browns, and the fingerboard was beginning to show wear. But when I played a single note, I was transfixed. The violin had a smooth sound that was strong and clear. Most instruments required coaxing, but this one was a music box that you wound up and set free. I was confident I could make it sing, and even if I played wrong notes, they wouldn't sound half bad.

As an extra bonus, Zoran had offered to fix my poor old Roth for free.

Rachel's head slipped down my arm, but she didn't notice. We'd been up all night packing, so naturally she was exhausted. She also had nothing to worry about. When Domingos told her everything had been taken care of, she'd believed him. That left the dirty work to me. Even if I could wiggle through the performance, I was still on a fool's mission. If Liza was determined to hide, she wouldn't do so in plain sight.

Chapter Eight

"How many times have you performed this piece?" asked the concertmaster.

"Just a few. I'm still getting the hang of it."

Willem Janssen laughed because he assumed I was kidding. He was a roly-poly gentleman who had reached middle-age gracefully, as if he'd expected it. Not only was he the concertmaster and the host of impromptu visiting musicians, but his wife was the principal second violinist. His son was the principal cellist. His daughter was the principal violist. From what I could observe, the family had only messed up by not producing their own bass player. Several of the other musicians had family connections within the group as well. Most had studied music conscientiously from a young age. As a result it came easily to them. The rehearsal was tranquil and relaxed because every single musician was well prepared.

Except for me. Mentally I was in the wrong place. I knew I could handle the music; I'd already proved that to myself. I felt confident playing on a borrowed violin that was finer than any I'd ever played before. The problem was my double mission to search for Liza.

If my fellow musicians noticed I was distracted, they were kind enough to blame jetlag just as Rachel had. I called on my acting abilities to imitate the world's most natural performer. Instead of carefully taping the music sheets together, I turned them one by one as if they were superfluous. I deliberately played every solo while looking at my colleagues rather than the music. I never once asked the conductor to repeat a passage on my account. Although he took the time to rework several measures, he was merely fine-tuning some of the dynamics. The musicians already played the piece well. The small ensemble of forty-five members produced a tight, exuberant sound.

They were also docile. They followed Schroeder's every move without question, and they knew the music well enough that they could look up and watch his beat without losing their place on the page. Schroeder demonstrated little passion, meaning he was nothing like Domingos, but he was competent and energetic. He knew the score intimately, so he cued important entrances, but the performers provided their own levels of depth. The few times I slowed down to emphasize a phrase or to exaggerate a prominent note, the others followed right along.

At the break I was released, yet I chose to hang around. I had the list of Liza's likely haunts in my pocked, but my best chance for information would come from within the orchestra. By watching the rest of the rehearsal, the others would assume I was enthusiastic about the concert, and hence I would earn brownie points. I would probably need them. Since Rachel thought I was staying on her account, my presence did double duty. In an extension of courtesy, Rachel had been given a seat in the last stand of the second violins, and she was cheerfully fighting her way through the music. She'd had classical training years earlier, but by now she too was used to playing by ear. Reading music was such a challenge that she kept her eyes focused on the page at all times, which gave me the chance to look around inconspicuously.

Yet I knew I was wasting my time. The musicians seemed perfectly normal. They were merely rehearsing for the next concert. Nothing was cause for alarm or analysis. Nothing was unexpected—although I might have been. It was another evening, another practice session.

Nothing more.

~

"Domingos told me how much he enjoyed conducting your orchestra," I said to Willem. Since the Janssen house was only a short walk from the theatre, we were on foot. Rachel and Willem's other family members had pulled ahead, so for the moment I had the concertmaster to myself.

"We appreciated working with Domingos one hundred percent," Willem said. "He brought our music to another

72

level."

"I'm sure he has faults, but they don't have to do with music."

"True, true."

Despite the cold air, walking through the quiet streets was liberating. Most of the houses were already dark, signs of residents who led lives that were as neat and organized as those of the musicians. Everything fit into place. No problems. No drama. No worries. Unlike me.

"In Tucson the orchestra members love him tremendously. What they don't love is his companion."

For a few seconds Willem didn't answer, so I waited. Usually, if you could train yourself to wait long enough, you received the information you needed. It was like being tickled. You had to wait it out to get the upper hand.

"The woman made herself hard to like," Willem said slowly. "Thanks to her I was pushed out of my chair for an entire year. I made such a fuss that they had to pay me the same salary they paid her! So she is playing with your orchestra in Arizona?"

"Last week she quit. Evidently the city didn't agree with her."

"Neither did Delft. But she was an unhappy person, and such people are the same no matter where they are. But never mind her. Tell me about that fine violin of yours."

For long minutes I extolled Zoran and his fine instruments. I figured that if I kept talking, I would throw Willem off guard long enough to scoop up the right kind of information. Thus, moments before we reached the house, I swung back into gear. "I understood that Liza was coming to Delft for a vacation."

Willem came to a halt so that he could emphasize his point. "Delft! That one? Not at all. Our beautiful city is too quiet for her in general, and in January it's much too cold. She is a woman for beaches by day, night clubs by night. After playing the concerts, of course."

73

"Of course."

Mentally I genuflected. I wasn't used to being sneaky, and I didn't like it. Nevertheless, I faked a shudder. "When Liza left, I was so pleased that I opened a bottle of wine and drank half of it in her honor."

"I drank a large beer! I admit that I did not like her."

"Except for Domingos, I haven't met anyone who does."

"Yes. But then, he's always an exception of one kind or another, isn't he? He willed us to play better, and we did. He started a youth program, one that has been very popular. He established a charity concert to boost awareness of the orchestra. In short, he always surprised us. I suppose the best conductors do."

"Domingos doesn't try to think outside the box. He does so naturally."

Willem clapped his hands. "Exactly! For that reason we tolerated the woman. Somehow she fit into his plan even though we couldn't understand how."

I understood the feeling. Knowing I wasn't alone was a consolation. "Moraes is in his own category."

"Yes, he is. No matter where we might be standing, he's on a different plane."

He was probably on a plane at that very moment. One that could fly.

~

"What have you seen so far?" Rachel asked.

"Nothing much. I meandered."

We'd left the Janssens' house after breakfast and were heading to the Markt, which was the main square. I'd already crisscrossed it a dozen times. While Rachel slept in, I'd visited three cafés and a hairdresser's. I was so wired I had to tell myself to slow down every time I opened my mouth. But my efforts had been wasted. I'd flashed Liza's picture around a dozen times, but none of the baristas or hairdressers could remember her. Maybe they didn't want to.

As we neared Nieuwe Kirche, the New Church, Rachel

74

stopped to take a picture of intersecting canals. At this time of the year they were dark and forbidding, so I couldn't tell what she was taking a picture of. Or maybe it was the contrast I didn't like. I only appreciated water I could jump into.

"You're not a very good tourist, Andy, if you didn't bother to look for landmarks."

"I was trying to get a feel for the place."

"I can't fault you for that. Isn't this the sweetest town?"

"Sweet."

I wrapped my borrowed scarf more tightly around my neck. Rachel had told me that she hated cold weather, but she was bouncing along beside me as if it were July. Then again, she'd studied the weather forecast and brought along a winter coat. I hadn't done the same. I didn't own a winter coat. I hadn't been out of Southern California in the winter, so I couldn't imagine a place where a forty-degree morning was a normal January day.

Rachel stopped for another shot. "We'll have to come back in the summer. I'm sure the town is delightful then."

While I was ready to dive into a warm shop at any moment, Rachel was a kid at an amusement park. Her eyes were wide open and her spirits were sky high. Travel agreed with her. I'd noticed this already: in Greece, where she summered, and in Mexico, where she visited family. I wasn't sure whether it agreed with me or not.

"Summer is months from now," I said.

"It's never too early to buy a plane ticket. We could start planning ahead."

I nodded without paying attention. Then I spotted a woman marching towards us. One who might have been Liza.

I couldn't tell for sure because the woman's head was down, and she was wearing a hat. Normally Liza wouldn't walk that way, but normally she wouldn't be walking in such a sharp wind.

As the woman passed us, she turned her head towards the side as if avoiding me. Or avoiding the wind. Hard to say. But she was the right size to be Liza. Fashionable black coat, high-heeled boots. Though the woman had long passed me, I couldn't take a chance on missing her.

"Rachel! I left my debit card at the ATM. You go ahead."

I doubled back as quickly as I could. I followed the woman for a block, but when she turned the corner, she was out of my sight for several moments. By the time I reached the corner myself, she'd vanished down a quiet street lined with residential houses.

Breathless, Rachel ran up behind me. "Andy, you've lost all sense of direction! The ATM is over to the east!"

For show, I felt around in my pocket. "I have it after all. I put my card in the wrong place."

"So you do have it?"

I wrestled the thing from my jeans, where it had been safely riding the whole time. "Yes."

"Wow. You're jet-lagging worse than I thought. Want to stop for a coffee?"

Another coffee would have sent me straight into cardiac arrest. "No, no. I'm okay. I have to power through. You know, let my body catch up with the time change."

She eyed me suspiciously. "I knew you got out of bed too early. Should we walk back to the Janssens'?"

"You wanted to go to some museum."

She tapped her purse. "It's back the other way. I saw a sign."

"Lead on, then."

I followed Rachel like a puppy. It was irrational to think that Liza would have come here. The other musicians were quiet and competent. I couldn't see Liza making friends with any of them. I could only imagine her relating to musicians who were as impetuous and wild as she was. But she wouldn't make friends. She would make acquaintances who were never more than one audition away from being rivals instead.

"You're sure you don't mind going to the museum with me?"

76

"Not at all."

My smartest strategy was to humor Rachel as much as possible, but what I really wanted was to get back to practicing. That way, if I fell all over the music, the Janssens would at least know I'd been trying.

"Don't tell me you're worried about the rehearsal," Rachel said.

The last thing I needed was a girlfriend who could read my mind, but for the moment I was stuck. "I'm worried about tonight's audience. I'm worried about making a fool out of myself. I'm worried about burning the bridges for Domingos. I'm worried about—"

Despite my much greater height, Rachel reached up and put her hand over my mouth. "Let's pretend I didn't ask. We can concentrate on the moment instead."

I nodded, but I kept thinking about Liza. Of course, I hadn't seen her at all. She wasn't anywhere near Delft. She probably wasn't in Europe. Why would she be? She was a murderer trying to hide. She wouldn't come to a quaint little town where she would stand out more than a coyote in a chicken coop. I was wasting my time. Domingos was wasting my time. Maybe he just wanted to get me out of town though I couldn't think why.

"There it is," Rachel said. "Straight ahead." She was referring to the Vermeer Centrum Delft. The city didn't own any paintings by its most famous son, so it had capitalized on its lack by creating a tourist attraction out of reproductions. Rachel steered me towards the entrance.

"They don't have any real paintings," I said. "Just fakes."

"Yes, but they have facsimiles of every one of Vermeer's works."

My sophomore year in college I'd taken a course in art history. I remembered that Manet had painted a dead bullfighter. I remembered that Picasso and his friends had invented Cubism. I remembered that Vermeer's entire output of paintings was a smaller number than my current age.

77

"I'm not sure a visit will be worth the entrance fee."

"I'll pay for it!" Rachel said as she dragged me inside.

At least the building was warm, which made it worth the price after all. We took a slow sweep of the main floor, comparing and admiring Vermeer's images. He had worked meticulously and slowly, perhaps with the help of some kind of camera obscura. I liked the gentle palate and the peaceful designs, and I liked that many of the models had posed as musicians. Although the artist had chosen different subjects, multiple paintings depicted the same room, probably one in his own house.

I appreciated the subtleties of Vermeer's creations. I admired his exacting style. But a career that consisted of painting similar scenes would be too contained. Like Delft itself. It was a town for homebodies. A town where people appreciated new kitchen gadgets or gossip about the library. The town was gentle, unassuming, charming—and even a little dull. Hence it couldn't possibly contain someone as unpredictable as Liza.

Chapter Nine

"La comida está horrible," Rachel whispered. *The food is terrible.* She smiled as she said it. "We can raid the refrigerator tonight when no one is looking."

She returned to her conversation with the other violinists, all of whom she'd made friends with. They'd been chatting nonstop ever since we'd reached the small beer hall that was the orchestra's favorite post-concert haunt. The group had a sacred tradition of celebrating each concert with a late-night dinner accompanied by several ales. While they expected their concerts to go well, minor mistakes would be forgotten over a few pints.

Except that I couldn't forget. I'd completely blown the second solo—I'd come in half a second late and then played out of tune. Schroeder had looked over at me, and for an uncomfortable second, we'd locked eyes. Then I remembered where I was and what I needed to play and hacked my way through the rest of the passage. I plunged through the remaining solos without listening to them. I was on a mission for Domingos. I wasn't here for myself. I hadn't asked to come.

Rachel reached past me to take another piece of rock-hard bread. *"How can they get away with selling this stuff?"*

Dry, stale bread was the least of my worries. During the concert, I'd noticed a woman who might have been Liza. She was sitting to the left of the stage about five rows in, which gave her a perfect view of the violin section. Given the lack of lighting and the distance, I couldn't tell for sure. But whereas most of the audience smiled as I played the solo passages, the woman showed no expression. She seemed to be looking through me. Directly after the concert, I'd gone to the foyer to find her. Nothing.

"Aren't you hungry?" Rachel asked. "I mean, we've had worse." She was munching through a wiener made of mystery meat and some green goop masquerading as a vegetable.

79

"No appetite." Though I wasn't going to mention it to Rachel, I was like the Centre Vermeer that didn't have any true paintings. "Tonight I made too many mistakes."

"Domingos has confidence in you for a reason. And you did okay tonight."

Not even Rachel, who was not above lying, could bring herself to say I'd done a good job. Instead she returned to her conversation with the others. Having had successful public-school educations, most of them spoke excellent English. They were curious about Rachel and me in genuine, non-threatening ways. Rachel was in top form squashing myths about the Old West as well as current conditions in Mexico. When the musicians asked about mariachi playing, she showed them videos on YouTube. The players were so caught up in the art form that they bombarded Rachel with questions, which she fielded with aplomb. This was one of her specialties. She could talk with almost anyone, and she made instant friends in the process.

Our fellow musicians were more congenial than I could have hoped for. Even the conductor was gracious; while the rest of us surveyed the menu, he made a point of making the rounds and congratulating the players one by one. He showed me the online newspaper review in which Antonio Cruz (my name had changed again) had wowed the audience, not only with the interpretation of the Russian composer's most famous piece but with a charming encore that left everyone dancing.

Indeed, the Latin tune *Jealousy* was a hit every time I played it, even in Delft.

"Are you sure you can't stay some more days?" asked Anna. "We've enjoyed having you so much, and you've barely arrived."

"Back to my violin students," Rachel said. "They might not deserve me, but they do pay!"

"You don't mind working with beginners?" asked Willem's daughter. Jannie was a sweet teenager, eager to please and intrigued by foreigners.

"Working with kids is part of the job no matter the pain," Rachel laughed.

"You know, you are much different than the other one," Anna said.

"Other one what?" Rachel asked.

My hair bristled. I wanted to press a magical pause button so that I could think quickly enough to prevent a disaster.

"The other Mexican violinist."

Rachel was quick. She turned away from me and instantly produced her broadest fake smile. "And who was that?"

Anna turned to her husband. "I disliked the woman so much I forgot her name. Willem?"

He shook his head. "Andy, you were asking about that woman last night. What was her name again?"

"Liza," Rachel said flatly. "You're talking about Liza."

"That's the one," Willem said. "But she's not one bit like you are. Is it because you are Mexican-American instead of Mexican?"

"Not really," Rachel said. "It's because Liza's a bitch."

Surprised by her candor, the Dutch musicians laughed so hard they nearly choked. Then they raised their glasses in yet another toast. Smiling brightly, Rachel did the same.

Chapter Ten

Our borrowed bedroom had a double bed and an excess of wooden furniture, including two tall dressers and a bookcase that stretched from the floor to the ceiling. The creaky wooden floors were cold, but the down comforter had kept me warm the night before.

Tonight was bound to be chillier. Given the uncomfortable way Rachel had squeezed my knuckles on our walk home, I was sure she had guessed why we were in Delft. The question was how she would react to the way I'd misled her. I had several options for addressing the situation but didn't like any of them. I could take the high road and apologize, but that meant admitting that I knew better. I could explain how Moraes had roped me in, but Rachel wouldn't be sympathetic to my weakness for the conductor. I could deny everything, but that would only buy me a few minutes' time.

Rachel was taking a shower in the bathroom down the hall when I heard a faint knock on the door. Jannie quickly gestured that she wanted to come in. Since the room belonged to her, I immediately stood aside. I assumed she wanted to retrieve socks or some other needed possession. Instead she pulled me over to the bed and sat beside me.

"Liza is my friend," Jannie said quietly, "but Papa and Mama don't know this. They both dislike her."

I was so surprised that I couldn't reply. Jannie took this to mean that I didn't approve of such a friendship.

"It's true she has a temper, and she always thinks she is the best. But she helped me."

Jannie flexed the fourth finger of her left hand. For many string players, the smaller, weaker finger caused problems.

"Liza showed me some extra exercises, and sometimes she stayed after rehearsal to train me. She always told me I could play more accurately, and eventually I did. But why are you asking about her?" Jannie pointed in the general direction of the bathroom. "Was she your girlfriend before Rachel?"

83

Teenagers. For them it was all about romance, and I loved them for it.

"Liza got mad at the conductor," I said, improvising. "She left town so fast that we're all worried about her."

Jannie nodded. She was sweet enough to be gullible, but I didn't want to scare her off by asking the wrong questions.

"Domingos is really, really sorry. He didn't mean to hurt her feelings."

"I see."

"You know how the maestro is. He has so many things going on that his schedule is crazy. He couldn't come to Delft, so he sent me."

"That makes sense."

"That's why I've been asking around," I said. I looked straight into Jannie's eyes. "We haven't been able to contact her. That's all we want to do. We want to make sure that she's all right."

I couldn't read Jannie's expression, so I threw in the only clincher I could think of. "Domingos loves her," I said softly. "He loves her and he's sorry and he wants to do anything he can to help."

Jannie patted the comforter. "Don't tell my parents, but I met with Liza a few days ago."

I tried not to act startled. "She's living in the Netherlands?"

"Oh, no. She stopped by."

Liza in Delft? I'd barely missed her. That meant two things: Domingos knew her much better than I had given him credit for, meaning well enough to be on the right track, and he hadn't wasted his money on a goose chase after all. Liza was merely faster than we were. She had more at stake.

Jannie continued patting the comforter as if the motion soothed her.

"She was right here in Delft?"

"In Amsterdam. I pretended that I was going shopping, but I went to see her."

84

I'd only missed Liza by half a week and an hour's drive. "Why had she come?"

"She doesn't trust banks, and she said her apartment wasn't safe. She always gave me her extra money for safekeeping."

To a teen this might not seem strange, but the request would put any sane adult on guard. "Last week she wanted it back?"

Jannie nodded. "Is she in trouble? She seemed nervous, but she wouldn't tell me anything."

Liza had murdered a board member, ruined a concert, and fled the country, but she only "seemed nervous." The woman was an even better actress than I expected. That made her independent and unpredictable. And lethal.

"Liza may have done something inappropriate. Maybe by accident. But there's no proof. No matter what she did, Domingos will do anything to help her."

"What can I do?"

"Do you have her address?"

"She never told me where she was going. I called this morning, but the phone number is out of service."

Naturally. Liza was ahead of all of us.

"Is she living somewhere in Europe?" I asked.

"I'm not sure. Maestro Moraes conducted in France, you know. I think Liza usually accompanied him."

"Can you think of any other place she might have gone?"

Jannie looked over at her bookshelves where she had taped postcards from around the world. "Liza always talked about how she was homesick for Mexico. She couldn't wait to return. She was aching inside. I could see that. So I understood why she was in a bad mood sometimes. She couldn't help it. I might have felt the same if I had to go away from Delft. So please, tell me how I can help her. I really want to."

In a brutal way, it was refreshing to converse with teens. If you could get them to talk to you at all, they didn't mince words. Nor did they shield listeners from particular versions of the truth. Consequently, you had to be prepared to handle what they shared. Even though I couldn't imagine Liza showing compassion for anything, let alone a homeland, I also knew what it felt like to be displaced. I longed for my old life in Southern California in almost the same way. Like it or not, I could understand some of Liza's reasoning.

"None of us can help her at the moment, but if she comes back, or if she contacts you again, would you let her know that I've been looking for her on Domingos' behalf?" I reached for a small notebook that Rachel carried in her purse and searched through it until I found a blank page. I scribbled down my email address and phone number and handed the paper to Jannie. "Don't hesitate to contact me if you'd like to. For any reason."

"All right."

I reclaimed the paper and added a second email address. "If you prefer, contact Domingos directly. With any information. Even if you think it's not important."

Jannie carefully folded the sheet in half. Then she stood and carefully shoved it deep into her back pocket.

"And Jannie?"

"Yes?"

"Thank you."

We heard Rachel coming down the hall, but by the time my traveling companion opened the door, Jannie was removing her nightshirt from a bottom drawer.

"Sorry to bother you," Jannie said.

"No worries," Rachel said cheerfully. She was fully dressed, but she wore her towel over her shoulder. "Thanks for loaning us your room."

Janie nodded as she headed out the door. "You're welcome any time. Good night."

I waited until Jannie had disappeared down the hall. "Cute kid, huh?"

Rachel slammed the door so loudly the neighbors in the house next door might have heard it. "How dare you not tell me?"

"Tell you what?"

"That we came here to hunt for Liza!"

I didn't attempt any kind of explanation. "I didn't tell you because I was afraid you'd be angry, which you are. So in a way, I was right."

She threw down the items she'd been holding. Her toothbrush skidded along the floor while her toiletries bounced and scattered. "What were you supposed to do? Come here and interrogate your fellow players?"

"Domingos asked me to come perform with them. At the same time, he wanted me to ask around a bit."

"Guess what I found out from my stand partner. *Scheherazade* wasn't originally on the program for this concert. There was a sudden change of plans."

"This can happen in any orchestra. Maybe they couldn't get the sheet music they needed. Maybe a rival orchestra was going to perform the same piece, so they switched things up."

"Or maybe some dope from the States showed up and wormed his way in. You're not here as a soloist, Andy Veracruz. They didn't need you and you didn't come here to save the day. You came to chase after Domingos' missing lover."

"I'm not sure they're lovers."

"A woman who is a murderer."

"I'm not sure she did anything wrong. Domingos says—"

Rachel closed her eyes as if she needed a break from seeing me. "I would shut up about Domingos if I were you. And why is Liza so damned important to him?"

"She once saved his life."

"What a coincidence! You might need someone to save yours."

I wanted to say anything to soften the situation, and perhaps being in a teen's room made me feel more youthful. Hence I tried the dumb-innocent approach. "It's true that I didn't tell you the whole story. Why does that matter?"

"And to think I felt proud of you. We're both pathetic." She held her arms before her, palms down, and jiggled her fingers. "Two marionettes on strings."

"Rachel, I didn't have a choice."

"Of course you did. There's always a choice. You lied by omission and pretended to be a hero. What kind of boyfriend are you?"

I knew I was making yet another mistake, but my mouth would not obey my brain. "What's the problem? You had a good time, didn't you? The Janssens have been lovely, haven't they?"

Ordinarily Rachel would have come around. On most occasions she was reasonable; in fact she usually bent over backwards to go along with whatever nonsense I'd come up with. But this time I'd dragged her away from a week of lessons and gigs on the pretense of a paid vacation rather than a missing woman chase. Evidently there was a difference.

Rachel approached me, her arms firmly crossed over her chest. "What did your precious Brazilian maestro tell the Janssens about you? How did he work things out with Schroeder?"

We were going backwards. Up until dinner, she'd been referring to the conductor as Domingos.

"He said Schroeder would be doing him a great favor."

"Oh, right. Because you need to kickstart your career as a soloist. No, wait! That's not personal enough. The TucAz is going to record *Scheherazade*, so you needed to practice performing it. Which was it?"

"Rachel, you're getting worked up over nothing. And Domingos didn't send me to chase after Liza. He wanted me to ask around. That's all."

She undressed by throwing her clothes in the direction of her suitcase. "You're a meddler, Andy Veracruz. A damned mariachi meddler." In one motion she pulled on a baseball jersey she used as pajamas. "I can't trust you if you don't tell me the things that are the most important. We're here because of Liza. Period. Why you didn't tell me that, I don't know."

"Like I said. I was afraid you'd get mad."

She raised her hand in a gesture that said something like, "Of course I'm mad, you moron." Then she fell silent, which was lots worse. She went over to her suitcase as if she needed, at that very moment, to rearrange her clothing.

I watched her helplessly. I couldn't think of anything to say that would ameliorate the situation. Angrily she shoved items from one side of the small bag to the other.

"How much?" Rachel finally asked.

"What do you mean?"

"How much did Moraes offer you for coming here?"

"Nothing."

She stood and paced. Since the room was small, she resembled a gerbil in a cage. That made me an exercise wheel.

"You agreed to come here for nothing," she said. "Sweet."

"Domingos paid for the tickets. Both of them."

"Except that you said they were frequent flier miles, so he didn't pay a damned thing. What about all our expenses?"

"He'll pay me back. But thanks to the Janssens, we'll hardly have any."

So far our hosts hadn't let us buy a single meal. We were riding on Domingos' tux tails. Everyone we talked to worshipped him. I could sympathize. They'd had a lot more time to come under his spell than I had.

Unfortunately for me, for the moment Rachel was immune to Domingos' many charms. She returned to her luggage. I watched as she took socks out of her suitcase, refolded them, and put them back in. It was the slow torture of watching a ticking bomb. One false move would detonate it.

"What else did he promise you, Andy?"

"Nothing."

She started folding underwear. "You're lying."

I took a deep breath. For the third time, I was in a foreign setting with Rachel, and for the third time, I wasn't sure if I would be sleeping on the proverbial couch—except that the

Janssens didn't have one. If necessary, perhaps I could find my way back to the station. Surely there would be trains to Schiphol Airport by five or six in the morning, meaning that I would only have five or six hours to wait alone by myself. I might even be able to change the airplane reservation so that Rachel wouldn't have to travel all the way back to the States while sitting next to me.

Or perhaps I should go somewhere else altogether. I could lose myself in some foreign country. I had a borrowed violin, a few clothes, my passport, and a credit card with a limit of five thousand dollars. If I had to, I could survive.

"I said, what else did he offer you?"

"Rachel, he begged. After all he's done for me, I couldn't let him down."

Rachel planted herself in front of me. "He hasn't done a damned thing for you compared to what you've done for him. The offer?"

How did I get myself into such messes? In the last few months my every action had turned into a complication without a solution. A black cloud was following me like a kite on a string, but I didn't have any scissors. I wondered how Joey would have reacted to the situation. Somehow he always knew how to navigate between impossible positions.

"You might as well go ahead and tell me."

"He didn't offer me anything, Rachel. He asked me to help him. Period."

"Lovely, Andy. I suppose that makes you his pet dog. He says 'jump' and you don't notice whether it's in front of a bus or not. It's a shame you won't be spending much more time in Tucson."

"Why do you say that?"

"Moraes? He can't keep still. Anyone can see that. You'll be right alongside him carrying his doggie bag."

"Rachel, that's not true."

"I wouldn't bring up the subject of truth if I were you."

"Domingos tricked me into this."

"He did not. You agree to it."

I'd been triangulated. Domingos had caught me off guard, and Rachel had seen through me. I didn't have an escape route. "He sounded so desperate that I agreed to help him."

That wasn't true either. Far from being desperate, he'd been confident I would go along with him.

Rachel sat at the edge of the bed like a snake guarding a hiking path. I knew not to get too close.

"You're willing to help Moraes no matter what," Rachel said. "It's me you never help."

"You don't need my assistance. You're entirely self-sufficient."

"That's true, Andy. And I must admit, I certainly don't need you."

My phone buzzed. Since only a few people had the number, and most of them would have been asleep, I reached over for my phone to see who it was.

"Domingos," I said. "Should I take it?"

"I could stop you?"

She glared as I answered. She continued glaring as I shared details over the phone, but I was buying time so that Rachel would cool down. Domingos, on the other hand, tuned out as soon as I started talking about the concert.

"What time zone are you in?" I asked, stalling.

"Eastern time, I guess. I'm in Miami spending a couple of days with some friends." Domingos' voice was as buoyant as it had been before he'd sailed from the podium mid-concert. "Any signs of You-Know-Who?" He asked it cheerfully, as if Liza were a trifle, someone to gossip about, a hot chick he hoped to date.

"I'm still working on that," I said slowly, trying to calculate whether or not Rachel could hear Domingos' words.

"Excellent. Glad to hear it. In the meantime, I need you to do me a favor."

I could have sworn I was hearing things. I was experiencing an intense form of déjà vu. Or maybe my own

91

insanity had caught up with me. "I thought I just did you a favor. Don't tell me I'm in a time warp."

He laughed heartily. "Is Rachel there?"

"Yes." I didn't mention that she was scowling.

"Put her on, would you? I need to know if she wants to visit Lyon."

I felt the hairs on the back of my neck rise to full attention. "Lyon?"

"They loved me there."

"Lyon?"

"For two years I went back and forth between Lyon and Delft. You'll see."

"How's that?"

"You're flying there Thursday morning."

"But I thought—"

"Why come home when you're having so much fun? Besides, next weekend you're the surprise soloist."

I bit off a hangnail so abruptly that I drew blood.

"Are you still there?" Domingos asked.

"I'm not sure."

"I booked you into a nice hotel in Amsterdam for a couple of days. You'll have time for sightseeing. I sent you an email with the details. Now, do you want the good news or the bad news?"

I looked at Rachel, who was eyeing me suspiciously, hands on her hips, ready for her next attack. "All your news is bad."

"Come! Where's your sense of spirit?"

"Sense of adventure, you mean. I never had one. I'm not that kind of guy."

"Andy, drop the negativity. It's unhealthy."

"News, you said?"

"The orchestra members are very excited about your arrival. They want to feature you for back-to-back concerts next weekend."

How did he talk whole orchestras into bending to his will

at a moment's notice? I tried to imagine the conversation. "Mr. Conductor and musicians of Lyon, I have this little issue. Would you mind...." The scenario was absurd, yet some version of it had taken place. Domingos was so skilled that he could hypnotize his victims over the phone. Or maybe he'd contacted them via Skype, which would have been worse. He was even more convincing with the help of visuals.

"Lyon," I said. "That's a much bigger town than Delft. Lots of pressure. Competition. They'll know right away that I'm a fake."

"Even if they think so, don't worry, they're very polite, so they won't say so. Just, look around for Liza, play your two concerts, and leave. Everything will be fine. I'll send you a list of places to look for her."

"You've already invested a lot of money. Why not cut your losses? It will cost you a mint to change our tickets."

"Remember, they're frequent flier miles. I only paid for the taxes."

"You still haven't explained why Liza is so important to you."

"Two things, Andy. First, she's accused of something she didn't do. Second, we go way back. She's my oldest friend. And the most brilliant. So please, Andy, instead of arguing with me, start making plans. Lyon is a beautiful city. You're sure to enjoy it. Rachel too."

An all-expense trip to France on top of an all-expense trip to Holland was too much to expect for a mere missing person. "Did Liza steal your bank accounts or something?"

"Oh, no. She's not dishonest."

"Of course she's dishonest!"

"You'll love Lyon, Andy. Trust me."

For a moment I put down the phone and surveyed the room. I'd had an amazing experience as a soloist in a foreign country. I'd made friends with Dutch people who were warm and genuine. Despite her very rough edges, Liza had helped a key member of the orchestra, one who was eternally grateful.

93

So while my good angel told me to keep arguing with Domingos, my bad angel told me to save the effort since I wouldn't win the argument anyway.

"What's the catch?"

Domingos waited so long to reply that I thought he'd hung up.

"Domingos! I'm sure there's a catch."

"As in Tucson, the orchestra performs the same concert twice, in this case on Friday and Saturday nights. Unlike Tucson, however, many of the patrons are so loyal that they attend both concerts."

"Lyon must be a dull town. But why should this problem concern me?"

"They want you to play different concertos each night."

"What?"

"You can do it, can't you? Prepare two concertos?"

"But—"

"And one more thing. They're not interested in *Scheherazade*."

Chapter Eleven

"Joey? How are you doing?"

It was barely eight a.m. in his time zone, but my brother snatched up the phone on the first ring. "What's wrong?"

Not only did my brother look like me, but he knew me inside and out. He knew how I reacted and how I thought. More specifically, he knew that if I was calling him this early, I was in some kind of trouble. Occasionally I'd found it inconvenient that he understood me so thoroughly, but my brother's acumen also came in handy. It meant we could take shortcuts when we talked to each other.

"It's not that kind of trouble. Long story."

"With you it always is. You're not in the hospital?"

"Not yet. I might be soon if it turns out that looks can kill."

"What?"

"Actually, Rachel is not my biggest problem."

"You're in jail?"

"Not technically."

"Am I going to work today, or do I need to call in sick for a week while I fly to the States?"

"It won't be quite that bad, but I do need a favor. A big one. I'm really sorry."

"I'm not. Your favors are never boring ones like 'Can I borrow money?' or 'Would you give me Uncle So-and-So's address?'"

I was proud of myself on that one account. Besides an occasional short-term loan, I never bothered my brother about the kinds of mundane things that drove most sane siblings crazy. My problems were circumstantial. Almost always, they were out of my control.

"Where are you, anyway?"

"Delft. Where I just played a concert."

Joey did not respond.

"I would have invited you, but it was a last-minute thing."

"Delft," Joey said.

"It's a pretty town. Rachel is enjoying it. She's out taking pictures."

"Pictures."

"It's about forty-five degrees right now, but as soon as the sun showed itself, she raced outside."

"Moraes worked in Delft?"

"Before Tucson. See—"

"Wait. Let me guess."There was a five-second silence. Then Joey sighed. "You're chasing that woman. The one who left mid-concert and threw the board member to his death."

"As it turns out, there's no proof that Liza actually killed him, so we shouldn't jump to harsh conclusions."

"She sounds like Yiolanda with a violin."

Yiolanda had caused so much trouble in California that I'd been forced to leave town. She'd been married to my boss, but she'd flirted mercilessly. Even though I'd resisted her, she'd taken advantage of me. "Liza isn't here although she was in the vicinity last week. That's why Rachel and I are being sent to Lyon."

"Of course. I should have guessed. And you're calling me why?"

"How's the shoulder?"

He'd been shot a few months earlier, but he'd been conscientious about rehab.

"Getting stronger every day." He paused. "Why?"

Even though Joey hadn't tried to find a mariachi to play with during his few months abroad, I knew he'd taken his violin with him so that he wouldn't get too rusty. "You've been practicing scales and all?"

"A little bit. Why?"

"Which concerto did you play for your college orchestra audition?"

Joey said nothing at all.

"You can't remember?" I asked. "I was thinking it was the one by Manuel Ponce."

96

I knew exactly which one it was. My brother and I had talked about the choice at length. Orchestra auditions were notoriously vigorous, but my brother's strategy had been a simple one. By playing a concerto that was relatively unfamiliar, he'd hoped his smaller mistakes would go unnoticed. They didn't, but he'd still won second chair, which placed him beside me.

"Andy, that was twenty years ago. Why do you ask?"

"But you practice the Ponce every once in a while, right? Play it for the kids?"

"Once in a while every six months or so. That's not very often."

"I'm sure the fingerings will come back to you." I wasn't sure at all, but I was channeling Domingos. To my surprise, reckless optimism was a thrill. No wonder the maestro engaged in it so often.

"Andy, what's going on?"

"I need you to come to Lyon to play that Ponce concerto with the orchestra on Saturday night."

"I'm supposed to play a solo with a professional orchestra?"

"Right."

"This Saturday."

"I'll pay for the flight."

"And the conductor happens to want a concerto by a Mexican composer?"

"He's not picky. You might choose something else."

"Why can't you play the Ponce yourself?"

"I won't have time to rehearse it."

"Ah. Busy sightseeing, no doubt." He was kidding. He knew I was a lousy tourist.

"I'll be practicing the concerto that I'll be performing on Friday night. That is, when I'm not surveilling endless cafés to hunt for Liza. I'm so wired from extra caffeine that I won't be able to sleep until next week. The baristas give me dirty looks, but I've resorting to asking for decaf."

Joey whistled. "Let me get this straight. You're supposed to be performing concertos in back-to-back concerts."

"Yes, but the conductor wants different concertos each night. Domingos told him I was a soloist."

"Five days of preparation won't be enough?" Again he was kidding. He'd studied the Ponce for a good three months.

"Not quite."

"You didn't mention this to Domingos?"

I remained silent.

"No, of course not," Joey said, answering himself. "You didn't want to admit that you couldn't prepare two solos within a week."

"Since my job in the TucAz depends on what he thinks of me—"

"Got it. You want me to cover one of the concerts."

"That's the idea."

"I suppose this means I would also be impersonating you."

"If you wouldn't mind."

"Andy, you know I never turn down an opportunity to make a fool of myself while pretending to be you."

"Yes, Joey. I know that."

It was something I had been counting on.

~

The easyJet plane was so small I couldn't sit straight without hitting my head. Rachel either didn't notice my discomfort or didn't care. She scooted past me to take the window seat, but I wasn't sure whether she wanted to watch the rain or to distance herself.

I shoved my backpack under my feet and tried to imagine what relaxing felt like. Domingos' latest phone call had thrown me into permanent red alert. The Lyon Orchestra had happily okayed the Ponce piece, but for the other surprise concerto they wanted something Brazilian. Hence Domingos had chosen Villa-Lobos' *Fantasia de Movimentos Mistos*, which was for violin and orchestra. I'd never played the piece, but since I'd won the TucAz position by sight-reading Villa-Lobos successfully, Domingos reasoned that I could handle it.

In terms of learning the piece, he was partway right. I'd listened to the composition, along with the rest of Villa-Lobos' music, a gazillion times. I couldn't have memorized it within a week, but Domingos assured me that I could refer to the written music as long as I played the piece beautifully. "Beautifully" was a stretch too, but I had a fighting chance of getting through it. That was the most I could promise. When I told Domingos the same, he laughed. He assured me that the conductor, Ferdinand Chaussée, owed him a really big favor. I refrained from asking what it was.

I fastened my seatbelt and practiced the music in my mind. Plenty of the passages demanded careful attention. The intervals in the first part, justly labeled *Torment*, were strange and unexpected—so much so that most of the orchestra members wouldn't know when I was playing mistakes. *Serenity* was accessible; any professional violinist could handle it. *Contentment* was so hard that it was for masochists who biked on the ledges of tall buildings. It was ridiculous. Despite the ear training, I wouldn't have any hope of playing it accurately. No matter how much or how well I practiced, I would have to skip notes during the performance. Lots of notes. Maybe most of them.

Rachel pressed her nose to the window as she vied for the best possible view.

"Think it's raining in Lyon?" I asked.

"It's not. I already checked." She wrestled a piece of paper from her back pocket and handed it to me. "Here is your emergency list."

I was exhausted from four long days of rehearsal punctuated by Rachel's enthusiastic reports of sightseeing as she dashed around Amsterdam without me. "I don't have room in my head for French right now."

"*Je ne parle pas français.* 'I don't speak French.' At least learn that one."

"Rachel."

"Say it."

I stumbled through two syllables before she repeated it for me effortlessly.

"Now this one. *Combien*—"

"Rachel, I can't handle any more input."

She shook her head. "Spanish and French are a lot alike. If you'd start concentrating rather than whining, you'd see what I mean."

"I'm maxed out right now."

"Don't blame that on me." She rattled the paper and pointed to the last phrase on her list. "Here. This one is easy. *Aidez-Moi.* Eh-day-MUAW. 'Help me.' You never know when you'll have an emergency."

I attempted the pronunciation but butchered all three syllables. Then I squeezed Rachel's arm as if that would draw us closer together emotionally. "I'm really glad you decided to come with me."

"I'm not sure who's crazier, you or Moraes."

"Either of us might qualify."

"As long as your dopey friend is paying for my first trip to France, I don't care."

"I'm not sure Domingos is my friend."

"Every masochist needs a minion master."

I was vaguely aware that she was referring to a cartoon, but she was right about my being a minion. Twelve-hour practice days had turned me into a slave. Even if I stayed completely focused, there was no way I'd be able to pull off a polished performance. With a little luck I might manage a sloppy, exuberant one.

"And your brother is coming for sure?" Rachel asked.

"He's been practicing. He's in."

"And I'm the only Mademoiselle, ha!" she sang, parodying a line from *Cabaret*. The orchestra was putting us up in a hotel. As long as Joey and I never left or returned together, no one besides us would know that my brother was in Lyon or that the three of us were sharing a room.

100

"Is Joey's wife an angel or what?" Rachel asked.

"Christina is the head angel. They give her special wings."

"Well, guess what? I'm not in her league."

"What are you trying to tell me?"

She turned back to the window. "Nothing."

Despite the rain, we departed on schedule. Eventually I drifted off. I dreamt that I was back in Squid Bay, back in my mariachi group, and back in my groove of dating temporary women I never made promises to. Life was a lot easier that way.

~

I would have walked right past him as we exited security, but Rachel immediately spotted the twenty-something waving the foot-long "Antonio Crus" sign. The letters had been written legibly and carefully in red marker.

"Look, Andy! They only misspelled the last half of your last name by one letter." She waltzed over to the young man, who was dressed casually in jeans and a sweat shirt, and gave him a European-style greeting that included kisses on both cheeks; then he surprised her by going for a third kiss.

I nearly expected him to bow. Maybe he'd seen *The Princess Bride* too many times. He'd been overcome by a sense of duty. Worse yet, he seemed so happy.

"Etoile Chaussée," he said with a flourish. *"Enchanté."*

"Que nous enchanté... también!" Rachel said, mixing French and Spanish. "We're happy to meet you too!"

Etoile grinned deeply. "This is our first time for guests from Arizona. All my friends have questions about the Old West."

"And I will make up all the answers as I go along!" Rachel laughed. She liked Etoile immediately, and I wasn't sure that was a good sign. While he was too young to be a serious threat to me, Rachel seemed way too enthusiastic about him. Or maybe she was acting.

I didn't have time to ponder the situation. Etoile whisked us outside where his sister was waiting behind the driver's wheel of a decade-old Renault. He tossed our bags into the trunk and herded us into the backseat while Marie cheerfully introduced herself. Since their dad was busy, she and her brother had been assigned the pleasant task of fetching us from the airport.

Rachel chatted away, testing the limits of our hosts' English. Yes, a wonderful time in Delft, pleasant flight, so happy to be here, etc., etc. Compliments rolled off Rachel's tongue as if she'd been practicing. Actually, she had been. From online sources she'd learned that Lyon had a strong tradition of music and a famous theatre with an old-style chandelier. Did the orchestra usually have good crowds? The Chaussée family was originally from Paris. Did they like living farther south?

I sat back and rested my eyelids while the highway whizzed by. I would have been nervous if I hadn't been so sleepy. Whereas Rachel rattled off intelligent questions about the art museum and the riverbanks, I was so disconnected that I didn't know how to find the city from the airport. I was thinking that the classy Renault was an improvement over the bumpy flight when I drifted off.

By the time I woke, Rachel was reaching over the headrest to pat the young man's shoulder, and they grinned conspiratorially. I'd obviously been the butt of delightful jokes. Marie winked at me in the rearview mirror, a co-conspirator. I was thankful that Rachel was no longer snarling at me, but I wasn't much happier to have her flirting with a much younger man and really, really enjoying it.

I was trying to think of some snappy comment as we reached the city center, where we had to slow down for a line of protesters.

"What are they demonstrating about?" Rachel asked.

"There's always somebody protesting against something," Etoile said dismissively. "Education. Politics. Labor. You name it."

"Last week there was a shooting on a farm not far from

here," Marie said as she shuddered. "Some lunatic. I guess they're all over."

"You can't protect yourself from craziness," Rachel said.

Etoile shook his head. "No. You have to be lucky enough not to be at the wrong place at the wrong time!"

All three giggled; it was the unrealistic nature of youth to refuse to think about the darker side of things. They were fortunate that they hadn't experienced enough hardships to think any other way. I hoped they would never have to. Some people didn't. They floated through life on the top of things, gracefully dodging obstacles while the rest of us took up the slack.

I told myself to lighten up, but I couldn't convince myself to do so. I should have been excited at the prospect of playing such a challenging concerto, but I knew that as soon as I saw shades of another imaginary Liza, my concentration would be shot all over again. The woman hadn't fit the scene in Delft, but wouldn't she have felt at home in a sophisticated French city? More importantly, would she have paid a quick visit to retrieve something she'd left behind?

My radar perked up as soon as we joined a one-way avenue that hugged the river. Tall trees lined either side. People dotted the sidewalks. Women especially. Blonde ones. Many had covered their heads with hats or scarves, but the sun was shining brightly, and the temperature might have been fifty. In this more moderate climate, Liza wouldn't bother to protect herself. Instead her hair would flap in the wind, and her heels would pierce through any chill.

"We hope you'll be comfortable," Marie said as we turned onto a side street. "Our uncle runs a small hotel, and they have a spare room this week. It's the smallest on the property, but it's the one that Domingos was willing to pay for!" The siblings laughed like thieves, and Rachel chimed in. The three of them were already in synch. Even if I tried to catch up, I would never be able to.

"We're kidding with you," said Etoile. "The room is

103

small, but the important thing is that it's on the top floor of the hotel where the loudest violin practicing won't disturb anyone. Not that I'm saying you need to practice."

"Andy loves to practice," Rachel said. "That's practically all he does. In fact we barely need a bed." Rachel put her foot over mine and applied pressure. Her comment contained no sexual innuendo. She was highlighting the fact that our calculations about staying at a big hotel with a large front desk full of anonymous clerks who didn't notice anyone's comings or goings would not match our reality. It wouldn't come close. Etoile's uncle would probably treat us like family. He'd know whether we were at the hotel or off exploring. And if we multiplied, he would notice that too.

"It's a beautiful day," said Marie. "We're happy to show you around."

"Andy will want to get straight to his practicing, but I'd be delighted to have a tour," Rachel said. "I hear there's a big Ferris wheel?"

"Only a few blocks away," said Marie.

"Are you sure you don't want to go sightseeing with us, Mr. Crus?" asked Etoile.

"Call him Andy," Rachel said, once again pawing the young man's shoulder. "We don't like formality, do we, dear?"

I shook my head. "We do not."

"Well, Andy," said Etoile, "won't you come?"

Rachel had backed me into a corner. She was still punishing me for misleading her, and this was a subtle way for her to fight back. Thus, I didn't bother consulting my own feelings. "Rachel is right. I'm very, very tired. First I need a nap. Then practice."

Rachel pounded on my shoulder until it hurt. "Andy, that doesn't sound like you at all. Usually you do the practicing first."

Chapter Twelve

Etoile was right; the room was so small that its only furniture was a double bed and a suitcase rack. It did have its own tiny bathroom, however, which was a convenience. Best of all, since the room was an isolated alcove, I could practice without disturbing anyone.

But I was plenty disturbed myself. The passages were stubborn, and they wouldn't be played smoothly without a fight. My so-called style was becoming more like an attack. Each passage sounded worse than the last. The fingerings that I'd carefully worked out were so complicated that I erased them and played intuitively instead, leaping to high notes with gusto rather than technique.

Part of the problem was my lack of concentration. One moment I chided myself for falling victim to Domingos' plans without a fight; the next I chided myself for rehearsing rather than hunting for Liza. Several times I swung open the door to the balcony, a narrow strip that ran the length of the room, but the railing was so rickety that I was afraid to lean on it. I limited myself to taking brief glimpses of the street below and the flock of rooftops all around.

I further tormented myself by imagining Rachel racing around with Etoile. Normally she only sought attention when performing. If other men noticed her, fine, and if not, equally fine. Etoile was the first man I'd noticed her flirting with besides me. I didn't like it.

Finally I put the violin to rest and hit the streets. I began by heading north and walking in the direction of the Beaux Arts Museum. The stately building hailed from a time when art was the focus of any cultured town. Two pillars flanked stairs leading up to the entrance. Banners announced a photography exhibition titled "Darkness Revealed." I wondered if such photos had any answers for me, but I didn't stop to find out. I kept walking.

The museum bordered the Place des Terreaux, the plaza

that contained City Hall and might therefore be labeled the main square. I pretended not to see the Subway sign—who needed American fast food in France? —but gravitated towards the fountain that graced the plaza. Rachel had explained that Fontaine Bartholdi was a masterpiece created by the artist of the Statue of Liberty, Frédéric Auguste Bartholdi, and that we shouldn't miss it.

Presumably Etoile had escorted her right there.

In the center of the fountain was a statue of Mother France at the reins of four stallions, which represented the country's most important rivers. Although bare-chested, Mother France wore a cloak that flowed in the wind behind her. A pair of portly cherubs stood at either side, ready to assist. She was so defiant and proud that she might have been Liza except that Liza would have been personified by the four wild beasts instead. Delft, Lyon, Mexico City, Tucson. Where would the wind have taken her by now?

A better question was where it was going to take me. For the past six months I'd embroiled myself in one mess after another. The situations were never my fault, but something inside me was unstable. As long as I'd worked the same job at the same restaurant, I'd been protected. I'd ignored troubling undercurrents as easily as I'd played everyone's favorite songs. Now that the foundations of my old life had crumbled, I was in freefall.

I reviewed the square from side to side, trying to profile the people who would live in France's third-largest city. I could imagine Domingos enjoying its cultured atmosphere. The architecture included intricate stonework from the late 1880s, giving the city a gentle touch, and the river accompanied the city as a mentor guiding a prized student. The city had easily made way for a crazy Brazilian. Whether or not it had done the same for a crazy Mexican, I wasn't sure.

Ignoring the droplets of water that hit my jacket, I stood with my back to the fountain and oriented myself using the square. I took Domingos' list of Liza's old haunts from my

106

pocket and calculated the most expedient way to hit several places in the shortest period of time.

The nearest entry on the list was a bakery, but the Boulangerie Lanterne was a madhouse. Instead of buying a croissant or two, customers were snatching up enough bread and sweets to feed a family of four for a week. I bravely waited my turn among the aggressive shoppers, but the matron behind the counter scowled when I asked for a single pastry. When I tried to show her Liza's picture on my cell phone, the woman pretended she couldn't see the screen.

I clutched my purchase and backed off, but when a younger worker came out from behind the counter to add scones to the show window, I stopped her.

"*S'il vous plaît, aidez-moi,*" I said, begging for help by pronouncing every syllable badly. "Do you know this woman?"

I slid my cell phone under her nose so quickly that she couldn't turn away, but she drew back, startled.

"I have to find her," I said. I switched to Spanish and said the same thing.

The woman shook her head. *"Voulez-vous un café?"*

No. I didn't any want coffee. A simple croissant was more than enough.

I wasted fifteen minutes finding L'Interlude Café; Domingos had told me the wrong side of the street, or maybe it had moved. The place was so crowded that I squeezed into a table, narrowly beating out a young romantic couple. When I invited them to join me, they readily accepted. They proceeded to kiss for the next twenty minutes until an elderly waiter reached our table. He recommended the hot chocolate, and I took his suggestion. But when he returned to the table and I asked him to focus on my cell phone for a single instant, he shook his head. He indicated that he needed reading glasses. Before I could borrow some for him, he was gone. And since he'd simultaneously served me the hot chocolate along with the receipt, I knew I'd have to trip him to get his attention a third time. For a while I considered doing so, but instead I savored the rich drink before moving on.

The next two cafés were along the riverbank, the *quai*. Neither were crowded, and the waiters made no excuses about poor eyesight. However, none of them remembered Liza. They might have disliked her. They might have wondered why I wanted to find her. But had they ever waited on Liza in person, they would have remembered.

I finished my tour with the H&M clothing store along the route to the Place de la République. The store was definitely Liza's style. The clothes were stylish and youthful. The above-average-height clerks wore heels as tall as Liza's. I walked among the blouses, wondering which clerk to approach. Instead the women decided for me; I saw an older supervisor send a younger woman my way to ask if I needed help.

I claimed to be shopping for a present for my wife. Since she often frequented this store, perhaps the clerk would recognize her and know her tastes? I quickly scrolled to Liza's picture, but the clerk shook her head. She couldn't recall the customer, but she could show me some handbags. Or scarves. Or jewelry.

To be polite, I let her show me a few dozen products. Then I claimed I was too overwhelmed to make a decision. Instead I would return the next day.

I had no intentions of coming back, of course. In the meantime I had work to do. It was high time to return to the hotel and practice being a soloist.

Chapter Thirteen

The rehearsal was held at the theatre, a grand old space with balcony boxes and wooden handrails. The chairs were a faded plush velvet that matched the theatre's heavy green curtains. Carpeting covered the floors, which had the ironic effect of dampening the sound.

Ferdinand Chaussée was as friendly a conductor as Steven Schroeder had been. I could understand why the men had been chosen to follow in Domingos' footsteps. They had high energy levels. They were upbeat. They were skilled conductors, yet they didn't panic when they heard wrong notes. They knew their musicians and their audiences. They knew the levels that were achievable and were satisfied with them. No wonder they led sane, peaceful lives.

I felt comfortable under Ferdinand's direction. He consulted me about a few options, but if he noticed that my preferred tempos were slower than the ones written in the score, he didn't mention the discrepancies. He probably appreciated the easier speeds because he was battling a weak viola section. Half the players were out with the flu, and whenever the principal violist stopped to blow his nose, the others hesitated before carrying on.

Occasionally I turned to exchange a glance with Rachel, but she paid zero attention to me. She'd been offered a seat at the back of the first violin section, but instead of concentrating on the music, she chatted with her stand partner. The elderly woman frequently gestured at other orchestra members. Then both women giggled as they set their bows to their strings.

My fellow performers and I didn't run into a serious hitch until we reached a difficult segue that led to the last measures of the final movement. We'd gone back to Measure 54 repeatedly so that we could practice the final page. By then I'd even memorized it. Ferdinand never lost his patience, but when the French horns came in late for third time, he stepped off the podium and did a couple of arm circles.

"Have you any suggestions?" he asked me. He'd spent a year in Great Britain, but any British phrasing was topped with a thick French accent.

"I could turn around and wait for them."

"You are the soloist. We are supposed to wait for you!" He pretended to be exasperated, but his eyes twinkled.

"That's all right. I'm not used to playing solos."

"And the French horns are not used to waiting!" He twirled around in a circle. "You could do like this." He twirled around the other way. "You could do like that."

The concertmaster, who was a young man, very precise, who no doubt played better than I did, stood and joined the huddle. "I will watch for Andy and come in with him. You cue the French horns, Ferdinand, and we will all end up in the right place."

We did as Tomás, the concertmaster, suggested. It took us another three tries to coordinate the passage, but throughout the ordeal Ferdinand was calm and collected. For my part, I was relieved that the problem lay with the orchestra rather than with me.

"We should practice this movement again," Ferdinand told me. "You don't mind?"

"Of course not."

We'd only managed a few measures when I thought I saw Liza. Although the lights had been turned up on stage, the rest of the theatre was dark, so I didn't have a clear view. A few people were listening in—Ferdinand's wife, a couple of spouses or companions, perhaps a janitor. For an ordinary rehearsal there was no reason to expect onlookers, but tonight a person with a large mop of blond hair scrutinized the stage.

I shook my head and shoulders in a physical double-take. It couldn't be Liza. She would have never sat quietly during a rehearsal. Instead she would have announced herself. She would have marched to the stage and demanded that I hand over the violin.

"Anything else?" Ferdinand asked.

110

I hadn't heard the question.

"Do you want to review anything else?" whispered Tomás.

"No, no, that's fine, I think," I stuttered.

While Ferdinand went on with the next piece, I left the stage, set my violin down in the nearest chair, and ran up the corridor, trying to approximate the row where I'd seen the blonde. I was ready to confront her; she was wreaking havoc with my personal life. She was widening the rift between Rachel and me. Why did she think she could get away with murder?

I took the stairs three at a time and dashed out into the lobby, but the woman—if she'd been there in the first place—was gone.

When my cell phone started vibrating, I wrestled it from my pocket. "Joey?"

"I'm still at Heathrow. My flight's been delayed twice. Rain. Lots of rain."

"In good conscience I should warn you not to come."

"Why not?"

"I think I'm being stalked."

Joey paused. "I thought you hadn't done anything wrong."

"I must have. I'm just not sure what."

~

"A votre santé!" shouted Tomás. The other musicians cheered and raised their glasses. Half the orchestra had descended on a local bar, where I was the only participant not enjoying a good laugh after the rehearsal. Between Villa-Lobos and the hint of Liza, I doubted my sanity. If Liza were here to pick up another stash, who would have kept the money for her?

I had voted to go straight to the hotel after the rehearsal, but Rachel had insisted that we join the crew, especially since Etoile and Marie had enthusiastically invited us. Rachel sat between them, giggling as she tried to use French and they tried to use colloquial English. If she'd noticed I was on edge, she would have blamed Villa-Lobos. Or me. Subconsciously

111

you want to see Liza, she might have told me. Thus you keep imagining her. That means it's completely your own fault.

"When Domingos was your conductor, I understand you had a female concertmaster," I said, butting in on three conversations at once. "Does anyone know what happened to her?"

"Who cares?" asked a violinist on my right-hand side.

"I hope she's far away," said another.

"Did she stay in France?" I asked.

"She was too lazy to learn any French," said a cellist. "Maybe she couldn't find her way to leave the country!"

"Are there any other decent music jobs around here? Church groups or anything like that?"

"Forget about that other violinist," said the first bass player. He moonlighted with the newspaper, so he was gathering information for a profile. "Instead tell me this: Who is your favorite composer?"

"Villa-Lobos!" I answered.

Jokingly, the musicians shouted complaints. They thought I was crazy for playing Villa-Lobos. He wasn't the hardest composer in the classical repertoire—if you really wanted to kill yourself you could play Paganini or Richard Strauss—but the Brazilian's music was certainly challenging. It combined complicated rhythms most musicians had never heard before with discordant passages that sounded wrong even when they were right.

"And your next favorite?" asked the oboist.

"Juan Gabriel."

Understandably, none had heard of the Mexican singer-songwriter. Instead we turned to matters at hand, meaning the next afternoon's rehearsal that would be followed by the Friday night concert. The following afternoon the musicians would rehearse the Ponce concerto for the final concert on Saturday night.

"How would you rank our orchestra?" asked Ferdinand.

"The best I've worked with!"

They nodded vigorously, thinking I was evading the question, but actually I was sincere. The group played extremely well. The players emphasized the dynamics more than the musicians in Delft, and they enjoyed an extra fifteen or twenty members, which gave them a strong, rich sound. While they took their music seriously, they also seemed like fast friends, which was equally important.

"Oh, yes, we're very skilled," Tomás said with a grin. "Remember *Cinquante quatre!* I'm going home with that number stuck in my head tonight." He turned to Ferdinand and imitated him. "Let's take it at—Fifty-four!"

The musicians raised their glasses for a toast. "Fifty-four!"

The conductor laughed harder than anyone. "I will not spend my evening thinking of that number. Instead I will remember the terrible silences!" He pointed to the French horn players, all of whom were sitting amongst us. "I conduct, and then there is nothing!"

Even the horn players laughed.

"Please," Tomás said, addressing me. "Help remove this number from my head. How do you say 'fifty-four' in Spanish?"

"Cinquenta y cuatro."

"Wonderful! It sounds much different from the French," Tomás said.

"Cinquenta y cuatro, cinquenta y cuatro," chanted Etoile. The others didn't need more prodding than that. In my honor they were soon happily singing a six-syllable song that they invented as they went along. Even though they were already wound up, Ferdinand insisted on another round of drinks. I appreciated their merriment. They represented the best kind of classical musicians: professionals who enjoyed their work and also their colleagues. I'd enjoyed the same luxury when I'd led the mariachi back in California, but the TucAz players had a long way to go to achieve the same camaraderie. With Liza gone, perhaps they stood a chance.

"Santé!" Rachel shouted, using the French version of

"cheers." By now she'd no doubt learned another twenty phrases in French. "Here's to our favorite number, *cinquenta y cuatro*!"

Again the musicians raised their glasses and clinked them together in exaggerated mirth. I had no choice but to join in and pretend I wished the evening would never end. But since I couldn't learn a single thing about Liza anyway, what I most wanted was to return to the hotel and keep practicing.

Chapter Fourteen

"That was a wonderful evening, Andy," Rachel said as we squeezed into our small hotel room. "You might still be thinking about Liza, but I forgot all about her. You should try it. You'll have a lot more fun that way."

"I'm sure you're right."

"But since you're so obsessed, you might as well tell me what you learned about her today."

"Nothing. But I thought I saw her in the theatre. Watching us. Watching me."

Rachel kicked off her shoes and plopped onto the double bed, which was the only place to sit. "Okay. She sneaked into the theatre and watched the rehearsal. And she would be stalking you out of envy because she would rather be playing herself?"

"I don't know, Rachel. I saw a woman watching the rehearsal. I thought it might have been Liza."

"Wouldn't the other musicians have noticed her? Wouldn't they have said something?"

"It was a sensation more than anything else. It probably wasn't her."

"Some people see things. Auras, stuff like that. You're not one of those people."

She was exactly right. I never spotted halos or anything else. I probably didn't have the sensitivity. Some days I barely noticed what was in front of me. Otherwise I'd have never made it to thirty-nine. Every time I paid attention to details, I got myself and everyone around me into more trouble than we could reasonably handle.

And yet, irrationally, I didn't like Rachel pointing out a shortcoming. "I don't sense spirits, Rachel, but I do sense people. And Liza is a real person, not a ghost."

"Seems like a ghost to me, but whatever. And I think the chance of your having seen her is about one sixteenth of one percent. But if she's anywhere in the vicinity, she'll come to the concert tomorrow night. I'd be careful back stage. And if I were you, I'd definitely stay away from staircases."

I couldn't blame Rachel for her sarcasm. I couldn't imagine Liza feeling at home in Lyon or with the fun-loving musicians I'd been partying with. They would have never warmed up to her. As if her attitude weren't bad enough, given her heavy accent when speaking English, I couldn't imagine how she would mangle French.

"What did you learn at the bar?" Rachel asked impatiently.

"About Lyon?"

She rolled her eyes. "It took you two hours to learn nothing?"

"I couldn't figure out a way to work Liza into the conversation."

I was lying. The others had asked questions so quickly that I'd never once been in charge of the conversation. Also, I didn't need another set of total strangers explaining how much they appreciated Moraes' understanding of music and inspired conducting but thoroughly disliked a concertmaster who snarled.

"You're a lousy detective, Andy, no matter how well you play Villa-Lobos."

I was beginning to think that my whole life meant choosing the wrong line at the grocery store. One small misstep grew into larger and larger problems. But I was rarely aware of making poor decisions at the time. It was in retrospect that every mistake was clear.

"Once we hit the bar, I couldn't keep my mind off the concerto. I kept replaying measures in my mind," I said.

"Bad excuse. We're on a mission. I worked harder to learn about Liza than you did, and trust me, it's not my lost cause."

I wanted to add that she didn't feel any of the same pressure I did, but I knew to keep quiet. I was only playing the concerto while Rachel was playing the entire concert, starting with Mendelssohn's lightning-fast overture from *A Midsummer*

Night's Dream.

"You were so busy chatting with your stand partner that you missed several entrances," I said. "What information did you come up with?"

"About Lyon?"

I pursed my lips, but naturally I couldn't complain.

"All right already. Don't take yourself so seriously. They hated her, loved him, couldn't figure out why she and Domingos were together."

"Maybe they love each other. Or did."

"Liza does not love," Rachel snapped. "Don't think for a second otherwise."

"Maybe she can't love and be a brilliant violinist at the same time. She reserves her emotions for her performances."

"Believe what you want to."

I didn't believe it either. Nor could I could believe I was halfway defending her. In actuality the person I was defending was Domingos. He was too talented to be a terrible judge of character. There had to be a side of Liza that I couldn't understand, or else Domingos had gross defects that I was blind to. Either way.

"Anyway, the musicians adored Domingos," Rachel said. "Funny, innovative, challenging. The conductor he replaced was an old man who, they said it, not me, was ready for the grave. Domingos was a defibrillator. But he came with baggage. Not the first year. Not until he had a longer contract. Then he slipped Liza in. The concertmaster got mad and left even though he'd played with the orchestra for over a decade."

"Ouch."

"No one liked him either, so the other musicians were glad to see him go. The advantage to having Liza was that she played several concertos, thus saving the expense of a soloist. Now the orchestra is in the black again. They were happy to let you play because, guess what, Domingos offered your services for free."

"Ah." A free soloist. No, it didn't happen. Not in the

117

classical world. I was probably the very first one. No wonder they hadn't complained about my playing. I was bonus entertainment. In the mariachi world I would have been livid. Under the present circumstances, I could relieve myself of the tiniest bit of pressure. No matter how I performed, the Lyonese would be getting their money's worth.

"But they decided they're going to pay you anyway," Rachel said. "It's supposed to be a surprise, so you'll have to pretend to be delighted about it."

"Good to know. But I suppose you didn't learn anything important about Liza either."

I regretted my words as soon as they left my mouth, but by then I was too late to change them.

Rachel got off the bed and started putting her shoes back on.

"Where are you going?"

"Out for a walk."

"Now?"

"Right this minute."

"What's the matter?"

She wrapped her scarf around her neck so tightly she might have strangled herself. "I don't want to spend another second with you."

I swallowed every piece of humility and started spitting out excuses as fast as bullets. "Rachel, I'm sorry. I'm under a lot of pressure. I'm not used to being a soloist. I have a lot more practicing to do. I haven't been able to concentrate."

Rachel whipped her coat over her shoulders. "Don't you dare underestimate me, Andy Veracruz. If you want to know the truth, Liza has a son."

I was so surprised that I forgot I'd just placed myself into the doghouse. I couldn't imagine a woman such as Liza as a tender mother hovering over a crib, picking up a wailing infant, changing diapers. "A son? Where is he?"

Rachel pulled on her hood as if it were a shield against stupidity. "She left him in Mexico."

118

"With a babysitter?"

Rachel looked at the ceiling as if it might provide an escape. "No, you dope. He stays with his grandparents."

"But who's the father?"

Rachel fastened her coat. "I'm sure I don't know. Maybe Liza doesn't either."

If I'd been faster, I would have scooted across the bed to prevent Rachel from leaving, but in the end it didn't matter. As Rachel reached for the door, someone knocked on it. Rachel didn't need to go out for a walk because a breath of fresh air strolled right into the room. It was Joey: my brother, my confidante, and, more importantly, my lookalike.

From her warm greeting, Rachel was a lot happier to see him than she was to stay with me.

~

I shouldn't have been surprised that my brother had learned more about Liza than I had. He was persistent, patient, and organized, which were three qualifications I lacked. He was also computer-savvy. He'd uncovered articles about Liza when she'd soloed in Lyon as well as in Tucson. Most critics agreed that her playing was anywhere from inspired to brilliant though frequently undisciplined. Joey hadn't yet located articles from Delft, but he'd found her name listed on a program from Mexico City dated ten years earlier. She hadn't been the concertmaster at that time. She'd only been the assistant concertmaster, which meant the player next in line.

"And before Mexico City?" I asked. Since we had no other options, we were all seated on the bed. Joey and I both awkwardly stretched our legs over the sides while Rachel sat comfortably between us.

Joey shook his head. "I can't find any records before then."

"Nobody starts as assistant concertmaster," Rachel said. "There was something earlier."

"I'm sure there was," Joey said. "I just don't know what. You didn't ask Moraes about all this?"

119

"He was evasive. My questions hit a sore spot."

"He also claimed Liza isn't guilty," Joey said. "Is he foolhardy or optimistic?"

"He breathes optimism like air," Rachel said. "For example, he thinks Andy can play anything."

I caught the jibe, but Joey pretended to take Rachel's comment at face value. That's why he always had a calming effect on me. He never overreacted while we were puzzling things out.

"Actually, my brother can play anything!" Joey laughed. "We won't talk about quality control. That's a different issue. But have you been following the Tucson newspaper online?"

Strangely, neither Rachel nor I had thought to do so. "Did it cover something about F.J. Gómez?" I asked.

"Evidently he has friends in high places. The obit says that he died of heart failure."

"A blade through the chest could cause heart failure all right!" Rachel laughed.

"The knife might have been for show," I reminded Rachel. "He probably broke his neck on the stairs."

"The newspaper article was three sentences long," Joey said. "Very suspicious. So maybe he was involved with money laundering. Drug running. He was born in Chihuahua but worked for a decade in the capital. He might have connected with *narcos* in either place."

Narcotraficantes. Drug runners.

"You don't think Liza killed him either," Rachel said. "What is it with guys and fake blondes?"

"Not so fast," Joey said. "I'm not ruling her out. But someone could have been following him. Someone who had nothing to do with Liza."

Rachel nodded. "He was a crotchety old man making a fight over stupid issues."

"I've been comparing orchestras on YouTube," Joey continued. "In Asia some of the female musicians wear different colored gowns: pinks and bright blues and reds and greens. I rather like the idea. In both Europe and South America, the women wear black, but the sleeve length varies. Some don't wear sleeves at all. Many wear jewelry. Others wear sashes or hair clips. The guidelines seem flexible."

"C.F. wanted to fight," Rachel said. "Or maybe he thought he was flirting."

"F.J.," I said.

"I don't have an opinion about your board member yet," Joey said. "But I'm not convinced Liza ran away."

Rachel shook her head so hard she shook the bed. "She was doing a hopscotch?"

"Think about what's going on in Mexico these days," Joey said. "You have to admit that kidnapping is popular. Liza might be a victim."

"I would feel sorry for the kidnappers," Rachel said. "Good try, Joey. But you're dead wrong."

"How do you know?"

"Everywhere we go, Andy keeps seeing her."

Chapter Fifteen

I woke when my brother turned over in his sleep and kicked me. I couldn't complain since it was Rachel who had volunteered to sleep on the floor. She and Joey were both dead to the world. It was barely seven a.m., and dawn hadn't yet broken. I took out the pages of music so that I could study silently. To my surprise, the passages were starting to come together. Years of listening to the piece—as well as the rest of Villa-Lobos' repertoire—had trained my ear. I was still struggling with the harder runs, but the previous night's rehearsal had helped me work through details.

The Villa-Lobos was much more complicated than anything else I'd ever performed, but by now I was starting to relax into it. I was exploring some of the nuances and matching my style to key passages. In short I was on the verge of owning it, which was exactly what I needed for an exciting and inspired performance.

I owed part of my success to my fellow orchestra members, all of whom had been friendly and supportive. Whereas some groups might resent a soloist, the Lyon musicians had welcomed me as much as the Delft musicians had. I attributed this gift to the legacy of Domingos' stint as a conductor. He had revolutionized the group, infused them with energy, and left them in competent hands.

Gingerly I fished through Joey's luggage and found a laptop. The password was predictable: the house number where we'd grown up. I wasn't used to searching the web, so I started the easy way by Googling the conductor. The Internet only revealed the biographical information I already knew: Born and raised in Río de Janeiro. Undergraduate work in Campinas. Graduate degree in conducting in Guadalajara. First job in Minas Gerais, Brazil. Then São Paolo. Then the conducting competition that had been his entryway to Europe. By now he'd guest-conducted all over. US gigs included Atlanta, Dallas, Brooklyn, Minneapolis, Tampa. The world-wide gigs included three European countries I'd never heard of. He'd conducted so many orchestras that he seemed to be in perpetual motion. Maybe he couldn't help it. Maybe he was running from something, but he didn't know what. Worse yet, maybe he did.

Despite the myriad of concrete details about Domingos' musical achievements, about his personal life I found nothing. By now he might have had a wife and a couple of preteens. Instead maybe he was obsessed with Liza. Maybe he'd been trying to tame her. At the end of the day, he couldn't live with her, couldn't live without her. Instead he hovered in a state of denial, with Liza being his one Achilles' heel.

I was too restless to stay in bed. I dressed quietly and left the room without waking my roommates. I continued with my list of Liza's favorite places. At the first café, the baristas were so young they still believed in Santa Claus. Someone Liza's age would have made no impression on them. At the second café an old man sitting near the cash register claimed he recognized Liza's picture, but he wanted five euros to remember more about her.

I was too irritated to pay. Instead I moved on, but the last places on my list, a chocolate shop and a bookstore, were both fruitless. Anyone who recognized Liza was keeping quiet about it.

~

Although I'd played well during the rehearsal, by evening I was jittery. It was common for a soloist to have only one or two rehearsals with the orchestra, but I might have voted for another five or six. There were too many rough edges, delicate spots where the orchestra gave way to the violin solos and vice versa.

Ferdinand didn't seem to notice. He stopped the rehearsal a good twenty minutes early and told everyone to rest up for the night's performance, but I didn't manage that either. I returned to the hotel with every intention of practicing, but since Rachel had gone out sightseeing with Joey, I was distracted. I wanted to be out with Rachel too, not stuck in a small room where I couldn't turn around without bumping into the wall.

By the time Rachel and I reached the concert hall that evening, the place was nearly three-quarters full. The air buzzed pleasantly as patrons took their seats. The musicians were pleased with the turnout, and Ferdinand was so cheerful that he was nearly giddy. As I listened to the Mendelssohn from the wings, I silently commended the musicians. They played precisely and with great enthusiasm, relishing the music rather than wading through it.

While the audience clapped enthusiastically, Ferdinand joined me off stage.

He wrung my hand for the fourth or fifth time that day and told me the performance would go off without a hitch. The rehearsal had gone well, so we had nothing to worry about. Such assurance was unnerving. Ferdinand probably hadn't heard of Murphy's Law, but I knew all about it.

When we started playing the concerto, I hit a sour note right off the bat. This was helpful. It was like getting a B in college; once your straight-A average was compromised, you could relax and simply do your best. As I quickly corrected the note, I automatically glanced at Ferdinand. Either he hadn't noticed the mistake, which was unlikely, or he knew to overlook it, which was the smartest strategy anyway. What was played was played. That was the beauty of live performance. The most painful passages only lasted a nanosecond. Since you couldn't fix them, you moved on.

I played the first movement, the *Torment*, as if truly tormented. I treated each phrase seriously, as if it hurt, as if I'd learned the passage while suffering the worst heartbreak. To add to the show, I wielded my bow with unnecessary flourish. I relied on a lesson I'd learned early on; if you acted as if you knew exactly what you were doing, most people would believe that you did. Anyone with enough musical training to know better would empathize.

I'd learned that valuable lesson from my first professional

music job. For the first couple of weeks I'd been in over my head, but I'd immediately developed my theatrical abilities. At first my efforts were acts of self-defense, but by acting the part, I became the part. I grew into it. The same was true for me now. I hadn't been up to the level of performing this concerto until this very moment. And now, between the audience's expectations and my own willpower, I forced myself to a higher level. I played as if I had terrible emotions inside that demanded to come out. The audience followed my every move. Some patrons swayed along with me. Even though the lights were so dim that I could only see the people in the front rows, I felt as if we were all one body, one mournful soul.

I took *Serenity* a little slower than Villa-Lobos called for, but I wanted to exercise a full vibrato and wring emotion from every note. I was proud of my vibrato—not because it was something I had practiced and then acquired, but because it was something I'd developed almost unconsciously and then learned how to take full advantage of. Fellow musicians noticed it because developing a melodious vibrato was one of the more devilish parts of learning to play the violin. People who started with the instrument late in life—meaning past the age of about ten—struggled to develop a smooth, natural sound.

I valued a melodious vibrato for several reasons. Since it mimicked the sound of the human voice, it was soothing. It masked inaccuracies in intonation. More importantly, the vibrations made the audience feel. That was always the goal—not playing everything just right, although you tried to do that, but affecting the audience on a visceral level. You wanted to reach into their souls and transport them to a higher plane. While they were listening, they might be anywhere else. They might be imagining an island paradise, a beautiful partner, times gone by. You didn't necessarily expect them to be thinking about the music. You set the stage by offering a fresh world of sound. The rest was up to them.

Joey embraced architecture for a surprisingly similar

reason. Architects designed the environments in which people lived, breathed, and acted out their lives. Homes gave people structure while music was the window dressing that colored their experience. Thus music and spatial design were part of the same packet of human comfort. As I played *Serenity*, I tried to convey that very notion. I was pretty sure I even managed it.

But, as always, serenity with me wasn't a condition. It was a moment. And it didn't stick around.

Chapter Sixteen

I might have enjoyed a relatively smooth concert. I was in the right mindset for it. But my luck didn't hold. It was as if I'd taken a shot of bourbon before the concert, and now, during the third movement, the alcohol set in and I became too relaxed.

Perhaps I should have expected such a reaction given the soothing sounds of the music itself. *Contentment* was the resolution, the place where the melodies stopped colliding and instead wound into themselves, satisfied. But the person who became too resolved was me. The movement had come together so well that I became overconfident. Smiling grandly, I sailed through a long passage without the help of the printed music. Instead of standing rigidly, I walked a few feet to the left and to the right. I was channeling Villa-Lobos in a way that was magical.

Then, out of the corner of my eye, I noticed a man who was vaguely familiar. Hispanic, probably Mexican. Brown skin. Big droopy moustache. But where had I seen him before? I told myself to pay no attention, but after a few more measures, my eyes disobeyed me and sought the man again. The theatre was too dark for me to discern his expression. I glanced away, waited for Ferdinand's cue, and then once again was drawn to the familiar figure. I walked a few steps in his direction, chided myself, retraced my steps to consult the music, and turned towards him again. He reined me in as a trout on a rod, drawing me closer with invisible twine.

Since we had several minutes left to play, I again ordered myself to concentrate. The harder I tried, however, the less I could control myself. I became a human pendulum gravitating towards the man, away from him, towards him, away.

As I walked away yet another time, I finally remembered. He was the protagonist in *Jailed by Love*. It was strange for a famous Mexican actor to attend a concert in Lyon, but that was the way of the world. Everything was becoming more universal. People crisscrossed the planet without thinking twice. They jet-setted around, never mind the carbon footprints. Nobody took those seriously. Not yet.

Suddenly I came to my senses, realized I'd been drifting, and started listening to the orchestra a half second before I needed to resume playing. Ferdinand smiled to himself, but I knew what he was thinking: Watch it. You're getting too comfortable. You're having too much fun.

But as I strolled back towards the man, I noticed that he was sitting completely alone. That was wrong. Such a famous actor would be flanked by companions or at least by fans.

Then the explanation smacked me on the side of the head so hard that I almost fell off the stage. The man was no Mexican actor. I hadn't seen him on a TV screen. I'd seen him in a photograph that featured a sailboat. He was Liza's lover, Miguel. And no matter how much he loved music, Villa-Lobos hadn't brought him to Lyon. Liza had.

I was so stunned by recognizing Miguel that I didn't give myself enough time to prepare for the penultimate solo entrance. I took giant strides to return to the center of the stage to consult the music. As I raised my violin, the tip of the instrument hit the music stand and knocked it off balance. I might have caught the stand, thus interrupting an important melodic line. Instead I watched as the flimsy strips of metal teetered, tottered, and then fell to the floor with a clang, scattering my pages across the stage. Three floated over the edge, landing in the audience.

The first violinists, who were the closest to me, stared in horror. Had I merely tipped over the stand, one of them would have picked it up. Had I taped my sheets together, someone would have retrieved them for me. Instead the loose pages fluttered downward in uncontrollable chaos.

I should have known better. Thanks to the wind, the same thing had happened to me several times when accompanying guest singers at outdoor mariachi concerts. Thanks to vigorous air conditioner, it had happened during my audition with Domingos. I had never dreamed that it would happen during an

130

orchestra concert thanks to my own lack of coordination.

My situation was desperate. I could have sloshed through the rest of the movement by memory, but if I missed an entrance or played wrong notes, I would confuse everyone, including Ferdinand. Since I didn't have the luxury of carefully weighing options, I acted on my gut instinct, just as when I'd filled in for Liza in *Scheherazade* or thrown down my violin to catch Domingos when he flew from the podium. Figuring that the loss of a few dozen measures would be minor in terms of total performance, I turned towards the orchestra and shouted *"¡Cinquenta y cuatro!"*

Ferdinand nodded. At the end of the phrase, miraculously, the orchestra jumped to Measure 54, and thus we arrived at the final stretch of music together. I was so panicked that Miguel went out of my head. I only had enough brain power to think about eighth notes. Luckily I was still functional. So was the orchestra. Since we'd gone over the ending so many times, we powered through the final chord progressions. We stayed together, ending the piece at exactly the same time.

As I took a bow with Ferdinand, the crowd applauded loudly. Many cheered. When I turned to thank my fellow musicians, half were holding up five fingers on one hand and four on the other. The rest were laughing so hard they were crying. The performance would go down in history as a near disaster. No matter how many soloists the orchestra featured in the future, I was the soloist they would remember.

Ferdinand and I went off stage long enough for him to congratulate me on my quick thinking and embrace me so enthusiastically I almost dropped my violin. Since the audience was still clapping, we returned to the stage for a bow. Then Ferdinand shouted "Encore!" The audience and musicians chimed in until I nodded.

"Aidez-moi. Je ne parle pas français," I said, using up the sum of my French to ask for help since I couldn't speak the language. I switched to Spanish and thanked everyone for such warm support. Then I started *"Rondinellas,"* Swallows, a

Mexican violin solo I'd performed hundreds of times. The piece had a combination of fast and slow passages that made it neither too fiery nor too showy. Although I closed my eyes to concentrate on my vibrato, the audience was right alongside me.

The applause was enthusiastic. I bowed in one direction and then in the other, but I didn't see Miguel. His seat had already been vacated.

~

By the time I reached the hotel, Joey was halfway through a juicy sandwich made with cheese and salami and some kind of white sauce. He'd been sitting on the bed watching a French sports channel, but he wasn't paying attention to it.

He stood and embraced me. "How did it go?"

"My performance was memorable."

He offered me what was left of his dinner, but I shook my head. "Not hungry."

"It was that bad?"

After I gave him the low-down, he started laughing. By then it was funny to me too. I had the image of hundreds of loose pages of music floating down in the audience as snowflakes. I might have been in a Bugs Bunny cartoon featuring me, Bugs Bunny.

Joey swallowed the last bit of bread and wiped his mouth. "You're sure you saw Miguel?"

"Almost sure. I packed up my violin and went straight to the lobby, hoping to spot him, but too many people stopped to congratulate me. I exited the theatre and circled it several times, but by then he'd disappeared."

"If he were there in the first place."

"I saw someone who looked like Miguel. Spitting image. That's all I can tell you."

"Why didn't you stay for the rest of the concert?"

"Too restless."

"Aren't the musicians expecting you to go out with them after the concert?"

"The least contact I have with them—"

" I know. The easier it is for me to pass as you." He pulled at a strand of his hair. "I borrowed scissors from the desk. Ready?"

We squeezed into the bathroom where, with a pair of kids' scissors, we tried to make Joey's haircut resemble mine. With a touch of black dye to mask the gray, he'd pass.

"I'm sorry you got stuck here alone all night," I said as I cut.

"Having a quiet night to practice was a luxury. By the way, in the newspaper there's a nice article about the guest artist from Mexico."

"Mexico, huh? How did they spell my name?"

"Andrew Veracruz. Not that anyone but Granny ever called you Andrew."

"I'm pretty sure it was the name she picked out."

"Ouch!"

"Sorry." I'd snipped a little too close to his ear.

I looked at Joey in the mirror, but who I was really seeing was the better version of myself, the "me" I wanted to be. How could we be so close and yet so different? How was it possible that we'd come from the same background, yet he had turned into a responsible family man who knew who he was and what his goals were while I was floundering among pieces of driftwood? Yes, as the older brother I'd witnessed my parents' marriage breaking down in a vivid way. That was true. And it was not my fault, not exactly, that I'd ended up without a steady mariachi job in a town that I hadn't planned on moving to. Yet on every level, Joey had picked a more reasonable path for his life than I had. He'd made better, more rational choices. He'd never once thrown caution to the wind except, of course, like now, when he was busy helping me.

"Andy, what's the real reason you didn't go out with the musicians?"

There he was again. Dissecting my secrets. Understanding me better than I understood myself.

133

"Etoile and Marie make me feel old. Rachel too."

"Rachel's almost our age."

"When we travel, she's like a ten-year-old on speed."

Joey shook his finger at the mirror. "If you don't keep up, she'll move on."

"Maybe she already has."

"No. But she's still miffed you didn't confess to being invited to Europe to chase Liza."

"She told you that?"

"She did."

Not only did Joey know me better than I knew myself, but evidently he knew my companion better as well. If I hadn't known that his intentions were honest, I might have been jealous. "Does she regret coming to Europe with me?"

"No. She's having a fine time."

"Then I don't see why she's mad."

Joey pointed to a final tuft of hair that I needed to trim. "You should use more psychology. You didn't tell her because you were afraid she might be angry. She interprets that as your not being mature enough to understand her feelings."

"I'm not sure what I need to do to make her happy again."

"Be honest with her, Andy. Share."

"Is that why you get along so well with Christina?"

Joey started laughing so hard I made an unfortunate slash through his bangs.

"My wife is more complicated than that. But talking to Rachel and listening to her, really listening, would be a healthy start."

That was my problem: the difference between men and women. Women didn't think the same way I did. They thought about houses, families, clothing styles. I thought about the next ten minutes.

"Don't get me wrong, bro,'" Joey said as he took a comb and examined my handiwork. "I love Christina. Very much. We're very happy. But if I were a single man, and I met Rachel, well, you get the idea."

He'd told me the same thing once before. While masquerading as me back in Squid Bay, he'd met Rachel before I had.

"Exactly what are you telling me?" I already knew, but I asked anyway.

"Try a little harder. No, a lot harder. For the rest of the trip, do whatever she wants."

"We're leaving the day after tomorrow."

Joey took the scissors from me and set them down. "So you don't have much time. But I'm sure you can manage it. You're charming in your own way."

"Are you sure?"

"Otherwise Rachel would have already left. With a little effort she'll forget you came all the way here to find another woman."

We gravitated back to the mattress and stretched out. "Rachel shouldn't be so upset."

"Maybe she thinks it's Domingos you're in love with."

"Domingos! But I'm not gay! I never—"

Joey held up his hand as if he could halt my nonsense with his palm. "You seem smitten. You rescue him from the hospital like an accomplice. Fly halfway around the world to perform a favor which, to be honest, might have gone very badly."

"You think I'm smitten as well! That's crazy! That's ridiculous!"

Again my calm, patient brother held up his hand. "Then tell me why you're under his spell."

I picked at the fuzz in the thick bedspread. Joey always asked me tough questions, the ones I didn't want to ask myself because they required too much introspection. "Domingos understands greatness in music. Not everybody does."

"And?"

"He gave me a job we both knew I wasn't prepared for."

"Most people have jobs like that. Why else?"

"I can't explain it, Joey. I admire him. He has a pure love of music."

135

"So do most musicians. Try again."

I'd never met anyone as dynamic as Domingos, which was one reason I couldn't explain him. I loved music too—I lived music. But he embodied it. When he conducted, he didn't wave a stick. His whole being transmitted meaning. Other conductors I'd worked with had been competent. Stephen had been very good. Ferdinand, superior. But Domingos took conducting to a level of perfection the others would never reach. It didn't have to do with musicianship. It had to do with soul, which was also why I couldn't figure out a reasonable way to communicate what I felt.

I shrugged. "I wish you could meet him."

"Why's that?"

"Then I wouldn't have to try to explain. But Joey, I'm lucky to have you."

"Don't I know it? But we're lucky to have one another."

"You're sure?"

"Of course I'm sure. Christina's brother is a real jerk."

Chapter Seventeen

While Joey spent Saturday morning practicing in our box of a hotel room, I let Rachel take me around sightseeing. We covered the Musée Lumière as well as the Roman amphitheatre. Normally I would have protested against so much culture, but I was in too good a mood. I'd surprised myself by playing a decent concert—and surprised myself more by not ruining things when my klutziness became a feature of the last movement. While the newspaper's music critic would have been justified in berating me for stumbling around, instead he praised the orchestra's ability to adapt to the technical difficulty of flying pages of music. He even had my name right. Meanwhile the musicians went to the orchestra's social media site to describe working with me as the "most fun they'd had in months." Several had already texted or emailed that Rachel and I should return as soon as possible, either as performers or guests. The musicians were looking forward to the evening's concert, and so were all their friends.

I was much less confident. Despite the practice we'd had as young adults, I wasn't sure Joey could manage the identity switch. As a violinist I was louder and played less cautiously. Whereas I constantly made adjustments, Joey stuck to his bowings and fingerings. We decided the best bet was for him to mention his love of French cognacs. If he seemed sluggish, his fellow musicians would assume they understood why. On the other hand, he'd performed the concerto for several wedding receptions. De facto he was better prepared to be a soloist than I had been. He was better prepared for most things.

But at least for one day, I was off the hook. I wouldn't be required to do anything of importance. Instead I could relax while Rachel escorted me around. Now that I had time to enjoy the city, I was pleased that Rachel and I had accidentally landed in Lyon. I was almost getting used to the fact that the circumstances changed unexpectedly at every turn. I still needed to restore Rachel's trust in me, but Joey's pep talk had given me new hope. Rachel's good will could be re-won over time. I couldn't blame her for being testy. I might have felt the same way had the tables been reversed except that such things didn't happen to regular people. They happened to me.

As a final nod to tourism, I agreed to accompany Rachel to the Ferris wheel in Place Bellecour, the large square on the Presqu'île, but I was relieved when it wasn't running. I wasn't squeamish about heights, but for the moment I preferred to have my feet firmly set on the ground. Instead Rachel and I had to settle for a peaceful stroll along the river banks. Thanks to the sweeping views and the cheerful sunlight, Rachel was lighthearted. While she wasn't thrilled with me, neither was she hostile. No doubt Joey had said kind words on my behalf, and she had halfway listened.

Three times I did double-takes when I saw short blondes wearing high heels, but the first turned out to be an elderly woman in her seventies. The second was younger, but still too old to be Liza. The third was the right shape and age, but her features were softer. It was merely the thought of Liza that was hovering. She was a bird in the wind, but she had migrated faster than we could chase her. Despite his reluctance to do so, Domingos would have to move on.

~

To avoid run-ins with other musicians or patrons, I had Rachel buy my concert ticket. I stalled inside a bookstore down the block until ten minutes before curtain time so that I could run in at the last minute. As directed, Rachel chose a seat at the rear of the theatre. Even with the house lights on, the other musicians wouldn't recognize me from such a distance, especially since I wore a heavy scarf that hid half my face. Attending the concert was still a risk, but I wanted to cheer Joey on. I also needed to study the performance so that I could turn into "myself" again for the inevitable after-party that Rachel would want to drag me to. She would be reluctant to leave Lyon. She was having much too much fun flirting with Etoile.

138

I slid into my last-row spot and was surprised to find enthusiastic concertgoers on either side of me. The house was substantially fuller than the night before. Evidently the townspeople paid attention to the newspaper and trusted its music critic. Once again I was thankful things had gone so well. In theory practicing always paid off, but in real life, it only paid off when the circumstances all lined up in your favor. That didn't happen all the time.

At eight o'clock sharp I expected Tomás to march out to the stage and initiate final tuning, but one minute went by and then another and another. Still no concertmaster. People were still trickling in, so evidently the theatre managers were holding the curtain in exchange for last-minute sales. No one seemed surprised or bothered by this. People sat in pairs or small groups, happily talking amongst themselves. Between the ornate balcony boxes and the sparkly chandelier, the theatre was a quaint, comfortable space. Why should anyone be in a hurry for the performance to begin?

I turned my attention to the musicians. A few were warming up, but the rest were chatting as if they were attending the concert instead of playing it. They had worked hard enough to deserve the mini-break. Joey had reported a smooth rehearsal. The entrances were clear, and the Ponce concerto was much easier than the Villa-Lobos was. The piece should practically play itself.

Tomás came out and asked for an A. The musicians tuned quickly; they were already satisfied with their instruments. Then Ferdinand came out. The musicians automatically stood, and the audience clapped enthusiastically. The man next to me shouted Ferdinand's name. So did some of the other townspeople. The conductor was the embodiment of the orchestra in a city that appreciated music. I relished his position.

However, Ferdinand did not pick up the baton. Instead he greeted the crowd and thanked them for coming. That much I caught. Then he delivered several quick sentences that I didn't understand at all. I wasn't even trying to; he'd made similar overtures to the patrons the night before. But suddenly everyone around me clapped thunderously. Offers of free tickets for the next performance, perhaps? Raffle tickets? The applause grew deafening. People hollered "bravo" with such enthusiasm that I wondered if the President of France were in the audience. I couldn't remember who the president was, however, or whether it was a man or a woman. I didn't have the tiniest grasp on the political situation and chided myself for being so unworldly.

Then Ferdinand walked off stage. For a moment I thought he might have forgotten his score. Instead he went out into the audience and took an empty seat in the middle of the front row.

I rubbed my eyes as if I were dreaming. Conductors didn't walk off stage. They didn't sit in their own audiences. The Lyon musicians were skilled, but they still needed a leader to keep the beat and help everyone start at the same time. Then a guest conductor sashayed onto the stage. One I knew. One named Domingos.

Chapter Eighteen

Domingos! I was too dumbfounded to think about logistics, how he'd arrived in Lyon, how far in advance he'd planned his attack, how he'd orchestrated such a surprise. I tried to catch Rachel's expression, but my view of her was blocked by her stand partner. I debated whether or not I should slip backstage to warn Joey. I might have texted him, but I was afraid he might have left the ringer on. No, by that point any damage would have already been done. Somewhere between the dressing room and the wings of the stage, Joey and Domingos would have already encountered one another. Joey may or may not have been quick-thinking enough to catch on.

My heart rate mimicked the tempo of Mendelssohn's killer overture. I had no idea how Domingos would react to the switch. Not only would I have to admit that I wasn't the performer Domingos thought I was, but I would also have to admit that I'd been dishonest enough to try to hide it from him. I wondered how soon I would be looking for a new job. But that was far from the immediate problem. I wasn't sure how Joey would get through the concert. He would be banking his performance on the rehearsal, but Domingos would be expecting Joey-as-me to understand his style of conducting as well as the other musicians did.

I tried to distract myself by watching their reactions, but they all seemed perfectly comfortable. Some were grinning. Others were watching Domingos, catching his eye, and smiling. He returned their communications. The shepherd was home with his flock, and everyone in the building was thrilled except for me, Joey, and maybe Rachel.

I had to consciously stop my leg from bopping up and down. As soon as the overture was over, I faked a coughing spell as an excuse to trip over ten people and get out into the aisle. Instead of leaving the hall, I stood behind the last row of seats so that I could exit the theatre if necessary. I wasn't sure I could watch the performance. I had no idea what would happen. Joey and I fooled many people, but we were no match for Domingos. The question was the timing. Would Domingos have recognized the switch at the first glance, the first words, or the first measures? The other question was my brother's reaction. Would his nerves paralyze him, or would he simply carry on?

I paced soundlessly on the carpet while reminding myself to breathe. The performance could go badly, or it could be a train wreck in an avalanche. I tried to imagine how I might have reacted in Domingos' shoes, but that was impossible. Domingos and I thought on different wavelengths. I couldn't follow his thinking because it zigzagged among countless tracks. Even when he was conducting a concert, I imagined that his mind flew off to several other places simultaneously. He was always a few steps ahead of himself, which put him a thousand miles in front of everybody else.

Neither Joey nor I were as far-thinking, but thanks to our mariachi work, we were used to last-minute changes. We were flexible. We'd played under the best circumstances, meaning at restaurants where we were fully rehearsed and fully comfortable. We'd also performed songs we barely knew with guest singers who could barely sing. We'd been in situations where we had to change keys mid-song, dodge waiters juggling stacks of plates, or interact with customers while singing. Within reason, we were skilled at going with the flow. The current situation, however, was outside all reason.

Domingos left the stage while the other first violinists shifted their chairs to make room for Joey. However, neither conductor nor soloist came out on stage. I glimpsed Rachel's legs, which were squirming. As the pregnant pause lengthened, I wondered who was having it out with whom. I wondered how I could repay Joey when I was already a billion favors behind.

Then my brother strode onto the stage. He came out quickly, but I could tell he was uncomfortable. The tux was a little loose on me, meaning that it was a little tight on him. He didn't turn to the audience until he got to the center of the

142

stage, but when he did, he grinned. The audience cheered politely; one person shouted *"¡Viva México!"*

Domingos followed closely behind, passed my brother to reach the podium, turned to the audience, and bowed deeply. No matter what the conductor was thinking, his body language said that he was thrilled to be with his audience. He nodded to Joey, who did a final tuning. Then the two men exchanged glances, Domingos raised his hands, and the orchestra started to play.

As had happened many times since childhood, my younger brother impressed me. He had been accurate in reporting that he would be able to play the concerto without much trouble. He'd rehearsed carefully and polished some of the more difficult passages. Zoran's violin was a finer instrument than either of us had ever used, and as Joey relaxed into his own performance, I could tell he was enjoying the sweetness of the melodious sound.

By the time Joey reached the end of the first movement, I was breathing normally. He had played most notes with a steady tempo. Thanks to his weakened shoulder, his playing lacked its normal bite, but he was in synch with the orchestra until the end of the movement. At that point he had to wait a millisecond for the musicians to catch up. With that action he distinguished himself from other soloists. They might not have waited.

Joey started the second movement with increased confidence. He took a step closer to the audience and smiled, comfortable with the music. They watched him intently, enraptured with the pleasing yet unfamiliar sounds. For her own solos Liza would have never chosen Mexican music. She would have insisted on Russian pieces that were more dramatic. She wouldn't have cared whether the audience wanted to hear them or not.

I leaned against the wall, and for a moment I closed my eyes. I registered details: a note I might have held longer myself, a moment when I might have switched to a fuller vibrato. But on balance I couldn't have been more pleased. My brother, the architect, was entertaining Lyon. Joey wasn't the finest violinist the townspeople had ever heard, but for this particular Saturday night, he offered an experience that, if not infinitely memorable, was certainly desirable.

Domingos was in fine form as well. He rocked and swayed, motioning for more sound from the basses and less from the winds and vice versa. He coaxed Joey into using more bow and more vibrato, creating a perfect musical waltz.

For the third movement I might have sneaked back into my seat, but as I leaned against the wall, I saw an odd glint from the nearest balcony box. It might have been my imagination. It might have been a strange moment when the light bounced off the railing in a funny way or maybe two light sources crossed one another.

I froze and watched for the glint. Then I saw it again. This time I rubbed my eyes. A glint of what? The reflection of someone's glasses? The reflection of a purse buckle or a jacket zipper? I left the hall and ran down the corridor to the door of the first balcony box. Carefully I took the handle. I turned the knob millimeter by millimeter. Finally I opened the door an inch. Then two. Then three.

A man was devouring a woman with kisses. Her hand, which was holding a program, was in the air. But she was not in distress. She was an older woman, but lithe, and the man was fully concentrated on making every kiss memorable. He was succeeding admirably. If anything, they would be praying that the concerto never end.

I returned to the main hall. This is the result of an active imagination, I told myself. You see things that don't exist. You see Liza. You see her lover. You see light sources. Knock it off. See what's there. Concentrate, for once, on the people who are closest and dearest to you.

By the time I returned to my spot against the back wall, Joey was at least halfway through the final movement. This too was going well. I noticed details such as the flute coming in too

144

soon, the trumpet cracking, and my brother playing high notes slightly flat. Overall such mistakes were small. But then I realized there were two balcony boxes. The glint was coming from the furthest one. This time I had made no mistake. I was seeing the glint of metal.

I ran down the corridor, passed the box with the necking couple, and reached the final door. I threw it open. A man about my age wearing black pants and a black jacket was hunched over the rail. He wasn't holding binoculars. He wasn't holding a cane or wearing Coke-bottle glasses. He was clutching a rifle.

The weapon was neither fancy nor new. It resembled rifles commonly used for deer hunting back in the US: a solid brown stock coupled with a black barrel. How had he smuggled it into the theatre? As to why, I could guess. He was aiming right at my brother.

"Aidez-moi!" I shouted as I ran for the figure. I plowed into him as if I were a football player, although I'd never played football. I had enough momentum to knock us both sideways. As we fell, the man pulled the trigger, perhaps by accident. The rifle went off, shooting through the chandelier and shattering glass onto the patrons below.

I struggled to my knees but then we both froze in martial arts stances. The man had black hair, big, bushy eyebrows, and pale blue eyes. His expression registered neither surprise nor confusion. He was a professional. He'd come to do a job, and any difficulties were everyday obstacles.

However, he'd counted on the relative protection of a secluded balcony box. He'd never expected anyone to notice him, and much less someone with such a vested interest in thwarting him. When the man brought the rifle to his chest, I lunged at him, grabbing onto the weapon with both hands.

"Let go!" I shouted.

The man grunted.

"Don't make me hurt you!" I shouted.

We push-pulled the rifle back and forth. I'd never trained

in self-defense, but I enjoyed several advantages. I'd taken the man by surprise, and I was half a foot taller than he was. Thanks to years of playing the violin at full volume, my arms were agile and strong. The man battled to hold onto his weapon, which allowed me to twist us around until his back was to the railing. It was him or me.

I reached my right leg backwards. When it touched the edge of the seats, I knew I had leverage. Summoning up all my strength in a single moment, I threw all my energy against the weapon. As I followed through, my rival did a backflip over the railing, kicking all the way.

I slumped backwards and fell to the floor. People started screaming, but I didn't look over the rail. My fight with the sniper kept playing in slow motion: rushing him, grabbing the rifle, struggling for control, overpowering him. Repeat. By the time the two security guards made their way to the balcony, I was stunned into immobility. They shouted at me, but I didn't know what they were saying. I didn't care. All I could think was that someone had tried to kill Joey and that I had saved him. I had acted without hesitation.

By then a dozen concertgoers rushed the booth. They bent to my side asking if I were all right. I nodded weakly. I wasn't hurt physically. When I heard the ambulance in the background, I knew it wasn't coming for me.

It took Rachel several minutes to squeeze through the huddle and join me on the floor. She threw her arms around my neck and thanked me for bravely risking my life to protect the orchestra. She kissed me as she cried, and I felt her wet tears hit my shirt one after the other.

I was touched by her reaction. I couldn't remember anyone ever crying over me before, and I was glad I had finally done something she could appreciate. I didn't have the heart to tell her that I was only trying to protect my brother.

Chapter Nineteen

Joey and I were escorted to the police station by two very young officers who had never dealt with pandemonium. While one drove, the other made quick calls on his cell phone, no doubt to superiors. During the short drive, my brother put together the details: the way the would-be sharpshooter had fallen on top of several people, the way pieces of the chandelier had shattered and flown in all directions, the way he and Domingos had continued for a dozen measures before they realized something had gone horribly wrong. Then the players panicked. They crashed into one another in their hurry to exit the stage. The patrons reacted similarly save for the dozens who whipped out cell phones and tried to call for help at the same time.

Once at the police station, we were escorted to a desk in the back corner. Soon all the officers crowded around, eager to hear the story. Neither aggressive nor demanding, they asked me to tell them what happened in infinite detail. I explained myself slowly, in English, while Etoile supplied the occasional words they didn't understand.

I had gone through the story a couple of times when the Chief of Police arrived. He'd been called in from a dinner party, and his moustache was still full of bread crumbs. The stately man waved everyone else out of the way and sat across from me. Once again I recounted what I remembered. Then the Chief of Police asked about the assailant. What language had he used? I didn't know; the man had grunted rather than spoken. What was the man's ethnicity? I didn't have a clue; the others could guess as much as I could. What was the man's attitude? He was calm and confident. He hadn't expected interference. He had never expected to fail.

One of the officers came over and tapped the Chief of Police on the shoulder. The hospital had called; the shooter had died from his injuries. I assumed he had broken his neck, but I didn't understand the medical jargon. Instead I understood the

147

urgency in the officers' voices.

I had forced a man over the balcony and killed him. I expected to be hauled straight to jail, but instead I suffered no consequences. No one even discussed the fact that I should have been on stage rather than in the audience. As far as the concertgoers were concerned, I had prevented a lunatic from assassinating their most beloved ex-conductor. The consequent good will I garnered was extraordinary. What with Domingos and Ferdinand vouching for me and exchanging quick words with any police officer who would listen, I was never once treated as a Person of Interest. I had become an accidental hero, and everyone in the station wanted to thank me.

The attention embarrassed me because I didn't feel like a hero. I hadn't tried to kill anyone. My reactions were instinctive: Stop the man with the rifle at all costs. In hindsight I might have wrestled away the weapon. I might have shouted to Joey and Domingos to take cover. Instead I'd used my height and agility to employ the easiest solution.

The next hours were grueling. Since they couldn't wrench any more useful information out of me, the officers interviewed the dozens of concertgoers who had trooped down to the station of their own accord. None remembered seeing the sniper. None of the theatre staff recognized him either. That left the police officers with the task of asking the same useless questions and getting the same useless answers. Finally the theatre manager arrived with a list of the evening's ticket sales. He had discovered an interesting fact: The ticket for the balcony booth had been purchased during the hour before the concert. In cash.

~

It was four in the morning by the time the police dismissed the lot of us and we adjourned to the hotel. Since we were starving, Ferdinand convinced his cousin—the only staff member on hand at the time—to open the kitchen for us. Ferdinand himself put together a makeshift meal for a select crew: he and his wife Michelle, Marie and Etoile, Rachel and

148

me, Joey and Domingos.

The enormity of the evening's events had been replaced with simple hunger. We devoured stale bread, cheeses, fruits, and cold cuts while we tried to make sense of things. What kind of crazy person would commit a random act of violence in a theatre? How could anyone be disgruntled enough to protest against classical music?

Since we couldn't find convincing answers, we focused on drinking. We polished off several bottles of red wine. As we recovered from the close-call, we let ourselves go, growing merrier by the minute. While our French hosts were delighted by Domingos' surprise visit (he'd arrived an hour before the concert), they were even more delighted that Joey and I were lookalikes. They were amused by our ruse down to the detail of sneaking in and out of the hotel room. They assumed that we'd substituted for one another as a joke rather than as a necessity.

"When did you catch on?" I asked Ferdinand.

He turned to Joey. "I didn't. I assumed that you were nervous, so you had a drink of some kind before the concert. That explained why you reacted so slowly. When Domingos greeted you backstage, you needed several seconds to cough up his name. I was afraid you were completely drunk and wouldn't be able to play the concert!"

Joey refilled Ferdinand's glass and then his own. "I'd seen your pictures from the orchestra websites. I recognized Domingos as well, but my brain kept telling me he was in Brazil!"

The group laughed heartily, especially the conductors.

"What about you, Domingos?" I asked. "When did you realize my brother was not me? And how?"

"A facial expression?" asked Rachel. "Andy is half an inch taller, if you're good with heights."

"I'm not," Domingos said. "But in case you ever want to trick another conductor, let me give you a tip. Learn to hold your violins in exactly the same way."

Involuntarily I made a motion of putting a violin to my

shoulder. Our teacher had been strict about where we placed our instruments; I would have assumed that Joey and I did so in the same way.

"My brother is sloppy when he's tired," Joey suggested.

Domingos laughed. "Guess again."

I'd worked harder on technique and had more dexterity, but I didn't want to say so.

"Andy plays with more bow?" asked Marie.

"More vibrato," said Etoile. "To cover up the wrong notes!"

Domingos clasped his hands. "Good guesses, but wrong. Do you give up?"

Everyone chimed in with suggestions. I tilted my head more. Joey played closer to the bridge. I used more rosin.

Domingos shook his head. "Joey, I knew you were an imposter when we were standing in the wings." He picked up a knife and a spoon. "Here is the violin," he said, holding up the spoon. "When Andy takes the bow with his left hand rather than his performance hand, he holds it about halfway." He demonstrated with the knife. "That means he puts his oily fingers on the hair. That's bad for the bow, but some violinists do it anyway."

"I don't," Joey said.

"Exactly. You are careful to hold your bow at the frog so that you avoid touching the bow hairs. *Voilà*."

"So you knew before I started playing."

"I did."

"Why didn't you say anything?" Joey asked.

"What is better than a double charade?" He turned to me. "Andy, why not admit that you didn't want to prepare two concertos at the same time?"

I shrugged. "I didn't want to let you down."

"Ha! I ask the nearly impossible, and you're afraid you don't do enough. But anyway, the solution was ingenious. If it hadn't been for our shooter friend, you would have fooled almost all of us. Of course, you might also be dead! Come.

150

Let's have another round."

"Domingos," I said, "you might have been killed tonight. How can you possibly be so cheerful?"

"Andy, I am almost forty-five. Even if I never wake up tomorrow, I've had a good life. I've done what I've wanted to. I've conducted orchestras all over the world and worked with some of the world's best musicians. Don't think I've run out of ambition! But I also recognize that I've been lucky. I've had a great life. And that's the way you have to think. Be thankful for what you've lived. *Lo bailado no se le quite*, as they say in Spanish. What you've danced, they don't take away. It's important to keep that in mind."

"But somebody might have come to the concert specifically to kill you," said Marie. "That would make me reflective."

"Perhaps I reflect too little! But terrorism is random. You shouldn't think about it. Why not? Because there is nothing you can do. You will never know how to avoid the wrong place at the wrong time even if you spend your life trying to calculate such a thing. Either you have good luck, or you don't. Nothing more."

Marie and Etoile jumped in with statistics about incidents in the region and also in Paris. Despite Domingos' warning about reflecting, they started doing precisely that. While they traded facts, I tried to get a word in edgewise, but Joey pulled on my arm and whispered, "They've decided the attack was random. Let's not change their minds."

It didn't take a genius to realize that Joey had the best strategy. Why should they know that it was probably Domingos himself who had at once delighted but endangered them or that Liza's lover had been stalking the theatre looking for signs of either of them? I tried to concentrate on the larger picture. I too had enjoyed a lucky life. I had a brother who would do anything for me. I had a companion. I had new musician friends in Europe. I was alive.

Finally the Chaussées took their leave, but Joey and I

made no attempt to move. Neither did Domingos or Rachel.

"We've almost killed this one," I said, holding up a bottle of cognac. "Final nightcap, anyone?"

Joey nodded. I poured each of us a shot.

Rachel turned to Domingos. "So exactly how many enemies did you make here in Lyon?"

Domingos laughed. "None that I know of."

"No jilted lovers?" Joey asked.

"Not so many. Only a dozen!"

"How about rival conductors?" I asked. "Everybody I talked to around here worships you. Even Ferdinand."

"This attack didn't have to do with music," Rachel said. "It's more personal."

Domingos exhaled slowly. "I know that. This doesn't have to do with me."

"Of course not," Rachel said. "It has to do with Liza."

"Exactly." Domingos regarded each of us in turn. "Please realize that I would never intentionally put anyone in danger, but it's possible I was followed."

"All the way from Brazil?"

"Presumably. But I've learned my lesson. I don't know where Liza is and neither does anyone else. The trail is dead in more ways than one."

"So now what?" I asked.

"We go back to Tucson. We pretend that nothing happened."

"Except that you don't have a concertmaster."

Domingos pointed at me with the tip of his index finger. "Sure I do."

"Me? I didn't audition for that chair. It wouldn't be fair."

"It's an emergency. You'll do."

"What about Philip? Or Kenny?"

"Those pussyfoots? They'd never accept the position. But you, Andy, you're too untrained to know what you're up against. You'll do fine."

"That's exactly the point! I don't have the training. I don't

152

have the experience. I don't—"

"Andy, the next time someone tries to assassinate me, you're the only one who will be brave enough to walk into the bullet."

Although he winked, I wasn't sure he was kidding.

"Another shot?" Joey asked, trying to make a joke as he held up the bottle.

"Not for me," Rachel said. "I'm off to bed."

Domingos stood. "Me too. I have an early flight. If I hurry I can sleep for three hours." He turned to Joey. "I'm in Room 304. There are two beds. Join me at whatever time. That is, unless you enjoy sleeping on the floor."

"Thanks."

"For Andy's brother? Anything!" He waved goodnight as he escorted Rachel out of the room.

"You played really well," I told my brother. "It's a shame you couldn't finish the concert."

"Ferdinand already invited me back. As soon as I reach London, I'll check my schedule."

Joey didn't sound excited. He sounded businesslike. The lighting in the room was dim, but I knew my brother better than anyone else in the world, probably even better than his wife did. I couldn't see his face clearly, but I could tell that he hadn't regained his sense of self.

"Bro,' what's wrong? You were confident, and you played with inspiration. You performed with an alternate conductor but never missed a beat. You should be ecstatic."

Joey took a deep breath. "Andy, what do you really think was going on tonight?"

"Ferdinand Chaussée isn't ambitious enough to have enemies. Domingos was clearly the target."

"Your reasoning?"

"I told you what happened in Tucson with the podium. Tonight's madman was hired, presumably by Miguel."

"Andy, no one here knew Domingos was coming."

"Miguel probably figured that either Domingos or Liza

153

would turn up. He would have been prepared for either scenario. Or having someone shoot me, Domingos' stand-in, might have been satisfaction enough."

"I think it's a long shot. You do too, or you would have mentioned it to the police."

"I couldn't think of anything concrete, and I didn't want to sound like an alarmist. But maybe someone was following Domingos. Maybe he mentioned something on World Friends. He's fond of social media."

"I already checked, Andy. There was nothing. He wanted to be a surprise."

"You're sure?"

"I checked three times. But your name was in an article that came out the day before the concert. There was also the review from last night."

"What are you saying?"

He leaned forward. "I have some bad news, but I wasn't sure Rachel needed to hear it."

The heater had been running all evening, but suddenly I noticed that it had turned off. "Oh?"

"Can you guess?"

"My old boss escaped from jail?"

"Released on a technicality."

"For a possible homicide?"

"In California all the jails are full. They're letting people go right and left. Don't be so surprised."

I asked despite knowing the answer. "So what are you saying?"

"Domingos wasn't the target. You were."

I went up to my room and lay in bed, but I didn't come close to sleeping. Me the target of a sniper? No. It wasn't possible. I had implicated my ex-boss in a murder, but I'd done so discreetly. He wouldn't have known I had anything to do with it. And he was frugal. He wouldn't have been flitting all around Europe looking for me. He would have waited until I was back in the US.

154

No, the attack had to do with Miguel, and Miguel had to do with Liza. That was the only reasonable explanation. But my mind kept playing "what if"? What if I hadn't seen the sniper in time? What if I hadn't made it to the balcony box? What if I'd been faced with the horrible task of calling Christina from the morgue? Instead Joey and I had been lucky. Extremely lucky. We may have been in the wrong place, but we were there at the right moment.

This time.

Chapter Twenty

Joey and Rachel and I were early getting to the Lyon–Saint-Exupéry Airport. We sailed through security and found seats in the nearest lounge. Rachel and I had an hour to spare. Joey had a longer time to wait, but he refused to sit down. He shifted from one foot to the other as he gazed at the myriad of shops advertising duty-free.

"Are you feeling all right?" I asked.

Joey took out his wallet. "I should have picked up something for Christina, but I didn't find anything I liked. I've got chocolate for the girls, but I don't always know what to do for my wife." He held out a fifty-euro note. "Rachel, would you mind? I mean, I don't mean to be sexist or anything, but—"

Rachel smiled as she took the bill. "I don't mind shopping around, but no guarantees."

I waited until she was out of earshot. "Usually you don't have any trouble buying for Christina." My brother was the only person I knew who had a stable relationship with a partner. He and Christina were in perfect synch, never had heated arguments, and, as far as I knew, kept no secrets. That meant they had a much more solid relationship than our parents ever had. "Are you guys having any trouble?"

Joey's tone changed completely. "Andy, my trouble, as usual, is you. What do you remember about the hitmen you met in Squid Bay?"

"I try not to remember anything about them."

"When you get back to Tucson, I want you to change your phone number."

"I did that last summer."

"Do it again."

"I see. You think I should get an Arizona number."

"No. Use some other state. You can order a cell phone online."

"You're not overreacting?"

"And another thing. You need a new name."

"But—"

"I mean for the concert programs in Tucson."

I paused. "The orchestra members know my name is Andy."

Joey raised his eyebrows. "Tell them that there's a famous musician from Mexico named Andy Veracruz and you don't want anyone to confuse the two of you."

"You want me to make up a last name?"

"Go with Crus. With an S. That's a stupid spelling anyway. Antonio Crus. No. Try Tony. That way neither of the initials will mirror your own."

Rachel waved as she passed us, empty-handed, and continued to a store opposite our waiting area.

I sat back against the uncomfortably hard plastic. "The musicians will think I'm vain. Or delusional."

"Tell them that this other Veracruz fellow made a terrible recording. That you need to distance yourself."

"What if you're overreacting?"

Joey sighed deeply. "Why do you think I moved my family to London?"

"Only temporarily."

He shrugged. "Still."

I'd claimed that we were perfectly safe in Squid Bay and that the hang-ups hadn't meant anything. Joey hadn't believed me. He reasoned that a murderer would have no qualms about a repeat performance. When Joey found a short-term contract in the U.K., he'd jumped on it.

"I thought you liked living in London. Theatre, museums, etc.," I said.

"That's beside the point. I don't believe in coincidence. You shouldn't either. A killer is released from jail, your name appears in an international newspaper, and a shooter comes to the theatre while he thinks you're performing. You can say what you want to, but that's no coincidence."

"Unless he was there for Domingos."

Joey shook his head. "You go right on kidding yourself. It's been nice knowing you."

My brother always reasoned things out more carefully than I did. Our whole lives, whenever I was busy interpreting a gut reaction, he was making lists of facts. I knew better than to discount him, but I wasn't ready to give in. "Going by another name would be like having two identities. I would have trouble remembering who I was. People would call out 'Tony' and I wouldn't answer. They would think I was ignoring them."

"You'd get used to it."

"It's confusing to be two people."

"You're a Gemini. You can deal with it. And you'd stay alive."

The shooter had undoubtedly come for Domingos. The man was well known and successful, so lots of people would be jealous of him. While I had indeed called 88-Crime to help identify a killer, that had been in California several months earlier. It was a minor detail, nothing more.

"I found a bracelet," Rachel said as she returned to us, "but I'm not sure it's right. Won't you come look?"

Joey smiled as he rose. "Thank you so much, Rachel. I'd love to see what you found."

While my girlfriend headed off with my brother, his words echoed in my head. Only some twenty hours separated the appearance of the online review of my Lyon performance and a shooter's attempts to kill a musician. Anybody using Google alerts might have seen the reference. In that case there was plenty of time to organize a hit even from a different continent. Planes flew from the US to Europe all day long, but the shooter might have come from anywhere. He seemed to have been working alone, but Joey-as-me would have been a simple target: a soloist at a concert in an otherwise peaceful town. It should have been perfect.

My next thought was only slightly less disconcerting. How long would it take an assassin's employer to learn that he had failed? I wasn't sure how routinely assassins checked in.

Maybe not very often.

~

We arrived in Tucson so late that we went straight to the TucAz rehearsal from the airport. Although he should have been suffering from jetlag, Domingos, who had arrived a couple of hours earlier, had an endless supply of adrenalin. I wondered if he spiked his Gatorades with caffeine. While I tried not to yawn, he conducted as if he'd had a full night's sleep and twenty hours to study the music. Several times I lost my place, and Philip had to point to the right spot. This should have been embarrassing, but instead I didn't care. I was too tired to be nervous. I played automatically.

As soon as the rehearsal was over, Domingos motioned for me to stay behind. I took extra time putting away my instrument so that the other musicians would clear out and I could talk to the conductor in private.

"I got off on the trio," I said. "I couldn't get the hang of the rhythm. I'm happy for you to let Philip be the concertmaster. Or Kenny. They're more studious. They're more prepared."

Domingos waved his hand. "They're scared shitless. We already went over all that. Forget about them."

"I played terribly tonight."

"Yes, yes. You were sight-reading and you were tired. Don't worry about it. But there is a small problem on the program for the next concert. The personnel manager sent the information to the printers before I could warn them, so Philip is listed as the concertmaster."

Saved by timing. "That's perfectly all right. The only people in Tucson who know me are Rachel and her sister, and they already know my name."

"I'm afraid the printers also failed to fix the misspellings, so you're still listed as Anthony Cruz."

"Domingos, I want to keep the mistakes."

"What?"

"See, there's this other Andy Veracruz who lives in Texas,

160

and he made this horrendous mariachi recording with the Schubert version of *Ave Maria*. I don't want to be associated with him. Ever."

Domingos watched me carefully but said nothing. After a few seconds, he surveyed the room. The janitor was still putting away the last chairs, and the clarinet player was taking apart the second of his instruments. Domingos pretended to organize the scores in his briefcase until we were alone.

"Andy, you're not the kind of guy to worry about a rival musician. As far as I know, you have no plans for making any mariachi recordings, although sometime in the future we might make one together."

I said nothing.

"When I Googled Andy Veracruz at the time of your audition, you were the only one I found."

"I would really like to change my name," I said almost inaudibly.

For a moment he held my eyes. Then a smile began at the corner of his mouth. "You got a woman pregnant?"

"Well—"

"I wondered why you left California so abruptly."

"But that's not what happened."

"Of course not! She got pregnant and claims you're the father. That can be damned uncomfortable. Believe me, I should know." He held up two fingers. "They tried it on me twice. The first time, the father was somebody else. The second time, the woman wasn't even pregnant. I know all about that kind of stuff. Some women will do anything for a free carpet ride. Not that I'm against women, mind you. It's a small percentage who try to take advantage. Unfortunately, the more famous you are, the more often you're a target."

"But—"

"Why do you think I don't date? That's why. I'm waiting until I'm old enough to enjoy women who've been through menopause." Although we were alone, he put his head closer to mine and whispered. "So what are you going to tell Rachel

161

about this name change?"

"There's this mariachi recording—"

"Okay, okay. I get it. So you want to be Anthony Cruz?"

"How about Tony?"

"Okay, then, Tony Cruz."

"Maybe even Crus. With an S."

He cocked his head. "Crus with one S. This is getting complicated. Maybe I'll call you T.C. for short. Nice to meet you. Are you going to change the name on your passport?"

I was sure he was kidding, which was why I pretended to take him seriously.

"I hadn't thought about a passport yet."

"You need to."

"Why?"

He turned on his cell phone. "Because we're going to Mexico after the next concert. I found a midnight flight."

"Mexico?"

"T.C., I have a zillion frequent flier miles. I can't use them all myself."

"I'll still be jet-lagging from Europe. I won't even have time to do laundry."

"Me either," Domingos said brightly. "So what?"

How could I argue against total confidence? My curiosity nudged me until I gave in. "Why would we want to go to Mexico?"

"Why not? It's a fine country. Nice people." He patted his stomach. "Great food. Forget about the fake enchiladas you find around here."

Domingos was not one pound overweight, and I was sure he never focused on food. Suddenly I felt tired. "Why else would we want to go to Mexico?"

He whipped out his phone, and for a moment I thought he was going to text someone important mid-conversation. Then he scrolled through some applications until he found his photo archive. He immediately located the picture of a woman. "Remind you of anyone?"

162

The woman wore sunglasses and her head was turned to the side, but her stance was unmistakable. "Liza."

"That's right, T.C. She was tagged in World Friends. I downloaded the photo right away, but within minutes she removed it. Recognize the place?"

She was crossing a pedestrian zone. Behind her was a colonial-style church with two towers, but it wasn't in the center of the square as in most Mexican towns. The church was on the corner, thus ruining the balance. "If I didn't know better, I'd say it was San Luís Potosí."

"You do know better. That's exactly where it is. See? You're exactly the man I need."

So Liza had surfaced in a thriving but otherwise forgettable Mexican city that was nearly a dozen hours north of the capital.

"You know the city well?" Domingos asked.

"No, but I've visited a time or two. My cousin's daughter lives there."

"Is she a musician?"

"Probably not."

"They have a great orchestra. Evidently half the players are from Russia. You have a cousin, you said?" Domingos asked.

"I have two in Aguascalientes. Brothers. But that's a couple of hours away."

"And a niece in San Luís."

"Technically she would be a second cousin."

"Terrific. Let's call her now."

"Why would we do that?"

"Because we're going to visit."

"I don't remember agreeing to go with you."

Domingos put his hand on my arm. "You will. So please call. Do you have the phone number with you?"

"She has a baby, so tonight it's too late. Why do you want me to contact her?"

Domingos stared at me as if I should have guessed the

163

answer, but I hadn't yet learned to think along his lines. "Because, Andy, we'll need a quiet place to stay."

"Are you sure that Liza is worth the trip?"

Domingos swept his hand from one side of the room to the other as if he were still running the rehearsal. "I am a conductor, Andy. A leader of people. Not everyone, of course. I don't lead the town in a parade. But I lead musicians, and those musicians lead people's hearts. Do I make mistakes? All the time. But I have never, ever not worked for the benefit of my orchestra and in turn for the benefit of my musicians. Is Liza worthy? She is the finest violinist I have ever worked with. Don't think I'm dissing you. You're coming along. But you're no Liza. It is my duty to help her. Is my mission a waste of time? Perhaps. But I'm not giving up without a fight. You are probably the only person who can help me. But I'm a realist, Andy. If you're not up to the challenge, I must accept this. Not everyone holds my values. But I know that you are a musician at heart. That means you care about people. You help improve the quality of their lives. I know good and well that you don't care about helping Liza, but I'm ready to bet my baton that you want to help me. So how about it?"

There were a lot of things I wanted to say. That Domingos was indeed crazy. That I was a musician because I loved music, not because I was a humanitarian. That it stroked my ego to sing a request. That down deep I was a selfish guy who wanted to make enough money to support himself and maybe deserve a lover. I wanted to voice objections, too, such as the fact that chasing after Liza was worse than trying to find a feather in a rainstorm. That she didn't want to be found. That we wouldn't know what to do once we'd found her. Objections zipped through my mind, but I didn't voice any. I didn't think about the logistics or Rachel or Joey or anyone else. I only had the energy to say four words. Since I'd used them with Domingos once before, they rang loudly in my head even before I uttered them.

"When do we leave?"

164

Chapter Twenty-One

The next evening, Domingos was in high spirits. He started rehearsing the Dvořák symphony with aplomb. At first I went along with him, making notations in the music so that I could remember to play softer or louder or to use different parts of the bow. Then a disturbing thought knocked me out of whack. If I had been the target in Lyon after all, we might be dealing with two would-be assassins rather than one. Whoever had messed with Domingos' podium might still be lurking in Tucson whereas the conductor assumed that all his problems had ended in France.

I was so caught up in my thoughts that I missed the repeat in the trio. Philip was off in space, so he missed it too. Kenny saved the section by plowing ahead exactly as he should have, and the other violinists were smart enough to follow him.

"You're thinking like a mariachi player!" Domingos said, grinning at me without missing a beat.

Within a couple of measures I found my place, but I had a new problem: I didn't know how to tell Domingos he was in danger. My concentration, rarely stellar anyway, was shattered. Domingos' attacker might be with us in the rehearsal hall. It was a short, nondescript building whose address didn't appear on the symphony homepage, but the location was hardly a secret. It was included on all the audition materials. Anyone nosing around on the website would have found it.

"Louder!" Domingos shouted when we reached a climactic moment.

I guessed at the notes while checking the room's EXIT signs. I wanted to be sure to know where they were. Running might be the only option.

When Domingos granted a break, I tried to approach him, but too many other musicians rushed the podium, nearly tripping me in the process. The bassoon player wanted to check on a crescendo, the bass player questioned a rest, etc., etc.

I bypassed the drinking fountain where many of the others

congregated and left the building. I wanted to convince myself that nothing was wrong. For several long moments I let my eyes grow accustomed to the night. Then I circled the building like a cat on the prowl.

A few yards away someone was burning wood. On the next street over, one motorist honked at another. Across the way, a street light hummed and blinked. Not a single thing seemed unusual, but that only made me feel more unsure.

I circled the building a second time for good measure. The same number of vehicles were in the parking lot. The building across the street was still dark.

The only thing that was active was my imagination. Maybe the expensive podium had been poor quality after all. Maybe the only possible danger was Liza, and she was miles away.

By the time I returned to the rehearsal room, Domingos had started without me. As soon as I picked up my violin and allowed Philip to show me where we were, I caught Domingos' eye. He winked, but I didn't smile back. I put my index finger to my lips and subtly pointed to him.

Domingos looked at me quizzically. He didn't understand that I wanted to talk to him in private. If he hadn't met Rachel, he might have thought I was flirting. I resigned myself to being stuck in a rehearsal without a better way to communicate with its leader, but every few seconds I checked the doors for signs of unexpected movement. When I saw a big stick out of the corner of my eye, I whirled around so fast I scared the janitor. His mop banged against the door jamb, but none of the other musicians noticed. Not even Domingos.

I was so worked up that the softest sounds in the percussion teased my imagination. Despite Domingos' cues, I missed one entrance after another. I played out of tune, and several times I ignored the dynamics so noticeably that the woman who was leading the second violinists gave me a dirty look. I ignored her and told myself that I was like a horse wearing blinders. If I could make it to the finish line, even in last place, I'd be okay.

The next minutes were painful. I told myself not to be distracted, but after every few measures I looked over my shoulder. Thanks to Philip and Kenny I survived, but my efforts had been mediocre. I didn't care.

Thanks to union rules, Domingos released us right on time, but again, he was immediately surrounded by musicians whose attention to detail bordered on neurotic. "At the beginning of the *Andante,* was it a *mezzo piano* or a *piano*?" asked the second clarinetist. Who cared? Didn't he realize the part was unimportant? Nobody could hear him over all the brass.

I hovered behind Domingos while he patiently addressed each ridiculous detail.

"Yes?" He sensed that I was behind him before he turned around.

I finally had him to myself, but several other musicians were still milling about.

"Tengo que hablarte." I have to talk to you.

"Díme." Tell me.

"A solas." Alone.

Domingos packed up his scores. "Walk with me. I have to Skype with Brazil in a few minutes, and I since I forgot my laptop, I have to hurry home."

I scrambled to put away my violin and catch up with him, but by then a percussionist was complaining about one of the timpani.

"Uh huh, uh huh," Domingos said dismissively. "I'll see to it at the next rehearsal." He turned to me. *"¿Qué tienes?"* What's up?

"Algunos tiempos." Some tempos.

"Tempos," Domingos nodded. "Do you remember where my house is?"

"Of course."

"Meet me there in half an hour."

Since I didn't quite trust my memory, I followed him,

ignoring speed limits and running lights the way he did. We blasted past the university, took a short cut through El Con Shopping Mall, and slid down a side street to reach his two-story stucco abode.

While he dashed inside, I walked up and down the street to kill a little time.

Domingos had chosen a quiet, residential area in the middle of town. The properties were well established and distinct. The yards were carefully landscaped with mesquite trees and cacti. Nearly all proudly displayed Protected by American Safety signs. They also boasted two-car garages, so by this time of night no cars were parked on the street.

I had the neighborhood all to myself.

~

After twenty minutes I went to Domingos' front door, but I didn't bother to knock. His voice boomed Portuguese, so I knew he was still Skyping. He wasn't shouting; his normal speaking voice was loud. As he continued his conversation, his volume rose. Since I couldn't catch more than a few isolated words, I concentrated on tone. One moment Domingos sounded angry, but then his laughter would erupt like water shooting from a fountain. And the pattern would repeat.

Finally there was a lull. Before I could knock, the door opened. Domingos was still talking, but he was carrying the laptop and saying *"sim, sim, sim"* while inviting me into the living room.

I might have guessed that the room would have a sleek, modern look. The walls and carpet were white. To the right a long white couch hugged the wall. To the left a baby grand stood before the picture window. The piano's music stand was covered with papers: some printed, some blank, some with handwritten notes. The bench was at an angle as if Domingos had abruptly left the keyboard to attend to something else.

The room included a museum's worth of memorabilia. The east wall was adorned with pictures: Domingos in a picture with the famous opera singer Placido Domingo, Domingos

168

conducting in a park during a sunny afternoon, Domingos rehearsing with students at a school. The north wall had a series of art prints with musical themes: a symphony hard at work, an emphatic conductor, violins floating through the air. The bright splotches of reds and yellows and greens added to the surroundings without overwhelming them. I went close enough to read the artist's name: Dufy.

Domingos closed the computer and indicated the comfortable plush couch. "Nightcap? You bothered to come all the way here, so we might as well drink something."

"A beer, if you've got one."

He returned with two glasses, two bottles, and a lime cut into wedges. I'd never heard of Oculto beer, but the design on the label included a skeleton. How was that supposed to be a marketing tool?

Domingos left again and returned with music scores. "Okay, Andy. I mean T.C. Which tempos are you worried about? Yes, I could take the finale slower in the symphony, but don't you prefer a challenge?"

No wonder musicians appreciated him. He was that concentrated. Despite an exhausting rehearsal, he was prepared to dive right into the tiniest details.

He opened the score and whipped through the pages as if he were racing himself. "I'm not quite sure how I feel about the beginning of the Second Movement. Did you think it was too abrupt?"

"Domingos, I didn't come about the music."

For a moment he raised his eyebrows as if a ghost were standing behind me. Then he calmly closed the score. "You don't want to go to San Luís Potosí."

"Domingos—"

He used his right palm as a stop sign. "Hear me out, Andy. I can understand your concern. Yes, Mexico is a danger right now. Corruption, kidnappings, you name it. But San Luís is a pleasant, tranquil town. You might say I should go by myself. You might be right. But I need your help, Andy. You're

169

observant. Look what happened in Lyon! You literally saved my life, which is why I'm asking you to help me now."

"Domingos—"

"If you don't want to leave right after the concert, we could wait until the next morning. I haven't bought the tickets yet."

"Forget about Mexico," I blurted out. "We need to change the venue for tomorrow's performance."

"What?"

"We have to perform someplace else."

He folded his arms over his chest.

"Don't you remember what happened at the last concert?" I asked.

"I agree. No more podiums. We can put the brass players on risers so that I can see them easily."

"That theatre is too dangerous."

Domingos studied my face as if searching for traces of lunacy. "Even if we could find a theatre, how could we move all our equipment? How could we warn the audience? Where do you think we are, Brazil?"

"There's probably a data base with phone numbers. We could put announcements on the radio."

"Many of our patrons are old, Andy. They can't stand change. They would be so irritated if they went to the wrong theatre that they would cancel their subscriptions. No, Andy. We can't risk it. That might work in other countries, but it won't work here. Anyway, what good would it do? Someone determined to follow me would manage it another way."

"This way they'd lose their advantage! Don't you see?"

Domingos sat back. "Andy, we're in Tucson now. You can relax."

I scooted to the edge of the couch. It was too short for me, and it was even a little short for Domingos. I assumed it had been picked out by a woman. One the size of Liza.

"You're in as much danger now as you were last week," I said. "That madman in Lyon? He wasn't after you."

"Who then? The mayor was sitting in the front row. That's not a good seat, but it's what he prefers. He doesn't walk well anymore. The owner of *Le Progres* was there as well. He, too, does not miss a concert. He was surrounded by his wife, a couple of his children, and I think some grandchildren. I've lost track of who is who. Then there was the university president. I can't remember his name; it's always his wife that I remember."

"No, Domingos. No person from Lyon."

"The target was the chandelier?"

"No, Domingos. I was."

"You!" The conductor stood. "You?" He laughed. "My friend, you're a pretty good violin player, but you're also delusional."

"You don't understand. Joey and I both had to leave California."

Domingos leaned forward. For the first time ever, I had his complete attention. "You both got women pregnant?"

"Not that I know of."

"What happened?"

"The usual. Found a dead body. Sent a man to jail."

He patted me on the shoulder so hard I almost bounced to the floor. "I see that you're concerned. I appreciate that. I'll ask the theatre to hire more security. Good?"

"Not good."

"In a couple of days we'll be out of the country. No one can find us in Mexico, right?"

All kinds of ruffians could find us, even the ones who weren't looking. The economy was still lousy because each president was worse than the last. People were desperate after years of drug cartels and dishonest officials. Anything could happen, especially to me.

"Down there we'll be anonymous," Domingos continued. "Nothing to worry about."

I had so many things to choose from that I wasn't sure where to start worrying.

171

"And don't concern yourself about the tickets. I'll get them for early Tuesday morning. That way you can spend a little time with Rachel. I enjoyed meeting her, you know. And she was great in Lyon. Everybody loved her. See if she'll come along to San Luís. It's a darling town. I'm sure she'll love it."

Before I could formulate a sentence, Domingos' computer started dinging more loudly than a fire truck. "This is going to be Brazil again," he said. "Do you want to wait around?"

Chapter Twenty-Two

Within ten minutes I'd made it to Rachel's, but I didn't immediately go inside. I was hoping she might be asleep, but all the lights in her apartment were on. She was as much of a night owl as I was. Hence I stalled; I didn't know what to tell her about Mexico. If I admitted I wanted to continue helping Domingos chase after a lost cause, she would be unhappy at best and furious at worst. So I sat in the car, Rachel's car, and delayed. I tried to think of any version of the story that would be a happy compromise between truth and folly. Rachel wasn't the jealous type, but she had no patience for Liza. I didn't blame her.

Yet I couldn't turn my back on Domingos. He was too confident that he was doing something righteous. If I didn't help him, I'd miss out on the opportunity to do the same. Somehow I needed to reset my gears. I'd thrown a man over the balcony and he'd died; now I owed the world a few good acts. Although I didn't trust Liza myself, it was just barely possible that her disappearance and F.J.'s death were coincidental. In that case Liza deserved our help.

She would reject it, of course. She wasn't the kind to accept the gentlest, most well-intentioned acts. She was the kind to get mad at a man who tried to hold open the door for her at a grocery store or who tried to lift her luggage to the overhead bin on a plane. Hence Domingos was going about things in the wrong way. While Liza might have helped him at some time in the past, she would never allow him to return the favor. There was no way he could change that.

What Domingos needed was to get Liza out of his system. She was the stumbling block that threatened his grandest dreams. If his only solution was to track her down long enough to be thoroughly humiliated, so be it. In a sense Domingos and I were both stuck. He wanted to help Liza; I wanted to help him. As soon as Domingos could find Liza long enough to be more thoroughly rejected than a groom left standing at the altar without a bride, the conductor and I could get on with our lives.

"Rachel?"

I entered the apartment slowly in case she'd left the lights on for my benefit, but Rachel was bent over her four-octave electric keyboard. A sheet of staff music lay on a clipboard before her. In terms of energy levels, she was on par with Domingos. She was constant activity. And music went through her head all the time. If she didn't stop to write it down, she feared it would float away from her.

"Sorry I didn't call," I said.

She erased a note, checked it against the keyboard, and wrote down a new one. "That's okay. I saw your cell in the kitchen, so I knew you didn't have it with you. The phone company should be paying you instead of the other way around."

"I meant to bring it."

She shook her head, mussing up her hair. "That's all right, Andy. Anyway, it's not so late."

"I was with Domingos." I kissed the top of her head. "What's the song about?"

She winked long enough for me to know that she was partially kidding. "The stupidity of men."

"Are you at a stopping point?"

"Not quite yet. Can it wait?"

"Sure."

I took my violin and went into the bedroom. Although I knew I was too distracted to learn anything, I took out the music and practiced mechanically. Chances were that during the concert, I wouldn't be able to concentrate. I would be too busy looking for Miguels or Lizas or hitmen. Hence I reviewed the hardest passages slowly to lock them into my memory. While my fingers exercised, I constructed logical arguments as to why I needed to go to San Luís Potosí. Baptize my niece's baby? Always a swell excuse. Surprise party for my cousin's 40th birthday? No one could argue. Music festival Domingos roped me into? Possibly annoying, but especially believable.

174

Instead I dodged the problem the easy way. I fell asleep while Rachel was still in the living room. When she came to bed herself, she didn't wake me up.

~

When our Saturday concert went off without a hitch, I used all my energy to worry about the Sunday matinee. Kenny had assured me that the musicians always made more mistakes during the repeat performance but had more fun playing it. On this occasion he was right. The winds missed an entrance in the otherwise straightforward overture, but Domingos found a way to fold them back in. Twice my stand partner was late turning the page, but I was able to improvise without losing a beat. Other small hitches didn't affect me, so I dismissed them. Domingos did the same. While he conducted, he was radiant. He demonstrated the joy of conducting as if he expected each concert to be his last. I remembered what he'd said about having lived a good life and tried to erase possible scenarios from my head, the ones where the chandelier fell on the conductor or a man on a rope sailed down from the rafters with a harpoon gun.

Strangely enough, such preoccupations improved my playing. I was too worried about imaginary assassins to be afraid of thirty-second notes or missed cues or erratic tempos. Because I had so many other things on my mind, I kept my eyes right on the page while I played by rote. Whenever I looked up from the music, I caught Domingos' beat while imagining phantoms in the dark space behind him. Surely there would be some. Maybe a whole squad.

I didn't express any additional worries to Domingos. I didn't have a chance to. Before the concert, he was swarmed by questions from musicians who were far more meticulous about the music than I was. At intermission he was swarmed with well-wishers. After the concert, the only way he escaped was by slipping out the back door.

The musicians reconvened at a yuppie hamburger joint that was blessedly peaceful at five in the afternoon. I would have skipped the socializing, but when Domingos extended a personal invitation, Rachel immediately accepted. She had less resistance against Domingos than I did, a fact I tucked away for future reference. When he pulled up a chair for her, she scooted next to him. Evidently he'd been forgiven for both Delft and Lyon.

"I enjoyed the concert tremendously," she said.

"I enjoyed conducting you in France. When will you audition for the TucAz?"

She shook her head. "I have too many conflicts with mariachi gigs."

"You compare Dvořák to mariachi?"

"No, but I get to sing more songs!" Rachel and I had discussed the topic extensively, but two facts were hard to overlook: She loved the mariachi, and it paid better than the symphony did.

"You appreciate the beauty created by the human voice," Domingos said cheerfully.

"I do. That's why I was so delighted to hear about your opera festival in San Luís Potosí."

Behind Rachel's back, I nodded so vigorously that my head might have popped off.

"My opera festival," Domingos said slowly, feeling his way. "I suppose Andy told you all about it."

"What a sweet idea! If the city has a budget for it, then why not? And it's kind of you to make Andy your assistant. A little extra money never hurts, right?"

"Assistant," Domingos repeated. "His Spanish is flawless, so whom else would I choose?"

Rachel reached for a menu. "Me, of course, though I'm sure Andy can manage. I admit to being miffed though."

Domingos seized her hand and kissed it like a madman until she started giggling so hard she started coughing.By then all the others at the table had noticed as well. "I'll do anything!" he cried. He dropped to his knees. "Command me!"

She pretended to pull him up by the hair. "The next time

you schedule a planning meeting down in San Luís, make sure to hold it when I can go along."

Domingos planted his hands on his chest as if making a solid vow. "I promise! You're keen to visit the city's museums, I suppose. Or to stroll down the long pedestrian sidewalks."

Rachel opened the foot-long menu and dug her face into it. "Actually, I'm keen to visit a couple of cousins who live up the road in Durango."

"Musicians?"

"Heavens no. Meli runs a taco joint, and Kique is a law student."

"I'm sure they'd enjoy San Luís."

"I'm sure they've already been there. But since you and Andy will be busy nonstop, I would have plenty of time to visit them at your expense."

When I'd visited Durango with Rachel a few months earlier, I'd had a terrible dizzy spell for no discernible reason. I had bad memories of the city in general, but I'd made friends with Rachel's cousins. Meli had welcomed me into her home, and Kique, whose nickname was pronounced KEY-kay, had kept me entertained. Kique was like a younger brother who was even more reckless and more observant than I. Unfortunately, we'd been catalysts for one another. We'd gotten into so much trouble pretending to be hotshots that Meli had to bail us out.

While Rachel studied the list of novelty burgers, I caught Domingos' eye. He mouthed the word "assistant." Then he shook his head like the indulgent father of a three-year-old.

Chapter Twenty-Three

When Rachel and I went to fetch Domingos at three a.m. on Tuesday morning, we were both wide awake. Conditioned night owls, neither of us had been to bed. We were used to late hours. We liked them.

After traveling along Fourth Street, I asked Rachel to turn up Bentley Avenue. Several lights illuminated Domingos' house, but next door an old white van was parked near the end of the driveway.

"Which house?" Rachel asked.

"Keep driving."

"I thought you said it was closer to Third than to Fourth."

"We passed the house. But keep going."

"Did you forget the address?"

"No."

"Now what?"

"Turn right at the end of the block and pull up along the curb."

"Andy, what's the matter?"

I didn't answer. I was listening for Domingos' voice on the other end of the cell phone.

"Andy!" he said cheerfully. "You're almost late. Misplace your passport?"

"Domingos, does your neighbor to the north have a van?"

"He's ninety-eight. He doesn't even have a golf cart."

"Relatives who check on him?"

"Not since I've known him."

"Do you have a back door?"

"You're making me nervous."

"Maybe you should be."

I described the van as much as possible. It was an older vehicle, but I didn't notice which state the license plate was from. I hadn't seen anybody in the driver's seat, but given the lack of traffic at that hour, any deviant would have had plenty of time to duck down.

Rachel fished out her own cell phone. "Should I call the police and say there's a suspicious vehicle?"

"I don't know," I said. "It might be nothing."

"Andy, I'm looking out the window right now," Domingos said. "I don't recognize the van. I'm sure I've never seen it before. Can you see it now?"

"Wait."

Rachel backed up a few feet.

"I'm watching from the end of the block."

"See if anyone gets out. In the meantime, give me three minutes. Then drive around to Stewart Avenue, which is the street behind mine. I can jump over the fence and go through the neighbor's yard. You can pick me up there."

"Andy, what's going on?" Rachel asked.

"My imagination." I kept my eyes glued to the van. For a sliver of a second, I thought I saw the brake lights go on. Then nothing.

We pulled around on Stewart just as Domingos threw his bag over the wall. He followed right behind.

"Any movement?" he asked as he hopped into the backseat.

"I'm not sure," I said.

"What do you think we should do?" he asked.

"Call the police," Rachel said. "Tell them you think there's suspicious activity in your neighborhood."

Domingos checked his watch. "Let's keep an eye on the van."

Rachel made a U-turn and pulled back around. All three of us watched the van, but we saw no activity.

"Now do we call the police?" Rachel asked.

"Wait," said Domingos.

But nothing happened. We sat for five, ten, fifteen minutes. Nothing. Instead there was only the darkness and the sounds of three people breathing as softly as possible.

Rachel broke the silence. "We need to leave."

"From here you can reach the airport in ten minutes,"

Domingos said.

"But then I'll be speeding, and instead of catching a burglar, I'll get a speeding ticket."

"We'll be fine," Domingos said.

"Festival organizers," Rachel sneered. "And to think I believed you."

We both turned to her.

"I know, I know. I was an idiot to listen to either one of you." She shook her finger at Domingos. "You were being followed when you went to France, and you're still being followed here in Tucson. I could have told you that employing Andy to help you run from trouble is a colossally stupid idea."

"I'm not running," Domingos said.

"Whatever."

"If anything, I'm running TO trouble."

"You shouldn't have chosen Andy as a running mate."

"He saved my life."

"With him around, you're going to need someone to keep saving you."

"Now!" Domingos said as he hit a button on his cell.

A figure had slipped out of the car and was heading for the front door.

"This is Domingos Moraes. I live at 432 N. Bentley Avenue. I'm leaving my house right now, but a suspicious white van keeps driving up and down my block. Do you mind sending a patrol car by?" Domingos rang off. "Okay, Rachel. We better leave."

"What about your house?" Rachel exclaimed. At that moment an alarm went off. A loud one.

"Go, go! It's out of our hands."

Rachel started the motor.

"I thought you didn't have an alarm," I said. "All the other houses have little warning signs."

"Such signs are no deterrent. Besides, I like the element of surprise. When you travel as much as I do, you have to protect yourself."

"Watch it!" I said as Rachel took a corner so fast I rammed into the passenger door.

"Festival organizers. I hate both of you," Rachel said. "I don't know what's wrong with me. I should have been onto you long before now. But if you're going to put me in danger, you damned well better warn me. Let me guess. Liza's ex-lover is still trying to track her down, and he's so angry he's ready to kill somebody. So your best plan is to run down to Mexico."

"That's not it at all," I said.

"I see. Liza called from San Luís Potosí, and she needs your help. Rather, she needs Domingos' help, and Domingos needs Andy's help. Is that a better version?"

"Rachel, I—"

"Quiet." She shook her head as she sped down Kino. She was so ready to dump us at the airport that she wasn't worried about a speeding ticket after all.

When we caught a red light, Rachel glared into her rearview mirror. "You're as bad as Andy. Worse. He may be a nincompoop, but I doubt if he volunteered his services. Instead you bullied him into going along with you."

Domingos shrugged and tried to smile, but he knew better than to say anything.

"I wondered why Andy didn't know the name of the hotel you're staying at," Rachel continued. "That's because there isn't one. Are you even going to San Luís Potosí? Not that I care."

"My niece lives there, so we thought we might economize by staying with her," I said.

"Economize. Yes, it's your foremost concern. Should I call the poor woman and warn her that her life will soon be in danger?"

I didn't answer.

"You have two cousins, I think you told me. Like you and your brother, one a musician and one an architect. Let me guess. You called them up and invited yourself to stay for a few days, but you didn't say why, did you?"

We'd already reached the airport, so I only had to muddle through a few more seconds. "Beto and Leonardo live in Aguascalientes. Beto's daughter lives in San Luís."

"How convenient."

Rachel didn't slow down for the speed bump, and I hit my head against the roof of the car so hard that my back cracked. I would have complained, but she screeched to a stop so quickly I had to use both hands against the dashboard.

"Rachel, I—"

"What did you tell your niece, Andy? What possible reason could you give for suddenly dropping in?"

I exited the car, but she did too. Instead of popping the trunk, she went around to the back of the car and leaned against it. "You're leaving without your luggage unless you tell me what's going on."

"You can't stay here." I indicated the airport guard, who was already heading our direction.

"It's up to you. Nothing in your bag besides a couple of shirts anyway."

Domingos put his arm around her shoulder before she could shake him off. "It's all my fault. I talked him into it. You can blame me. Really."

She shook loose. "I blame you all right, but it takes two to tango, and I don't mean that in the usual way. I suppose your precious Liza is in San Luís?" she asked Domingos.

He nodded. "We have proof this time."

"Aha. So now I understand perfectly. You drag my boyfriend to Mexico to help you hunt for your favorite piece of trailer trash. No, wait, she doesn't have a trailer."

The guard had been hovering, but to her credit, as soon as she heard "trailer trash" she backed away.

"Why is Liza so damned important?" Rachel asked.

We said nothing.

"Tell me!"

"Domingos thought she could help with this opera festival, and—"

183

Rachel threw her arms in the air. I knew what this meant. It was an Italian sign of contempt. I'd seen her use it before; after all, she was half Italian. She opened the trunk with such a motion that it bounced shut again. She opened it a second time, more carefully. She picked up my bag and hurled it to the sidewalk. Before I could stop her, she did the same with Domingos.'

"You're both stupider than bricks. Liza probably hates both of you, and you better not expect a warm reception. But let me tell you one thing right now, Andy Veracruz. If you come back all shot up, don't expect me to nurse you back to health."

She hopped in the car and drove a foot. Then she slammed on her brakes, got back out, and marched towards me. She pointed her right hand at me as if it held a gun. "And let me tell you another thing. Don't you dare call my cousins. They have their own problems."

I hurried towards the airport entrance.

"Andy Veracruz! Did you hear me?"

I faced Rachel while I scurried backwards. "Too late."

"You called Kique?"

I came so close to the automatic doors that they opened. "He said to call him whenever I needed help." When I'd explained the situation a few hours earlier, he'd agreed to meet me in San Luís as soon as he could get away. I knew Rachel wouldn't approve, which was why I hadn't told her.

"Andy!"

I blew her a kiss and shot through the doors. "Run," I told Domingos as we headed straight for security.

"Who's Kique?" Domingos asked.

"Trust me. He's your new best friend."

~

We were pushing our way to the back of the plane when the police called Domingos. Could he come down to the police station? No, he was on an airplane minutes from takeoff. Was he aware that someone had tried to break into his house? No,

184

he was not.

"Mind if I take the window?" he whispered when we reached our row.

"Not at all."

While the rest of the passengers sorted out their carry-ons, Domingos chatted with the police as easily as if he were discussing a restaurant menu. He mentioned nothing about being followed. Instead he focused the police's attention on a possible robbery. Three of his neighbors had been burglarized within the year. Since Domingos traveled so often, he was a natural target.

"They've apprehended someone," he explained as our plane started down the runway. "A man about forty years old. No papers on him. Mexican, probably. They're not sure."

"They caught the guy in your house?"

"He never made it inside. The police spotted him as he was leaving the neighborhood. And guess what? A light was out on his license plate. When the officers tried to stop him, he ran. Bad move."

"What do you think he was after?"

"News about Liza, of course. Or perhaps Liza herself." He said it matter-of-factly as if he sincerely believed it.

"Maybe he was a simple thief."

"What was he going to do, stuff my baby grand in that rattletrap of a van? No, Andy. He wanted Liza. He would have demanded that I disclose her whereabouts, and since I don't have them, he would have beaten me up instead. So, Andy, you saved my neck. Again. You and Rachel both."

"Domingos, why do you obsess over Liza?"

"She's brilliant."

I shook my head. "She's your lover. Or she was."

He smiled. "We did some of our musical training together."

"What else?"

"She made me a better conductor. She brings out my best because she has the greatest passion."

185

We paused while the flight attendant told us how to be safe. I didn't bother to mention that I was safer in a plane with one engine than I had been all day running loose in a town where Liza once lived.

"Don't get me wrong," Domingos continued. "You too have the passion although perhaps not yet the skill. I heard about the concerts in Delft and Lyon. Both conductors said the same thing. You played with great sincerity and energy. They enjoyed working with you. So did the other musicians. Did you miss a few notes? Yes. Did they notice? Ferdinand did. So what?"

I knew what Domingos was trying to do. He wanted to distract me from the subject at hand much the way he had been gently guiding the police. "And your relationship to Liza?"

"I told you already. We go way back. She's my oldest friend."

"So what?"

"I feel bad for her. She had a rough childhood."

"Most of us did."

"No. Most of us don't come close."

"Sexual abuse, then?"

"A close friend died when she was young, and she hasn't recovered. She obsesses about the brevity of life, the randomness. The little girl died in a car accident, and it wasn't a drunken driver or anything like that. The tire blew up and the father lost control of the car. Anyway, never mind. It was a long time ago."

"There has to be more."

"Her little brother almost drowned before her eyes. The boy was too small to remember the incident, but to Liza it was traumatic."

"What else?"

"Andy, you ask so many questions!"

"I'm going to keep asking."

Although it wasn't yet allowed, Domingos reclined the seat as far as it would go. "Yes, yes. I'll tell you everything.

186

But first, Andy, be kind. Let me take a little nap."

Domingos turned away from me, using his jacket against the window as a pillow. I tried to settle into my seat, but my knees were almost to my chin and the cushions had a funny odor. I couldn't have slept on that flight if I'd taken sleeping pills.

No one else had a chance to sleep either. Almost immediately, Domingos started snoring louder than a helicopter.

Chapter Twenty-Four

The sun was bright, but the air was so cool that I shifted from one foot to the other. I'd brought a jacket, but the temperature was about fifty, which was chillier than I expected.

Domingos seemed perfectly comfortable even though he wasn't dressed any more warmly than I was. "Are you sure your niece is coming for us?"

We'd been standing at the curb outside the airport for twenty minutes, but there was still no sign of Laura, the niece I hadn't seen for several years.

"I told you we should have stayed at a hotel." That way I would have already been comfortably resting.

"Maybe she forgot."

I rubbed my eyes. I needed either coffee or a nap, whichever came first. "She's on Mexican time."

Domingos grinned. "So is everybody else. You have the address, right? We can grab a cab."

We were still in line when a Volkswagen screeched to a halt in front of us. A young woman sprang from the car and rushed me.

"Tío Andy!"

Laura gave me an exuberant hug, probably a bigger one than I would have given her if she'd called me at the last minute and begged for free lodging for herself and two friends. "It's so good to see you!" she said in Spanish.

"It's good to see you too." I peered into the car. "And you're not alone."

A small child frowned at me from the passenger seat. A baby slept in a car seat in the back.

"Sorry you had to wait. I couldn't get Max into the car. By then Nenita was sleeping. Tío Andy, you can sit in front with Max."

I wasn't good with kids. This had been confirmed when I'd traveled to Durango a few months earlier. And now, given that Max was firmly planted in the passenger seat, I had no idea what to do.

"Dále espacio a tu tío," Laura told him. "Give your uncle some room."

The child showed no sign of moving. We were already at a standoff.

"Andy, take my *mala*," Domingos said.

I frowned enough for Domingos to notice I was doing so. The correct Spanish word for suitcase was *maleta*. Also, I wasn't a porter.

"May I?" Domingos pushed past me, scooped up Max, slid into the front seat, and plopped the child onto his lap. "And what's your name, you fine young man?" Domingos asked in perfect Spanish.

Momentarily the child was paralyzed, but then he introduced himself as Maximiliano Emilio Pineda Veracruz. He and Domingos were already friends. Meanwhile I was the porter after all. I shoved our luggage into the trunk. Then I crawled into the backseat with the sleeping child where I was safe.

"Andy tells me he was at your wedding," Domingos said.

Laura pulled away from the curb. "We were so happy he could make it. And now look what happened! Two children already."

"And a third one on the way?" Domingos asked brightly.

"Not yet." She patted her stomach. "Maybe soon."

Domingos engaged Laura in one topic after another: the way Max treated the baby, problems with losing weight after a pregnancy, the difficulties of adjusting to life as a stay-at-home mom. Domingos was a chameleon, diving into a new situation and mastering the environment. He might have been talking to a group of plumbers or professors or any other group. He immediately found a way to the center.

This was a skill I lacked. I knew how to talk to musicians and their fans, so Laura was a stretch for me. Yet Domingos jumped right into her life. While I noticed the dust and the traffic, the crisscrossing power lines and the pickup trucks with

190

workers riding in the cab, Laura happily chatted away as if Domingos were the relative instead of me.

But I knew Domingos well enough to know his questions weren't idle. He eventually steered the conversation to city matters. He slipped in questions about the local orchestra so gracefully that no one would have expected an agenda. At first I didn't catch on myself. Had she attended any recent orchestra concerts? No. Why not? Always busy with the baby. Her mother-in-law never missed a performance, though. We could ask her. Domingos claimed that the fake festival meetings—we had decided that the cover story was as good as any—would be held at the School of Music. Is that where the orchestra rehearsed? The website had been vague about details although it stated quite clearly that the concert schedule could change suddenly and without warning.

Laura wouldn't know the details. She didn't have time for music. She barely had time to sleep! Since the downtown was full of one-way streets, she couldn't drive us past the School of Music, but we would find it easily because it faced a large park. All we had to do was head down Universidad and turn left when we reached Las Alamedas. She herself lived close to the downtown area although she lived on the west side of it rather than the east side. But the School of Music was easily within walking distance. Very convenient.

I congratulated myself. Laura hadn't forgotten to pick us up after all. No matter how small and uncomfortable her house was, the address would be anonymous. We could relax. No one knew where we were. We could melt into the background. Despite boasting nearly a million inhabitants, San Luís itself could disappear right into the belly of Mexico. It didn't have sights that were famous enough to attract international visitors, and it was too far from Mexico City to be a preferred getaway. Its colonial buildings were quaint, but many of the Northern Mexican towns had similar architecture. Hence most visitors would be conducting business or attending to family. That made the city a perfect hiding spot.

"How's your husband doing?" I asked.

Laura maneuvered into the center lane even though traffic surrounded us. "Arnulfo is fine, but his mother is struggling."

"That's something we all go through," I said casually. "It's one of the hardest things, watching our parents get old. Eventually, they pass on." It was the cycle of life. Time marched on without you. That was something you could count on.

"That's the thing. Arnulfo's mother. She's too stubborn, I mean. She won't pass on. She's healthier than I am."

We passed a line of small shops, but currently there were a dozen vendors and not one buyer. Several shopkeepers were already closing for the afternoon siesta. I was ready to join them.

"She's sharp," Laura continued, "but she can barely walk. She gets around, but whenever possible she prefers to have someone wait on her. That way she feels special."

No matter what Domingos wanted to do, I would insist on a nap. And then maybe some tasty tacos made out of *carne asada*, roasted meat. In Tucson I lowered my standards long enough to eat what passed for Mexican food, but I never enjoyed it.

"Because of Nana I haven't been able to go visit my own mother." Laura turned to Domingos. "My folks live in Aguascalientes. It's only a couple of hours away."

"You've been stuck," Domingos said as he bounced Max on his knee.

"Exactly! That's why your visit is a godsend."

"Thanks for hosting us," said Domingos. "We're grateful."

"We know you're here on business, but we were hoping you'd help out. Actually, Dad said you'd be happy to."

"Of course," I said. "Did you want some advice on remodeling?"

"Oh, no. We don't have that kind of cash. But with you and the maestro staying at the house, Arnulfo and I can go visit my parents."

"What?"

"You don't have to worry about Nana. We have a maid who comes in during the day. Her name is Maria. You'll like her. And Nana is no problem at night. She sleeps straight through. But we need someone to be in the house during the evening."

"But—"

"Dad insisted that you wouldn't mind."

Domingos shot me a killer look. Then he turned to Laura. "Why would we mind? We have to attend a few meetings with other music teachers. No big deal."

Laura sped around an XOXO, a small convenience store, and slowed down when she reached the third house. She popped the automatic control for the gate and drove up the short driveway. A young man with three jam-packed duffel bags was standing beside the front door. As soon as Laura turned off the motor, Arnulfo snatched our bags from the trunk and replaced them with his own.

Then Arnulfo surprised Domingos with a huge embrace. "Good to see you, Tío Andy."

Domingos stepped aside as smoothly as a matador as I extricated myself from the small car.

"Oh, of course! Tío Andy!" Arnulfo hugged me tightly. "We're so excited you could come and stay with us. Stay as long as you want!"

Laura push-pulled me towards the house. "I'll explain a couple of things and then we can be off. We really appreciate it. We can't tell you how much."

"But Arnulfo's mother—"

"She's in her room taking a nap. You don't have to worry about her until this evening."

Laura dragged me into a kitchen with a large oval table. In its center, a once-white plastic container held silverware while another held a stack of napkins which had folded over like wilted tree branches. At the far end, three plates of sweets had been wrapped with cellophane. A fly sat on the third one, but Laura swooshed it away.

She handed me a set of keys that had been lying on the counter. "I think I have everything set up for you, but you can always call."

"But—"

"You have Dad's number. If I don't answer my cell phone, call him."

She gave me another hug. For good measure, I suppose, she hugged Domingos too. Then she rushed out of the house. Her husband was already in the driver's seat, and the car was already running.

Domingos leaned against the door jamb and waved as they hurried off. "Nice gal," he grinned. "Accommodating."

"I told you we should have stayed at a hotel," I said.

"Yes, Andy. But you didn't tell me why."

~

I didn't score a nap. Domingos immediately dragged me out of the house. We headed directly for the School of Music, which was a stately structure two blocks east of the Plaza de Armas. The building had tall arches, high columns, and a big wooden door that hung open. Inside, rehearsal rooms bordered a large patio that was decorated with planters and dwarf palm trees. Students hurried back and forth or huddled in small groups. Domingos and I approached several. The students all agreed that the orchestra rehearsed from six to eight, but they weren't sure which days.

Since it wasn't yet five, Domingos and I consoled ourselves by walking down to a place inappropriately named The Italian Coffee Company where I ordered an espresso that was more expensive than a Starbucks' version and not nearly as tasty. We picked a table at the front and watched the street. Cars streamed by, but their owners waited patiently for pedestrians and cyclists to dart among them. The sidewalks were alive with townspeople: mothers with their children, business people carrying briefcases, teens looking for other teens.

While I squirmed to stay awake, Domingos calmly took in every detail. He seemed as comfortable in San Luís as he'd been in the hospital in Tucson or the police station in Lyon. When he caught the eyes of passersby, he smiled. Most of the time they smiled right back.

"Mexico feels like home to you, doesn't it?" I asked.

"After spending four years in Guadalajara? Yes."

"Guadalajara?"

"The Fermatta Music Academy."

Guadalajara was mariachi country. While Mexico City was close competition, the groups in the smaller, gentler city were vibrant and competitive. Years earlier I'd spent a week there with Joey. We went from one restaurant to another absorbing everything we could. While other cities scaled back on live music, Guadalajara was a mariachi musician's paradise.

When I'd auditioned for his orchestra, Domingos had questioned me about my rough playing. He pointed out that I lacked the refinement of nearly all the other competitors, but I had a better ear and played with more spirit. When I blamed my rudimentary style on mariachi playing, he seemed to understand. At the time I hadn't believed him, but knowing that he'd lived in Guadalajara changed the picture. He would have learned about the folk art whether he wanted to or not. Importantly for me, he would have known that mariachi was a high-class musical form. He might have interacted with some of the most skilled players. No wonder Domingos recognized and appreciated the way I played.

"How was your Spanish when you arrived?" I asked.

Domingos didn't take his eyes off the street. "As a Portuguese speaker, I could pick it up."

"Why choose Guadalajara? It's a long way from Brazil."

"I won a scholarship and got a full ride. That was a deal I couldn't turn down."

"You and Liza were in school together?"

"She started a year before I did."

"She also had a scholarship?"

"No. She was offered a teaching job that allowed her to study and work at the same time."

I could imagine Liza's daily life: violin lessons, practice in a soundproof room, practice, more practice, more lessons, more practice. In contrast, much of my training had been on the job. I didn't have time to be a perfectionist. Instead I had to improvise.

"Was Liza a model student?"

"Not always. She has a son, you know."

I spoke without thinking. "Yours?"

Domingos turned sharply, and for a moment I thought he was deeply offended. "No, Andy. Not mine. A best friend's. But he was killed."

Involuntarily I shrank back. For a moment I visualized Liza dressed in black as she hovered over a coffin. No wonder she was mad at the world. I would have been too. So far I'd been lucky in life. My parents were gone, but they'd both reached their seventies. I'd lost a friend to violence, but she'd been a friend's wife, not my life companion. Hence I couldn't imagine how Liza might have felt.

"Violent circumstances?" I asked softly.

"You could say that."

Mexico City was full of violent crimes. Kidnapping had become a sport, and although the rich had been the original targets, the practice was trickling down to the upper middle class. But the most common crime in the city involved the trafficking of drugs, mostly to dealers in the US. Drugs meant big money, and countless people were reckless enough to try to edge their way into the process.

"Was Liza's lover a drug runner?"

"No, Andy. He was not. He was a mariachi player who drank too much at a gig and accidentally smashed himself into a wall."

For a moment I started to smile. Then I realized that he wasn't kidding. I scooted back a couple of inches. Domingos

196

rarely spoke seriously of anything besides music. Generally, he avoided negativity at every turn. He didn't allow bad thoughts to slow him down in any way. I immediately wanted the regular Domingos back again.

But I didn't have any trouble at all imagining the circumstances. Drinking was a hazard that came with the territory. Outside of masses, nearly every mariachi gig took place in a setting that included alcohol. The players who made music a career either learned moderation or quit drinking altogether. Otherwise they didn't survive.

No wonder Liza had snarled at me when I mentioned being a mariachi player. She wasn't dissing me and my folk music because it wasn't serious. Instead she was blocking out her worst memories. For a moment I regretted thinking of her so harshly. No one deserved to lose a partner in such a senseless way.

"I'm sorry to hear it," I said sincerely. "How did Liza cope?"

"She lost her way for a while. Her in-laws helped with the boy. Teo was only a year or so at the time."

"What about Liza's parents?"

"They live further south. Too far away to be much help. Liza's salvation was the violin. Her concentration doubled. No, it quadrupled. She started practicing six hours a day, sometimes eight. She interacted with everyone else—including the boy—as little as possible."

I couldn't see Liza as any kind of mother, let alone a good one, but there was one way she could shirk motherly responsibilities and nearly be pardoned for it. "She sold her soul to her violin."

"Yes, Andy. She was that mad. There she was with a baby in a world that had exploded around her. She didn't know what to do with herself, so she poured everything into playing."

I imagined a slightly younger Liza, one who was ready to burst into flame every moment of every day. "You stayed close?"

197

"I spent weeks consoling her. We often practiced together. Liza's very analytical, you know. We would make videos of one another and critique them. She made me a better conductor. I made her a better violinist. She did, indeed, become a fine violinist. She landed a job with the opera. That satisfied her for a while."

I thought about a boy growing up with a mother who loved an instrument more than she could ever love him. "Why didn't she take her son to Tucson?"

"She said she couldn't arrange for a passport."

"That's not what you think?"

"No. I assume she didn't want to take him away from doting grandparents." Domingos pointed across the street. "Look."

Even at a distance of two hundred feet, Liza was easy to spot. She marched towards the rehearsal as if she owned the street, her precious violin flung over her shoulder.

I started to get up.

"Wait."

"We came here to talk to her!"

"We did. But we know where she's going. We should corner her at the school rather than out on the street, don't you think?"

While I agreed with Domingos, we were the ones who ended up with the surprise. By the time we returned to the School of Music, the orchestra was rehearsing. They sounded reasonable for a student-heavy orchestra. The conductor was a sprightly fifty-year-old, and he waved his arms cheerfully in strict tempo. The musicians sat on the edge of their chairs, alert yet relaxed. But one thing was noticeably missing. The chair for the concertmaster was empty.

~

We headed to the house disgusted with one another. Liza had slipped through our fingers. We'd searched through the School of Music; perhaps she was giving lessons. Perhaps she'd decided to rehearse on her own. No. She'd vanished.

198

Maybe she hadn't arrived. Maybe she'd spotted us and run.

Nana was waiting for us by the door. "I've been alone all afternoon!" she cried as we entered the house. She was a rotund old lady who had been squashed by time. While her actions were slow, her mouth wasn't. "I've called that no-good son of mine five times and he doesn't answer."

Of course Arnulfo hadn't answered. He was too busy partying at Beto's house, where I might have been myself.

"I might have died and no one would have noticed!"

"She's just like my mother," Domingos said under his breath. Then he went into his act, the one where he was so solicitous that finally Nana admitted that she'd been perfectly all right on her own for a while. Now that Domingos and I had arrived, what could we do for her?

For the next half hour Nana had us running all around the house making her a quesadilla and preparing her brandy and Coke ("My sleeping pill!") and locating her TV remote and her lost glasses. When she finally went to bed, Domingos and I settled into the family room because it was the farthest away from her.

Domingos crushed his first empty can of Tecate. "You know what's going to happen, don't you, Andy?"

I took a second Tecate for myself, cut half a lime, and dripped juice on the lid. Then I added salt. "We're going to make another beer run?"

"She's going to need help getting to the bathroom. Approximately one hour after you've gone to bed."

"In that case you can help her."

"Not me. I'll be sound asleep."

And snoring. Which meant I would be lying awake.

I'd already texted my niece to let her know that she didn't need to worry about her mother-in-law. She'd texted me right back. She knew that Nana was in good hands and she wasn't worried at all. My cousin Beto said hi. So did my cousin Leonardo. They were so grateful my friend and I were staying with Arnulfo's mother, etc., etc., etc. I could imagine them all laughing and partying in the background. They knew what we were up against.

Domingos and I reviewed the afternoon's progress. By approaching some of the orchestra players, we'd learned that a woman named Elizabetta had recently been hired as concertmaster. She played pretty well. This was the first rehearsal she'd missed. Presumably she'd be back the next day.

"You were going to tell me more about Liza," I said.

"The long version or the short one?"

I pointed to the dark TV screen. "I'm not sure how to work the remote. The long version will be fine."

Domingos hunched up his shoulders. "After Nando passed, Liza threw herself into her studies like a maniac. Practiced until her fingers hurt so much she was taking painkillers every night. She improved. Tremendously. She soloed with a few local orchestras and kept practicing as if her life depended on it. Maybe it did."

I'd always played the violin by choice. I'd never once felt as though my life depended on it. Maybe I hadn't suffered enough. Relatively speaking, playing the violin had come easily to me. I naturally had a good ear. My fingers were long but not too long. My wrists were flexible, and my shoulders didn't get sore unless I was doing a marathon with Villa-Lobos. I'd practiced long hours in high school and college trying to improve my technique, and I'd spent even more hours learning the mariachi repertoire, but the process had never seemed onerous. I'd nearly always enjoyed the challenge.

Liza's apprenticeship was beginning to make sense to me. No wonder she was fierce and aggressive. She'd worked hard to reach her highest possible level. She wasn't willing to accept anything less.

"When you were hired to conduct in Delft, you took her with you?" I asked.

"Not right away. She wouldn't have been satisfied being one of the regular violinists. She wanted to be concertmaster. I had to establish myself before I could offer her such a

200

position."

"And Lyon?"

"That was more delicate because of the old concertmaster, but I finally managed it."

"Liza didn't appreciate either job," I said.

"I wouldn't say that."

"She had trouble making friends."

"Europe wasn't a good fit for Liza," Domingos said. "She never felt comfortable."

I couldn't imagine why not. She should have been thrilled to live in Europe. Joey and I had spent a month there one summer while we were still in college. In every European city we'd visited, we'd been surrounded by cultured people who spoke two or three languages, considered musical training a normal part of growing up, and expected at least six weeks' vacation every summer. I would have moved in a heartbeat. "She thought she was too good for the whole Continent?"

Domingos looked up so sharply that he bumped his head on a lampshade. "You don't understand Liza. Until you do, you shouldn't judge her."

"She didn't get along in Europe, and I'm the one who shouldn't judge her?"

"She had her reasons."

"I'm listening."

"She missed Mexico. She missed her son. Europe was too cold for her. She didn't speak French or Dutch."

"You don't either."

"I speak enough bad French to keep everyone laughing. At any rate she met this Mexican guy at a cultural event that we played for. A businessman. Maybe she was homesick, but they hit it off and started seeing each other. Flew back and forth a couple of times to visit one another. Then Liza gave up Lyon and went to Mexico City."

"Where is she from originally?"

"Further south."

Mexico City was far down into Mexico if you were

driving, but a lot more of the country stretched below the capital.

"I need some help and I need it right now!" yelled Nana.

"I didn't hear anything," said Domingos as he headed for the kitchen.

When Nana yelled a third time, I headed down the hall.

Chapter Twenty-Five

"Liza saw us and evaded us," I said for the eighth time.

"She did not see us. I know her well. I would have detected the look of surprise in her eyes."

Domingos wasn't giving the concertmaster enough credit. If she could change her plans mid-concert, she could change them while walking across town. But I didn't mention this to Domingos. I would wait until I had better proof.

Meanwhile I would try to enjoy the surroundings. Domingos and I were seated on a bench in the Plaza de Armas. The main square was typical for a Mexican city. Although the cathedral was off-center, the other features were predictable. Long rectangular government buildings hugged the sides. A gazebo large enough to hold a small band reigned in the center. Areas of greenery were interspersed with pathways. A variety of trees provided wisps of shade.

Rather than hurrying around, we let the town come to us. People approached from all directions as if the townspeople spent their spare time walking from one end of the square to the other. I couldn't blame them. The Plaza de Armas was situated along a pedestrian walkway that stretched dozens of blocks from north to south. Had I been a tourist, I would have been content to spend the day walking up and down Calle Zaragoza myself.

By situating ourselves in the Plaza de Armas, we had the best possible chance of spotting Liza. If she lived west, north, or south of the square, she would probably pass through it to reach the School of Music.

We studied the women who marched by while trying to appear nonchalant. Liza might have thought to change her hair color or to parade around in casual shoes, but she wouldn't have been able to mask her height or her stride.

In theory our task was that simple.

"We've been here for over an hour," I said.

Domingos grinned. "Feel free to go back to the house to

203

stay with Nana."

While Nana had been duly charmed by Domingos, she had no warm feelings for me. I was a Mexican who lived in the US and was too stuck on himself to make frequent trips to visit family. Domingos had a clean slate. He was a guest. He spoke Spanish even though he was a foreigner. That made him golden.

I might have braved Nana regardless, but I was too antsy to stay at the house. Sitting in the heart of town was more productive. Liza would zip through the main square sooner or later. Evidently later. Days later.

"Maybe she takes cabs," I said.

"Maybe."

The town was full of green taxis that cruised around searching for customers. I could imagine Liza flagging a driver with a sharp glance that pierced through the front windshield. The woman hardly seemed like the walking type, and the plaza was too provincial to meet her approval. And hot. The air temperature was moderate, but the sun beat its way onto the pavement. So far Domingos and I had moved three times to stay in the shade.

Domingos checked his cell phone. "Think this friend of yours will be on time?"

Kique was driving in from Durango, which was several hours away. Because it was easy to find, I'd asked him to meet us in the plaza. "Give or take."

"My Mexican friends are always late. Sometimes hours late."

I feigned nonchalance. "If he were running late, he would have called."

"Talking about me?"

I was so startled I jumped from the bench. While Domingos and I had been chatting, Kique had sneaked up behind us. So much for surveillance.

As the dark brown twenty-something doubled over with laughter, his straight black hair fell down over his long nose. I chided myself. I should have expected such a trick from a law student with a sense of humor, especially one clad in jeans and a T-shirt from a fake Texan university. He knew a lot about current affairs both in and out of Mexico, but he couldn't stay serious for more than a few minutes at a time. Since I was the brother he'd never had, I was a prime target. He wasn't as tall as I was, but he was stronger. As he gave me a bear hug, I worried about my ribs.

"¡Menso!" he cried as he squeezed me. The word meant something like "idiot," but I knew he meant it in an affectionate way.

"Good to see you too," I sputtered.

"So you got us into another mess. Has Rachel forgiven you for the last one?"

"I've taken up residence in the doghouse." I turned to the conductor. "Meet Domingos. I assure you that this is his fault."

As he gave Domingos the once-over, Kique nodded approval. I knew what he was doing; he was mentally comparing the background information I'd provided against his own observations. Kique was both easygoing and smart. He analyzed people and situations with equal acumen. Instead of getting sidetracked by details, he saw the overall picture. His reflexes were as razor-sharp as those of a martial artist. Most importantly, in a time of crisis, he remained calm, which meant that he could react quickly and efficiently.

"We know Liza is here in San Luís," Domingos said. "We merely have to find her." He took out his cell phone and scrolled through until he found the picture of Liza in the main square.

"But she's hiding from her ex-lover," Kique said.

"She might be," said Domingos.

"Or the relatives of that guy she killed in Tucson?"

"She did not kill F.J," Domingos said quietly.

"Right," Kique said. "She threw him down the stairs so that he could break his neck and then placed a knife in his chest for safekeeping. It could happen. Who else would be chasing her?"

"Jealous musicians," Domingos said.

"Musicians? You guys are always too worried about hurting your hands to do anything violent."

I flexed my wrists. I wasn't about to admit it, but Kique was right. I needed my fingers. All of them.

"You don't understand," Domingos said sadly. "Liza has an artistic temperament. She makes enemies without trying to. She outplays her fellow musicians, and she isn't always kind about it."

Kique nodded as if assembling facts for an impossible law case. "What's it to you?"
"I've been explaining this to Andy for a week. She's my best friend. And I need to protect her."

Kique watched as a young woman strutted past and batted her eyes at him. "At all costs?"

"Yes. At all costs."

Kique squeezed between us on the bench. "Basically, your life is screwed until you can straighten out hers."

"Right," Domingos said. "Otherwise I'll never have any peace. And neither will Andy."

"What the hell. Peace is overrated." Kique spoke flatly, as if he were serious.

"You didn't bring Meli with you?" I asked.

"Did you need me to?"

"I'm not sure yet."

"Meli is my sister," Kique told Domingos. "She runs a taco joint, but she doubles as a hitman. Hitwoman."

"Everyone needs a sister like that!" Domingos said.

"Absolutely." Kique leaned back, taking in the square. "So what's our game plan?"

Neither Domingos nor I answered.

"Terrific. I got here just in time."

~

I led Domingos into a small practice room while the orchestra slowly assembled for the afternoon session. We

206

placed Kique in the lobby. Nobody would notice him because he blended in perfectly among the music students. The reality was that he had a terrible ear, could play only three chords on the guitar, and couldn't sing more than one song. But nobody would guess that from looking at him.

Domingos paced while the musicians arrived. We cracked the door open a few inches but stayed out of sight. Once we caught up with Liza, we didn't want her to squirm away. If we waylaid her as the rehearsal ended, she would be vulnerable. We could finally grill her about what she had done and why.

Every few minutes Kique texted us that she wasn't going to show and that we might as well go eat something, but we ignored him. As it turned out, we didn't need Kique as a lookout after all. Domingos and I both heard Liza at the same time. She strode through the patio as if she were mad at it, slamming down her heels as she pushed through the space.

Kique joined us in the practice room. "So that's Liza."

"That's her all right," I said.

"You're wasting your time looking for an angry musician."

"What do you mean?" Domingos asked.

"She's wearing stilettos. To a rehearsal."

"Liza is short," Domingos said. "She's self-conscious about it."

"And her dress barely covers her butt."

"What's your point, Kique?" I asked.

"So Liza has a rotten personality and musicians don't like her. Big deal."

Domingos held up his hand. "Stop. The music world is cutthroat. A hundred candidates vie for the same position. The players become maniacs."

"Trust me when I say that I don't know about music," Kique said. "But women I know something about."

In the background the oboe player sounded an A, and the orchestra started tuning.

"Consider your orchestra in Tucson," Kique said. "Do any

of the women show up for rehearsals dressed like Liza?"

"Well—"

"Of course not," Kique said.

"She likes to dress well," Domingos said. "That doesn't mean anything."

Kique shook his head. "The way women dress always means something."

"Liza is focused on the music," said Domingos.

"No. She's focused on Liza," said Kique. "But don't take my word for it."

The orchestra started playing. The result was so loud that we automatically stopped talking. It was also quite awful, mainly because several musicians had started at different places or maybe on different movements.

The maestro beat his baton on the music stand and asked the musicians to start over. After three measures, he stopped them again, shouting something about intonation.

He asked them to retune. Then he explained the timing to them, beating out the tempo with his baton.

The orchestra began a third time. Despite mistakes in the brass, the strings, and the winds, the conductor let the musicians keep going. They butchered their way through the first few measures. I wondered if they were all sight-reading.

Domingos shook his head and shielded his eyes with his hands.

"What's the matter?"

"Liza's playing," he said.

"What's wrong with it?" asked Kique.

"I've never heard her play that badly."

~

"What's the matter with you guys?" Kique asked when he returned to the practice room. He'd gone to fetch sodas, but Domingos and I had been too lazy to accompany him.

"Not a thing," said Domingos. "I feel great. You, Andy?"

"I feel great too. Comfortable bed last night. Soft." And for once, Domingos hadn't bothered me. I'd fallen asleep during the one moment he wasn't snoring, and I'd been sotired that I'd slept straight through until morning.

Kique sat down and shook his head. "¡*Mensos!* You guys are beyond help."

Domingos cocked his head. "Okay, so we're not as young as you are, but—"

"I thought you were going to follow Liza after the rehearsal."

"That's why we're waiting," I said.

Kique shook his head. "The musicians already left."

"No, no," Domingos said. "They're taking a break."

"Funny. They took their instruments with them. The janitor is straightening their chairs."

Domingos and I rushed to the doorway of the rehearsal room. Indeed, the musicians had cleared out. Most orchestra rehearsals lasted between two and three hours. This one had lasted less than sixty minutes.

This was terribly, terribly wrong. From the sound of things, the musicians needed all the rehearsing they could get.

Chapter Twenty-Six

Nana opened the front door as Kique reached for it. "Who the hell are you?"

"I'm the hired help."

"You don't look like much help to me."

"Nana, meet Kique," I said. "He's a good friend of mine."

"So he came to freeload too?"

"Why not?" Kique said, slipping by Nana and entering the living room. "I hear it's a beautiful house."

Nana followed him into the room. "I did choose the furnishings myself." Then she turned. "I tried to call you, Andy!"

"I forgot to take my phone."

"I know!" She reached into her apron and handed it to me. "Some help you are! And my maid goes home early on Wednesdays."

"Are you hungry?" Domingos asked. "I'm good in the kitchen."

"You? Maybe." She shook her finger at me. "Not this one. He's as worthless as his cousin, which is why my daughter-in-law is such a disappointment. Although I admit, she's better than her dad."

"That's why I asked Kique to come," I said. "So that he can stay with you when we have to leave."

I wasn't up to dealing with Nana on my own, so I herded everyone into the kitchen. Whether Domingos could cook or not was immaterial. His antics diverted Nana's attention. Watching her boss him around was amusing. Didn't he know what a *comal* was? Even Brazilians ought to know which cooking gadget was especially made for warming up tortillas. Why didn't he roll the limes across the counter before cutting them? That way he could get more juice.

From a safe distance at the kitchen table, Kique and I watched Nana command Domingos as a sorcerer commanding an apprentice. He paid no attention to her advice, cheerfully combining available contents from the refrigerator. As Domingos' stir-fry surprise grew larger and he threw in spices as if he knew what he were doing, Nana's complaints against us weakened. She relaxed despite herself as her nostrils detected pleasant combinations of fried oils and vegetables. Attention was all she really wanted, and now that Domingos was catering to her, she cooled down.

I narrowly resisted taking blackmail pictures that I could have shared with the TucAz musicians. None of them would have imagined Domingos flying around the kitchen as easily as he did on the podium. They would have been particularly tickled by the faded apron Nana insisted on tying around his waist. I sat steadfastly at the table so that I wouldn't have to don an antique, stained apron myself.

By the time we started eating the anonymous concoction, we could only concentrate on filling one tortilla after another. Maybe we were exceptionally hungry, but the mix of frijoles and mystery meat and overly ripe vegetables pleased us immensely. For a moment Nana forgot that she was old and weak and abandoned.

"You are nothing like your friends here," Nana told Domingos.

Behind the woman's back, Kique gestured as if to say, "What does she mean by that?"

"They're lazy and unimaginative," Nana continued. She shook her finger at me. "Like your no-good cousin."

"Beto can't be that bad," I said.

"When my son and Laura moved in here, the house was a mess. Beto came to help them move, but do you know how he helped? He sat on that couch and kept track of the soccer score. Claimed it was some big game. Wouldn't help my son lift a single piece of furniture."

"You can pay people to do that, Nana," I said.

"Why should you when people are taking up space right under your noses?"

Kique wiggled his fingers. "Violinists. So delicate."

"Not delicate. Lazy. And he's too busy to keep a decent job."

My poor cousin seemed to be up for target practice. "He's a musician," I said. "He works funny hours."

"A musician, huh? Then how did he buy a new car and a new house in the same year? He's up to something."

I was too hungry to be interested in someone else's finances. "Maybe he got a good deal."

"No. All of a sudden he has cash on his hands. Too much cash."

"You think he robbed a bank, Nana?" I laughed.

"No, of course not. He's not clever enough. Instead he's selling drugs."

"Beto? No way. He wouldn't do that. I'm sure of it." I was lying. I wasn't sure at all. When it was offered to him, Beto always took the easy way out. That's why he was a mediocre musician. He wasn't bad, but he didn't work hard at anything besides, occasionally, pleasing his wife. But lately the financial world had been in crisis. The usual money that people threw away on live music was harder to come by. I had noticed the problem in California, but Beto would have noticed it much more than I had. Worse, he was satisfied to make enough money to scrape by but not enough to get ahead or save for retirement. I could imagine him doing a drug run for a friend for the promise of quick cash. But it wouldn't have stopped with one run. He would have liked the money so much that he would have been willing to do it again.

"Who cares about Beto?" Domingos asked. "You know about culture. Tell us about the symphony. Laura said you had season tickets?"

Nana laughed. A piece of meat was stuck to the lower part of her chin, and every time she spoke, the blob slid down a millimeter. "Silly man! We don't need tickets. The symphony is free."

"But you attend regularly?"

"We don't miss a concert. My friend Lupe picks me up.

She still has a car."

"She's not scared to drive at night?" Domingos asked.

Nana laughed so hard she knocked over her water glass, and Kique scrambled to contain the liquid to the table. I took a paper towel and dabbed up excess water, but Nana was calm. She didn't mind calamities as long as she'd caused them herself.

"Silly! We don't go on Friday nights. We go to the matinees on Sunday afternoons."

"Of course," Domingos said as if endorsing their choice. "And what do you think of the concertmaster?"

Nana shuddered. "It's a woman. Can you imagine? A woman leading fifty men!"

"Does she do a good job?"

Nana pursed her lips. "She receives a lot of attention. If that means she's doing a good job, then she's perfect."

~

Kique looked up from his iPad. He was ensconced in a comfortable armchair while Domingos and I had sprawled out on the couch. "You guys kill me. You chase a woman all over Europe, follow her to Mexico, and then let her walk right by you."

Domingos and I couldn't believe it ourselves. The sensation was like rushing around the house searching for the sunglasses on top of your head. We both felt unbelievably stupid. Hence after we'd gotten Nana settled down for the night, we'd started consoling ourselves with a twelve-pack of Dos Equis. So far the remedy wasn't working.

"Please don't apply to be prison guards," Kique continued. "The inmates wouldn't bother to run away. They would parade right past you."

Domingos pretended to laugh, but his face showed lines of worry. "I've never dismissed musicians from a rehearsal more than ten minutes early. There are always details that need more work."

Kique tapped his screen. "Remind me not to take a job in

214

your orchestra. It would be too much pressure. Not that I play any instruments."

"I still don't see how the musicians slipped past us," I said.

"They used a back exit," said Domingos.

"Some must have left through the front door," I said glumly. I'd been kicking myself for several hours, but it hadn't done any good. Domingos and I hadn't managed a new plan of action. He'd been waxing nostalgic about his days in Mexico, how comfortable he'd felt in a Latin environment that was similar to his native Brazil. He'd put time into learning Spanish, but the language had come relatively easily. He was from another country, but his fellow students had been interested in his origins and supportive of his efforts. He'd been fortunate to have such a smooth experience. Then Nando had died and everything fell apart.

"Let's face it," Kique said. "Liza figured out you were here and doesn't want to talk."

Domingos softened his voice. "I have to warn her that she's in danger."

"You can't text her?" I asked.

"Her cell is out of service."

"Email?"

"I can't write loudly enough to make her understand."

Kique punched a cushion so deliberately I knew that somewhere inside he was angry. "Danger is relative. Some people like living on the edge."

"This is the wrong kind of edge to live on," Domingos said. "When I talk to her, I'll make her understand."

Kique opened another can of beer. "You're as bad as Andy. He loves a lost cause. But come. You said she played badly in the rehearsal. What makes you say so?"

"She was off-key and off-tempo."

"Maybe you were hearing the other violins," Kique said.

"No. They were rehearsing *Don Juan*. She was playing the solos."

215

"Maybe she let somebody else play."

"Only on her deathbed. But it was her. I would recognize the sound of that violin anywhere."

"Without seeing it?" Kique asked.

I nodded. "It's a special instrument. One with a terrific sound. Better tone. More vibrancy. I recognized it myself."

Kique made a gliding motion with his hand. "And yet you let her skate right past you."

"You should talk," I said. "You went 'around the corner' for a soda and came back an hour later."

Kique shrugged. "I was doing research. I found a mariachi playing at a restaurant. I stayed and listened for a while."

"Oh, right," I said. "Research."

"Did you talk to the musicians?" Domingos said. "They might have given you a lead."

"Mariachi players?" I spread my arms as far apart as they would go. "They're in one world. Classical musicians are in another."

"They might know something," Domingos said. "Don't rule them out categorically."

"Exactly," Kique said. "That's why I asked about their schedule. They'll be at the same restaurant tomorrow. We can question them."

"Sure," I said. "Comic relief."

Kique pretended not to hear me. He salted a lime and sucked the juice from it. "You already told me about Liza's husband. Tell me about her lovers."

"The violin always came first," Domingos said. "Nando was an interlude. He was the first man she went crazy over. His death changed everything."

"And after Nando?"

Domingos shrugged.

"Lots of lovers," Kique said.

"Musicians are passionate," said Domingos. "It shouldn't surprise you."

"No serious boyfriends?"

216

"None that lasted. After a few months she would give them up and start over. That way she could concentrate on her playing."

"What was so special about the Mexican she met in Lyon?" I asked.

"Nothing. She was unhappy living in Europe, so when he sweet-talked her, she fell for it. She was being way too naïve. I told her so, but she didn't listen."

Of course not. Liza would only listen to someone who told her exactly what she wanted to hear. It wouldn't have been difficult to fool her.

Domingos nodded at the air. "Miguel told her how talented she was. How beautiful. He offered her a way to get back to Mexico, which meant a way to be close to her son."

"She could have moved back to Mexico at any time," I said.

"Liza couldn't stand the thought of being ordinary. She wanted to be concertmaster. Miguel said he'd use his contacts to help."

I couldn't imagine Liza falling for a man, but I could easily imagine her falling for an ideal. In her mind, at least, she'd worked harder than anybody. Hence she deserved more than anybody. If Miguel were the means to her end, so be it. Her line of thinking was dangerous, but it wasn't uncommon.

"What went wrong?" Kique asked.

"I believe Miguel used his contacts to keep her out," Domingos said slowly. "She auditioned for the chamber ensemble, the orchestra, the opera. Every time it was a different story. 'You need to work on rhythm,' or 'You need to work on intonation,' or 'You need to work on bowing.' She would call me and cry."

I assumed Domingos cried along with her. Maybe Liza had never fallen in love with him, but somewhere along the line, Domingos had fallen in love with her. Maybe he couldn't help himself. Maybe she gave him the depth to conduct pain.

"So she didn't play at all?" I asked.

217

"Miguel wanted her to do some recordings, but she was never satisfied."

"Why not?" Kique asked. "Poor equipment?"

"She felt that she wasn't good enough. She's a perfectionist, but Miguel intended to put CDs on the market as quickly as possible. He was creating his own label, so he wanted her to record one set of concertos after another. She didn't have enough hours in the day to satisfy her own standards and still meet his schedule."

I imagined an additional disconnect. Liza thrived on attention. She craved the oohs and ahs that came from a live audience. A sterile recording studio wouldn't provide the same excitement. Hence Liza wouldn't play to the top of her abilities. As much as I hated to admit that we had any similarities, I knew that in a similar situation, I would react in the same way.

"Who is this guy?" Kique asked.

"Nobody interesting. A businessman."

"Which one?"

"Miguel Sánchez de Avila."

Kique slammed down his beer can so fast that half the contents bounced out. "The investment tycoon?"

I sat up straight. Kique wasn't impressed by famous personalities per se. What impressed him was power. The wrong kind.

Domingos watched Kique carefully. "How did you know about him?"

"He's one of the richest men in Mexico!"

"I suppose."

"He owns half of Mexico City."

"You're exaggerating," Domingos said.

"And he's a noted humanitarian. Last year he won an award for his donations to the arts. Of course, he's rich enough, so he can afford it."

"Yes. He's donating profits from his recordings. Hence, in part, his interest in Liza."

218

"Recently I read an article about him," Kique said. "How he doubled his money in eight short years. He's a business genius. Or a cheat. Or both. And I'm pretty sure he's married. How could Liza be dumb enough to fall for him?"

Domingos was silent for so long I assumed he would lash out at Kique. Instead the man's eyes sank inward.

"I don't see the problem," I said quickly, trying to act as a bridge. "And let's back up a step. Why wouldn't this guy want her to be concertmaster?"

"You've heard the song, Andy." To my surprise, Domingos whistled the first bars of *"La calandria,"* a metaphorical song about a bird in a cage. I'd never met a non-Mexican who was familiar with the lyrics, but they fit the situation perfectly. Miguel wanted Liza to be the little violinist in his recording studio. De facto, Liza would have made a terrible bird. She would have flung herself against the cage so hard that she would have broken her wings.

"He wanted her to concentrate on recordings," I said.

"Yes. There was a certain logic to his plan."

"I'm surprised Liza would go along with it," I said.

"She was hoodwinked by her emotions. She loved him at first. Or thought she did," Domingos said.

"And then?" Kique asked.

"Eventually she realized she wasn't in control."

Kique shrugged. "She was a business investment. She should have realized that."

"She was practical," Domingos said quickly. "She wanted to support her son."

"But you weren't practical at all, were you, Domingos?" I asked. "You took the job in Tucson to be close to Liza. You took a pay cut. You left Europe, for crying out loud."

Domingos shuddered, and I suddenly felt bad for insulting him.

"The TucAz is a good opportunity for me," Domingos said softly, "but, yes, I wanted to be nearby. I kept telling Liza to come play for me. Finally she did."

219

"Liza was the mistress of Miguel Sánchez de Avila," Kique said slowly. "She thought she could run away from him?"

"She claimed he wouldn't care."

Kique crushed an empty beer can, making a loud crunching sound. "About her, no. About his reputation, maybe. But I admit, it's ingenious of her to hide in Mexico."

"How so?" I asked.

"That's the last place Miguel would look."

Chapter Twenty-Seven

"Are you sure they said they'd be playing today?" Domingos asked. We were seated in the sparse outdoor patio of Carnitas Buenas, the restaurant around the corner from the School of Music. "It's already three-fifteen. You said they started at three."

Kique smiled. "Don't you have such a thing as Brazilian time?"

Domingos picked up a menu. "When it's something important, we come on time. Maybe early. We take ourselves seriously."

"So do mariachi players, but it's against code to admit to it," I said. "They might lose face. They're like the students who sit in the last row and wouldn't be caught dead raising their hands."

"Speaking of teachers, did you remember to call Rachel?" Domingos asked.

Whoops. No, I hadn't. I reached for my cell phone and turned it on. I'd meant to call the night before, but the first time I remembered she would have been teaching, and the second time I remembered it was already three a.m.

Before I could complete the call, I heard the familiar jingle of mariachi players in costume. Four twenty-somethings came into view. They carried the typical instruments: a *guitarrón*, which was like a string bass but carried across the chest, a *vihuela*, which was a small rhythm instrument about the size of a mandolin, a trumpet, and a violin. The men wore traditional black *trajes*, specially-made suits with silver-plated buttons running up and down their pant legs. The jackets had silver buttons on the chest and at the end of the sleeves. The men also wore white shirts and black boots and special red ties called *moños*, which were like floppy versions of bow ties.

"What should we say to them?" Domingos asked.

"Nothing yet," I said. "Let them warm up."

The musicians nodded to us casually and disappeared

around the corner. We weren't their target audience. They were hoping for couples, or rather, for young men trying to make an impression on their dates, or perhaps men who were out of their lovers' good graces and trying to get back into them.

The musicians started playing *Alejandra*, a popular old waltz, but I shook my head after three seconds.

"What's the matter?" asked Kique.

"They're not mariachi players," I said. "Listen closely."

"What's the problem?" asked Domingos.

The musicians were out of my line of sight, but I could hear every note clearly. "Can't you guess?"

Kique shrugged. "They sound good to me."

"To me too," said Domingos.

"Exactly! The problem is that there is no problem. They're too smooth."

Domingos raised his eyebrows. "Come again?"

"They're playing with dynamics."

"What's a dynamic?" asked Kique.

"How loudly or softly you're playing," said Domingos. "Andy, you're right, but I don't follow."

"They're classically trained. They're polished. Listen to the violin player. His intonation is exact and his vibrato is controlled."

"Maybe the musicians in this town have superior training," said Domingos.

"No."

The group worked its way in our direction because a young couple had sat down nearby. The woman wanted to hear *La barca*, *The Boat*, a romantic bolero that didn't have a mariachi version per se. I'd sung the tune a few times myself—anything to please the customers—but the modern Luis Miguel version that people were familiar with was instrumented for orchestra, and thus awkward to perform with only four players.

The quartet didn't attempt the song at all. They merely apologized. Strike One. A bona fide mariachi group was supposed to have a complete repertoire, but I understood the

222

problem intimately. People asked for non-mariachi songs all the time, and they took it personally if you couldn't comply.

The group struck out again on the very next request. The woman asked for *Ojitos traidores*, *Traitorous Eyes*, a fast number in a minor key. It was probably among the first hundred I'd learned.

"Go help them out," said Kique.

I shook my head. "They'll be okay."

The mariachi players talked amongst themselves, but they concluded that they couldn't play the song. Strike Two. What else might the couple like to hear? A Juan Gabriel song, the woman said. The one about staying in the same city in case the lover comes back looking for her. The players looked from one to the other. No one knew the words. They couldn't even remember the name of the song.

Kique dug his fingers into my shoulder. "Come on, Andy. This is painful."

The situation was not unusual. The mariachi repertoire was so ridiculously large that not even the best groups could cover all the requests. The learning process was never-ending. That was part of the charm.

Audibly, but not loudly, I sang the first two words, which were *Probablemente ya*, "probably already."

The musicians turned towards me. I held up five fingers, indicating the key of G. As I stood and neared the musicians, I motioned for the vihuela player to strum the chord six times, which was a shortened way to start the song. For a moment the man stared at me as if I'd come from Antarctica in an ostrich suit. Then he caught on and played the rhythm I had dictated.

I'd sung Juan Gabriel's tribute to breakup angst many times. It was at once a lament and a shred of hope: Probably you've already forgotten me, but in case you come back to look for me, I'll be right here waiting.

As I started singing, the woman clapped enthusiastically, and her companion beckoned me to come closer. While I did so, the musicians scrambled. The song used a typical chord progression, but only the vihuela player was familiar with the tune. I already knew what that meant: Neither the trumpeter nor the violinist would be able to play the bridge. When we got close to the end of the verse, I signaled for the latter to hand over his instrument. He did so without hesitation, silently thanking me as I played for him.

By the time we started the second half of the song, the woman had put her hand in the man's lap. Both of them listened to us intently, and for a fleeting moment I could be happy for the simple pleasures in life such as delighting a loving couple by punctuating their afternoon.

"Bravo!" they cried when we finished.

"Tantas gracias," the mariachi players said in chorus. *Thanks a lot.*

I addressed the *guitarrón* player. "Can you play *Ojitos traidores*?"

He nodded in a "yes and no" kind of way.

The fast, haunting song had always been one of my favorites. "Key of A minor," I said. I put the borrowed violin to my shoulder and sailed through the intro without missing a note. As I sang, I signaled the chords to my rookie companions, who scrambled to keep up.

The couple nodded appreciatively. For a moment I was back at Noche Azul Restaurant, back with my mariachi group, back in control of my life. Then we reached the end of the song, and the illusion vanished.

Next the couple asked for *El rey, The King,* a standard any mariachi band would know even if its repertoire only included five numbers. I handed the violin back to its owner, who was still nonplussed but grateful, and returned to my friends.

Domingos and Kique took turns ribbing me about showing off until the musicians took a break and swarmed our table. They introduced themselves and thanked me for helping them out.

"Where do you play?" asked David, pronounced "Da-VEED," who was the *guitarrón* player. "You know all the songs."

"I knew all the songs today," I said. "Sit with us. Would you like a beer or something?"

Horacio loosened his bow as he nodded yes, but David shook his head. "We better not. We have rehearsal a little later."

"For the orchestra," I said.

"How did you know that?" asked Aidán, the trumpet player. He took a close look at Kique. "Weren't you at the School of Music yesterday?"

"And you guys were late getting to rehearsal."

Lalo, the *vihuela* player, hung his head. "If we have a good customer, we stay overtime. Maestro Alfredo gives us the chance."

"The classical world doesn't pay well down here, does it?" I asked.

They shook their heads. Classical music paid terribly. They'd only taken up the mariachi thing to help them get through the month.

"We see that you have a new concertmaster," said Kique. "What do you think of her?"

Horacio shielded his eyes with his hands. Aidán used his trumpet to do the same. The others didn't speak.

"That bad?" I asked.

"She's always harping at us," said Aidán. "I mean the whole orchestra, not only the violins. Trying to prove that she's the only real musician in the room."

Horacio cut in. "She waltzes in last month, needs a job, insists on an audition, and then insists on the top chair. Must have slept with Maestro Alfredo, right? She's good and all that, but nobody's perfect."

"It's her prima donna attitude that I can't stand," said Lalo. "She plays okay."

"Do any of you guys know where she lives?" Kique asked.

The four men recoiled as if we'd pulled a rattlesnake from

225

under the table. Domingos started to speak, but I gently placed my foot on his. I wasn't sure which direction Kique was going, but I was sure he had a plan.

"Why do you want to know?" asked Lalo. "You don't want to date her. Believe me."

Kique lowered his voice. "Can you keep something to yourselves?"

They nodded.

"That bitch owes me money."

The men oohed and moved in closer.

"Last week I was at the School of Music waiting for a friend and she comes up all flustered that she needs new strings but the rehearsal is about to start and can I please, please, please go buy them for her. And I do. Crazy, huh?"

Everyone nodded, anxious for him to continue. Especially me and Domingos.

"Then I get back to the School of Music and she claims she doesn't have any cash. But she begs me to come back the next day so she can pay me. And stupid me, I come back. And guess what? She doesn't show. So I'm thinking thanks a lot, right?

"Right," said David.

"So I go look for her the next time. And she's all apologetic, oh, she meant to bring money but she didn't and all that. So today I'm following her home. If she doesn't have any money, she can give me a watch or something. That's only fair."

"You're absolutely right," said Horacio.

"Except she's such a bitch that if she sees me, she'll probably sneak out the back. So if I knew where she lived, I could wait for her there."

"I don't even want to know where she lives," said Lalo, "but she's renting a house from a relative of one of the French horn players. When we get to the rehearsal, I'll be happy to point him out to you."

"See, Andy," Kique told me as if we'd been betting on it.

226

"I told you I could get my money back. All you need is a little faith." He winked at the musicians. "And a few friends."

~

"She's not going to show," Kique said an hour later. "No way."

Kique and Domingos and I were sitting behind a six-foot planter at the School of Music. We were positioned so that Kique could see everyone going in and out of the rehearsal room but where Domingos and I were both shielded by potted palms. We hadn't given up our hope of taking Liza by surprise.

"Why are you negative all of a sudden?" I asked.

Kique put his hands on his stomach. "She's not coming. I can feel it."

"I have the same gut feeling," Domingos said. "Unfortunately, my gut is usually right."

I peeked at the patio, but the scene was nearly identical to the one the day before. In the far corner a choir teacher was going through a scale with a trio of singers. Several students seated on a bench were watching a video on a tablet. Two more students were near the entrance taking selfies. Others lazily crisscrossed the area. Hints of other instruments—a piano, a trombone, a flute—floated through the air like a whisper in the breeze.

"I'm not feeling anything at all," I said. "Does that make me callous or practical?"

"It makes you vulnerable," Kique said.

"To what?"

"Not now," he said, "but in a few seconds look behind you. Watch the entrance."

Domingos stood. "Is Liza out there?"

"Sit down! We're trying to be subtle, remember? But no, Liza is not there."

Slowly Domingos sat, a jack-in-the-box ready to explode at any minute.

I waited a few seconds. The entrance had intricate carvings along its arch, but the effect was hardly unusual. Any number of nearby buildings displayed similar designs.

"Nice stonework," I said. "It's typical for mid-Mexico. The colonial style—"

"Andy, forget the building. Watch who's passing by."

The entrance was so high that it afforded a clear view of the street beyond. At this hour of the day, there were plenty of passersby. In a moment's time, I saw a couple of guys, a lady with a stroller, several ten-year-olds, a young woman, and a candy vendor. "And?"

"A couple of guys keep walking past the entrance," Kique said. They're looking for something. Or someone."

"They might have followed us here," Domingos said.

"No. They were outside the School of Music when we arrived. That was twenty minutes ago. Look."

Two men passed by. They wore boots and jeans, but they wouldn't have been mistaken for music students. Not only were they lots older, but they had a different demeanor. They were more determined.

"Ever seen them before?" I asked Domingos.

"Of course not, Andy. I've never been here before."

"They're not local," said Kique.

"How do you know that?"

"If they were, they'd know how to blend."

Horacio and his friends shot through the entrance and hurried towards the rehearsal room, waving to us briefly as they scooted by. They'd changed to street clothes, but their *trajes* stuck out of their bags at odd angles.

"That's a very understanding conductor," said Domingos.

"It's a conductor who understands the circumstances," I said. "In Mexico being a musician means making sacrifices. You never make quite enough money. You're never quite comfortable. Instead you spend your life on the edge, hoping for the best."

"But you never lived down here, right?" Domingos asked.

"I get reports from Cousin Beto. He gets by, but he doesn't get ahead."

"His daughter seems to be doing all right," said Kique.

"She was smart enough not to follow in his footsteps."

Domingos raised his arms. "Surely you don't think all these students are doomed."

"Music is a luxury. If they want to break poverty level, they'll have to branch out."

"Look," Kique said.

The two pacers had entered the building. Once they reached the patio, they didn't know what to do. For a minute or two they stood in the middle. Then the shorter one ducked inside the orchestra's rehearsal room. As he came back out, he shook his head. Then they both returned to the street.

"They can't find Liza either," Kique said.

Domingos tried to smile. "You don't know for sure that they're looking for her."

"They're not carrying instruments," I said, "and they walked right past the vocalists. What do you think they are, electricians?"

"They could be music lovers. Or reporters who've come to do an interview."

Kique rubbed his forehead as if he could wipe away nonsense with his fingers. "I told you already. This doesn't have to do with music. It's more personal. You have to consider the bigger picture."

"There is no bigger picture," said Domingos.

"Ten-minute break," shouted the conductor. Players immediately filed into the patio, stretching their legs and chatting with one another.

"Come on," I said. "Let's go find that French horn player."

"Don't you think we should wait for the end of the rehearsal?" Domingos asked.

I didn't need to answer. Kique had already headed towards the brass.

Chapter Twenty-Eight

Liza must have made a nuisance of herself. The French horn player gave out her address before we explained why we wanted it. He also gave us all the pertinent details. His aunt owned a large house as well as a guest house, but she spent most of her time with a daughter who lived in Laredo. The property was near the corner of Abasolo and Parrodi, which was only a few blocks from the School of Music. The dwelling stood on a lot shared by neighboring houses. At night the driveway leading into the lot was protected by a metal chain gate, but during the day people were always coming and going. As long as we arrived before dark, we could stroll right in. The guest house was one or two buildings to the left of the gate.

Since we wanted to avoid as many residents as possible, we stalled by going back to Laura's to pick up the car. After we returned, we cruised the area until the street was quiet and the gate was locked. That suited us fine. We might have waited until someone came home and opened it. Kique and I could have made up some excuse about being the cousin of so-and-so or the nephews of such-and-such. Given our convincing Mexican Spanish, as long as we remained loose and cool, people would have believed us. But we didn't have that much patience. Since the gate was only six-feet high, we scaled it instead, faintly rattling the metal as we did so.

The driveway led into a graveled area that served as a parking lot for all the residents' vehicles.

"Think one belongs to Liza?" I asked Domingos.

"The School of Music is within walking distance. I'm sure Liza was aware of that when she rented the house."

"She doesn't seem like the walking type," I said. "All those high heels."

"Make no mistake," Domingos said. "If she had enough money, she would have bought a car. She would have made it a priority."

"Would she have bought any of these?" Kique asked.

Domingos glanced at the model nearest us. Then he walked down the row, ignoring the pickups but checking each car. "These are all too old," he said.

"You're sure?" I asked.

"I'm pretty sure."

Beyond the gravel lay a ring of houses. Lights showed in several of the windows, but no one took notice of us. There was good reason for this. It was the hour of *Encarcelado por amor, Jailed by Love*, the *telenovela* featuring Miguel's lookalike. On a warmer night we would have heard echoes of the soap opera through every single living room window.

We easily identified the guest house, which was the only one-story building in the bunch. The structure was illuminated by a tiny porch light, but the inside was dark, the curtains were drawn, and the windows were barred. The only sign of personality was a wall hanging on the front door. The faded blue-green owl had been crafted with yarn and a bottle of glue. Its chest was vaguely yellow. Giant sunglasses protected its big eyes. The decoration didn't match anything I knew about Liza. It was the kind of present you displayed because your youngest nieces had made it for you, and you couldn't stand to disappoint them. Such sentimentality didn't fit what I knew about Liza either.

Kique tested the bars on the front window. "The metal is for show. That's definitely a possibility." Then he tried the door handle, roughly twisting it from side to side. "This will be even easier." He took out a Swiss pocket knife and hunted for the right attachment.

"Don't bother," Domingos said. He took the wall hanging from the door. It dangled from a rod that had rubber tips at either end. He pried open one of the tips, and then turned the rod upside down. Out fell a metal key.

"She always locks herself out," Domingos explained. "After rescuing her in the middle of the night, twice, I gave her this owl so that she could hide a key for emergency situations. She takes the owl with her wherever she lives. It's the first thing she packs."

I shook my head. I lost many things, but house keys I held onto. "Seems like a dangerous plan to me."

"Who's really safe anyway?" asked Domingos. "Anyway, it saves her money on locksmiths." He opened the door, found a light switch, and flipped it on. "Coming?"

Kique and I automatically recoiled. The air was musty, as if the house had been locked up for weeks on end and the dust had started reproducing itself.

"You guys check," Kique said. "I'll stay here and keep an eye out."

Kique was making an excuse, but I didn't blame him. I wanted to stay outside myself. Nonetheless, I followed Domingos into a sparse living room with a concrete floor and a tiny rug. The walls were a rusty orange. Neither the couch nor the matching easy chairs looked inviting because the cushions were lumpy, and the blue corduroy was discolored from years of sweaty butts. The one light bulb, the old style, hung down from the ceiling, naked. Maybe Liza had chosen a low wattage on purpose. Seeing the room in brighter light would have only made it more depressing.

Behind the easy chairs was a flimsy metal music stand littered with symphony parts. Two black music folders lay at its feet. The stand faced the window, and I imagined that Liza daydreamed from time to time during tedious rehearsal sessions.

The heavy air made me feel uneasy. Maybe it was mold. When I got close to the walls, I could see that the paint was peeling and chipping off. Bunches of chips had fallen on the floor. In a modern art museum they might have been considered artistic, but I doubted that Liza had noticed. She wouldn't have looked down far enough to see the floor.

Despite the brisk air, I opened a window. "How about a little oxygen?"

"Good idea."

Domingos stood in the middle of the room as if he could

233

imagine Liza inside it. Despite the convenient location, this didn't seem like the kind of living space she would choose. It seemed like a hideout where you could crash if necessary. The house was so crummy that it would drain away your energy for anything else.

The bedroom was arguably more cheerful than the living room. The area was as sparse, but there were signs of a woman. A silk nightie lay on an unmade double bed, clothes hung on a rack, a vanity displayed hair ties, and a small cardboard box overflowed with fancy shoes. The mustiness prevailed, however. I opened the window in this room as well, and cold drafts rushed in.

Domingos stood before the clothes rack that was jammed with dresses and blouses. Finally he separated two of the hangers and fingered a black garment. "Remember this?"

It was the dress that Liza had cut the fake diamond from, the dress that may have cost F.J. his life. On the slender metal wire, the rag looked innocent.

"That outfit is hard to forget."

"Right. My most memorable concert."

"Mine too."

Domingos went to the vanity and opened each drawer.

"What are you thinking?"

He was fingering lingerie. "I miss her."

"Right. For the moment that's beside the point."

He went to the bed and dropped to his knees so that he could feel around underneath.

I could already imagine what he was looking for. Back in California, I'd always hidden my violin under the bed. I didn't like the implications. Either I wasn't clever enough to find an original hiding place, or Liza and I shared another similarity.

"There's a herd of dust down here," Domingos said. He used his cell phone to shine a light under the bed. The only object was a violin case.

He started coughing and had to come up for air.

"Well?"

234

"She's still in town. She would have never left without her baby."

"Does she always hide it under her bed?"

"When it fits."

We continued to the kitchen, which was also lit with one single bulb, but this room was distinct. It smelled worse than the other rooms combined. Double doors hid a pantry to the left. Smudges decorated the wall to the right. Straight ahead, a counter contained an empty milk carton and a sack of pork rinds. The stove was clean; I assumed Liza had never used it. Ripe bananas filled a wooden bowl above the refrigerator. Dirty plates towered in the sink. A dish towel cluttered the floor. Had I been Liza, I wouldn't have come home either.

I went straight to the window, which was over the sink, and threw it all the way open. "Does Liza have something against fresh air?"

"She hates to be cold." He sighed as he took in the details of the grungy room. "But she's always been a terrible housekeeper."

"Next to her I'm a professional maid."

Domingos opened the refrigerator and scowled at the contents. "Oh, God. I might have guessed. Do you see a garbage can?"

Under the sink I found a pile of empty plastic sacks. I held one open while Domingos started with the bottom shelf of the fridge and worked his way up. He threw away baggies with half-eaten sandwiches, dead tomatoes, and a head of decaying cabbage. After checking the expiration date, he threw out the assorted containers of yogurt. He opened a jar of salsa, smelled it, and put it back in the refrigerator. He was doing the same with a bottle of salad dressing when my cell phone rang.

Domingos added a container of grapes to the pile of garbage. "Answer later. It's probably Rachel."

I set down the sack and checked the number. Country code: 52, meaning Mexico. City code, 6188, meaning Durango. "What?" I asked Kique.

235

"Turn off the light and get out. You can use the front door, but hurry. Then go around to the back of the house. Wait for my signal."

"What?"

He hung up.

Domingos motioned for me to hold open the sack. "Come on! We're almost done."

I flung the sack towards the corner. "We're leaving."

"But Andy—"

I jerked his arm so hard that he stumbled. "Now."

I pushed him through the front door and gestured for him to go around the side of the house. I'd forgotten about the light. I started to go back, but when someone rattled the metal gate that led into the parking lot, I joined Domingos.

"Where are you, bitch!" yelled a voice in Spanish.

"We'll find you!"

Domingos and I listened while two heavyset men worked to climb the gate. They didn't make it on the first try. By then we had scooted around to the back of the house where a conglomeration of weeds and bushes vied for dominance. I wondered if San Luís had any snakes right before crouching in the bushes and pulling Domingos down with me.

"What about Liza?" Domingos whispered.

"Be glad she's not home."

The two men made it over the gate. They stood silently for a few moments before spotting the guest house and heading our way. Together they banged on the door with full force while shouting "Liza." From the dull thuds, I assumed that one of the men rammed the door with his shoulder. Then one was smart enough to test the door handle and walk right in.

Domingos tried to peek through the window, but I grabbed his jacket and pulled him back down. At the same time my cell phone beeped.

"Meet me out on the street," read Kique's text.

Domingos and I ran for the gate as quietly as possible. We scaled it the same way. By the time we made it to Abasolo,

236

Kique was waiting with the engine running. I hadn't closed the passenger door when he rocketed off, narrowly missing a Ford truck that had been parked in a sloppy diagonal.

"What happened?" Domingos asked from the backseat. "Who were they?"

Kique checked the rearview mirror, but nobody was following us. "The guys we saw at the School of Music. I told you something was wrong about them."

"They followed us here?" I asked.

"I don't think so."

"Why not?"

"If they thought they had company, they wouldn't have made so much noise."

Kique drove several blocks in silence.

"Now what?" asked Domingos.

"We go back to Liza's and we wait," said Kique.

"What if they're still around? Oh. They came by car?"

"Pickup."

"You caught the number on the license plate?"

Had the conductor not looked like a ghost, Kique would have razzed him. Under normal circumstances he would have razzed me too, but the situation was far from normal. "Yes, Domingos. But that won't do us any good."

"Why not?"

"It's registered in Mexico City. The police will wash their hands of it."

"Surely they won't ignore a break-in?" Domingos asked.

"Did you remember to lock the door?"

Domingos fished around in his pocket and produced Liza's spare key. "No. Andy rushed me out of the house."

Kique's eyes didn't leave the road. "So it wasn't a break-in. It was a walk-in. That's different."

We continued down a couple of dark blocks before making a circle and heading back to Liza's. The houses we passed were closed up and quiet. Everyone else in town was in bed. Good choice.

"Notice anything important about the men?" Kique asked me.

"Mexican," I said.

"Anything else?"

"They were so out of shape that they could barely get themselves over that gate."

Kique nodded patiently. "That much I already know." He turned onto Parrodi and parked across from the lot's entryway, but the pickup was already gone.

Domingos started to get out of the car.

"No," Kique said.

Domingos continued to open the door. "I want to see if they did any damage."

"The house doesn't matter. Get back in the car."

I'd never heard anyone tell Domingos what to do before. Then again, Kique wasn't an awestruck musician. He was a project manager.

"They might have stolen the violin," Domingos continued.

Kique stared straight ahead. "They weren't here for the violin."

I took out my worry beads and started twirling them. "So what should we do?"

Kique stretched his legs. "I told you already. We wait."

But we didn't. After an hour we were so sleepy that Liza might have walked right past us. Or maybe she already had.

238

Chapter Twenty-Nine

Laura's mother-in-law was thoroughly disappointed in us. Not only had we failed to visit the mask museum, the art center, and the Silva Federico Museum, but we hadn't toured the cathedral. Didn't we know that San Luís was a town of cultural treasures? We were no better than farm animals. On top of our cultural deficiencies, we'd left her alone all evening AGAIN. Her daughter-in-law had assured her that we would keep her company. After all, she was an old woman, and something might happen to her at any time. She might have a heart attack. She might have a stroke. She might need a glass of water.

I was saved by Arnulfo's guitar. Although Nana reminded me every few minutes that my voice was not as beautiful as her son's, she appreciated the fact that I could sing every song she asked for. Tunes from the time of the revolution? No problem. I knew all the verses to *Adelita*, and I only mixed up a few of the words. Pedro Infante's hits from famous movies? I could sing them faster than she could name them. The best of Vicente Fernández? They might have been written on the back of my hand. I even enjoyed singing them.

Finally Nana toddled off to bed with Domingos not far behind, but I was more awake than I'd been all day. How would I ever play another concert without being distracted by thoughts of escape artists and snipers? In contrast, a surprise visit from a Martian or two would be a cakewalk.

"You sounded good," Kique said without looking up from his iPad.

"Didn't think you were listening."

"You probably shouldn't think!"

"Find anything important?"

He nodded. "A friend sent me the notes from today's lectures."

"I'm sorry you had to miss your classes."

"Believe me, they're boring. Getting the notes is good enough."

"Do you like law school?"

He set down the device. "I like thinking that I can make a difference. That's probably naïve."

"Either way, it's better to think that way."

"I'm not sure it makes any difference. Mexico is so jammed up that there's no going back. The gap between the rich and poor gets wider because big companies go after the little guys. They wind up on the street asking for handouts."

On the way into San Luís from the airport, we'd seen ads for Walmart and Sam's Club. How many little businesses had those chains destroyed?

"I suppose Miguel Sánchez de Avila is the quintessential corporate type who gobbles people up," I said.

"That's why he keeps getting richer. Over the past twelve months, he's acquired sixty-three small companies. Squeezed them right out of business. Put people out of work left and right."

Reprehensible, certainly, but probably not illegal. Or surprising. "Women?"

"He's married to Anna Isabella García Rojas. Rich family. Property owners."

"Did you find any gossip about Miguel and Liza?"

"No, although he's been linked to several mistresses in the past. Why would he go for Liza?"

"She's a brilliant musician."

"Yeah, yeah. Somebody told me that brilliant musicians are a dollar a dozen."

The someone Kique was referring to was me. On balance I still agreed with myself, but I might have been exaggerating. "Liza combines expertise with passion. That makes her an exceptionally fine performer."

"But she skips rehearsals."

"Not usually. She must have sensed someone was following her and known enough to run."

Kique shook his head. "From what you've said, she's not people smart."

240

"Maybe she got lucky."

"Is Domingos sleeping with her?"

"He says he's not."

"And you believe him?"

"He says that she saved his life. That she made him a great conductor. In the competitive world of classical music, it's hard to find friends."

"What about you, Andy?"

"I'm not sure who my friends are either."

Kique's eyes pierced me, but his voice was calm. Tenacious. Patient. "What else?"

"You're going to be a good lawyer," I said.

"That's not what I asked."

"I'm living with your cousin."

Had Kique's eyes been lasers, they would have pierced me. "That's still not what I asked."

"I wouldn't sleep with Liza if she paid me herself."

"Good." He turned back to his iPad.

For a moment I listened to the sounds of the night: the buzz of the lamp, the minute hand of the wall clock, distant traffic. Normal, soothing sounds that signaled the end of the day. For a moment I had the sensation that it was a normal night. Then I remembered where I was and why.

"Do you think I'd ask for your help if I had anything going with Liza?"

Kique didn't look up. "I had to be sure."

"I love your cousin."

"Uh huh."

"You don't believe me?"

"I believe you love her in your own way."

The condemnation stung because it was so accurate. In California I'd dated without getting serious. I never found a woman who could sympathize with my music schedule, and thus I could make an escape. A relationship with Rachel was more challenging because it could actually work.

"I'm not sure my way of loving will be enough," I said.

Kique flipped his iPad shut as if it pained him to do so. "You're right. You'll have to decide to be all in or all out." He put two fingers to his forehead and then pointed those same fingers at mine. "No worries. We're friends either way."

Kique understood reluctance. He didn't condemn me for it. Then again, he was in his twenties, so he still had plenty of time.

"Do you think Rachel wants to get married?" I asked.

"Not necessarily."

"What then?"

"She's heading towards forty."

I already knew what Kique was thinking: the "f" word. Family. But I was terrible with children. I would be a bad influence. I wouldn't know what to do. I would panic when it cried. Excuses flew through my head like raindrops in a monsoon.

"I'm not sure I'm good enough to help her with that," I said.

"I'm not sure you are either."

~

Hours later I was still lying in bed awake. I knew the time because every few minutes I checked the bright orange letters on the guest room alarm clock. 3:36 a.m. 4:07. 5:25. A kid?! I wasn't cut out for it. I couldn't handle it. My brother managed beautifully because he was so different than I was. More patient. Responsible. Neat. I would be all wrong.

Kique entered the room and turned on the light. "Andy, wake up."

"What's the matter?"

"Get dressed."

"Where are you going?"

"To wake up Domingos."

I wasn't quick enough to protest, but it didn't matter. Domingos woke instantly. "What happened?" he asked as he joined us in the family room.

Kique showed us his iPad and tapped the left side of the

242

screen. "We went to Liza's guest house by going through the gate on Parrodi. That's the only way a car can enter." Then he tapped the right side. "But a person could have easily entered from Calle de la Esperanza."

Domingos snapped his fingers. "She might have slipped in while we were waiting in the car."

"Exactly."

"I can't believe we didn't think of it," Domingos said.

Kique nodded. "Google Maps. Very handy. Ready?"

We trooped out to Kique's car. When the maestro claimed the passenger seat, I didn't protest. He was all nerves. His neck muscles were taut. He didn't allow himself any regrets, but I knew he was thinking that we'd missed our window of opportunity. Liza might have left town. She was clever enough to have done so without leaving many clues.

Earlier in the evening the streets had been quiet, but now they were so deserted that they were otherworldly. We were the only people in town who were awake, and the black sky proved that dawn was far off. Normal people were sound asleep at this time. So were criminals.

Domingos tapped on the glove compartment. "Have any candy or anything?"

"Maybe. You can check."

Domingos shuffled through the maps and papers. "Why do you have three cell phones in here?"

"Andy always loses his."

"I wouldn't say 'always,'" I said.

Kique's eyes didn't leave the road. "Almost always."

"Oh, God," said Domingos.

"What's the matter?" I asked.

He pulled out a revolver, held it up, and stuffed it back into the glove compartment. "Your friend also has a gun."

Kique shrugged. "I like to be prepared."

"Aren't you overdoing it?" Domingos asked.

"No."

Although we circled Liza's block, we didn't see the

243

pickup. We parked across the street and walked towards the gate. This time we didn't have to scale it. The gate was already open.

"Careful," Domingos whispered. "Somebody must be out here."

Kique pointed to a rock that held the gate in place. "No. Someone works an early shift." He surveyed the other houses, all of which were dark. "We still have some time."

We went straight to Liza's house and quietly pushed our way inside. Kique guided us around with a pocket flashlight. The music stand was lying on its side, perhaps the victim of a savage kick, and loose pages were scattered across the floor. Otherwise the room was undisturbed. So was the kitchen. The items we had collected in the garbage sack were strewn across the floor, but a stray animal might have done the damage.

Liza's assailants wouldn't have spent much time in the house. Despite several hours of fresh air, the smell was still bad. I was surprised because I assumed Liza was a woman of finer taste. Or maybe she had no sense of smell. Some people didn't. Sometimes that came in handy.

"Liza?" Domingos called softly.

The bedroom was untouched. The same clothes were on the rack. The violin was still under the bed, which was still unmade.

"Where would Liza sleep besides in her own bed?" Kique asked.

For a second I thought Domingos would explode. His neck veins bulged and he took in a giant breath, giving him the illusion of more height. "She likes men, generally."

"So she might have gone out?" Kique asked.

Suddenly Domingos sounded tired. "Let's be honest. She might have stayed in."

"There are plenty of hotels in this city," I said. "She might have taken a room."

"Right," Domingos said, but he didn't mean it. I too thought the scenario unlikely. Liza would have found a cheaper

244

solution. One that was personal.

Domingos returned to the kitchen and started gathering the garbage all over again. Kique and I helped him without saying a word. When the bag was full, Kique took it outside.

I followed Domingos back out to the living room. He stared at the walls as if they could tell him something. Since they wouldn't, he felt defeated. He was used to finding things out right away. He was used to manipulating his world and everyone in it, but Liza didn't cooperate. She was in her own world, and she ruled it more ruthlessly than Domingos ruled his.

I couldn't think of any way to help him. Instead I went back to the bedroom and took out the violin. The reddish tinge was too flashy, but it fit Liza. I plucked a single string and was surprised by the resonance. Even the sound of a plain open string had a magical quality. No wonder Liza produced beauty with the instrument.

Turning the violin over, I studied it from all angles. It had been made from fine woods, probably spruce and cherry. The normal F-stops, the holes that let the instrument sing, were a bit bigger than usual. The scroll was a delicate curlicue, nothing too fancy, but individual enough to be original. As I slid my left hand up and down the neck, I realized that the violin was smaller than most by a quarter or maybe an eighth of an inch. The size would make it easier to play, especially for musicians with smaller hands, because it would require shorter shifts along the fingerboard. As I fingered a three-octave scale, I realized that playing such an instrument would also be easier for me.

Feeling like a trespasser, I took out the bow. It had a nice medium weight and a solid grip. When I held the bow up to the light bulb, I could see the letters "iot-H" along the side. It was probably a French brand in the several-thousand-dollar range, which made it about average. Given the fine violin, the bow wouldn't matter. For the most part, neither would the musician.

Rachel would have been jealous of such an instrument.

245

Rachel! I'd promised to call her the night before. I'd completely forgotten. I started to get out my cell phone, but then I realized I'd forgotten that too.

"Andy?" Domingos called to me from the other room. "She might have switched violins and left a cheap substitute in its place."

"No. This is the instrument she had in Tucson."

Domingos came to the bedroom door. "You're sure?"

As softly as possible, I played the first notes of the theme from *Scheherazade*. The sounds were so beautiful that I played a few more. I couldn't help myself. The instrument was like a breeze dancing over a field of flowers, and for a moment I imagined myself a soloist at a huge concert hall. The violin handled so easily it practically played itself.

Kique rushed in. "Was that you playing?"

Since I was still holding the violin, I didn't have to answer.

"What's the matter?" Domingos asked.

"Nothing. Andy has improved. A lot." He left us alone again.

"So," Domingos said. "You've improved."

I held up the violin. "Anybody can play well with this instrument. I understand that Zoran made it?"

"A few years ago. It won an international luthier's contest. It's one of a kind."

"How did you convince Zoran to sell it to you?"

Domingos smiled. "He owed me a favor."

I smiled too. The conductor had just confirmed buying it. "This instrument is golden."

"I know."

"It has soul. It's like a window to the world."

"That too."

I'd never picked up a piece of wood that I had less desire to put back down. Playing such an instrument was a privilege. An honor. For a few seconds I cradled the violin as if I owned it. Then I realized I looked stupid cradling a violin and put it back in the case.

"I'm surprised she leaves this instrument in the house," I said.

Domingos slid his hands down his cheeks. "She wouldn't have. Not on purpose. Do you know what that means?"

I didn't want to say she might be dead. Domingos didn't want to say it either. Instead we said nothing at all.

Chapter Thirty

"Why are you guys always doing nothing?" Nana asked.
"You're the same as Beto. You stay out all hours of the night,
and when you should be out sightseeing, you sit around like
bums."

It was early evening, and the bums and I were on the patio
trying to get drunk. We'd guarded both entrances to Liza's
until late morning hoping the woman would come home for a
change of clothes. Nothing. We'd gone to the School of Music
half an hour before rehearsal. Not a single musician showed up.
The janitor had no idea why the orchestra wasn't rehearsing.
She didn't care. It wasn't her day to clean the rehearsal room.

"We were supposed to finalize some paperwork with the
orchestra members, but we didn't manage it."

"Why not?" Nana asked. "They didn't offer you enough
money?"

"We couldn't find them," Kique said. He acted as
disgusted as possible.

"We went to their rehearsal, but it must have been
cancelled," I said. "And we have to fly out tomorrow morning.
But don't worry. You won't be alone for long. Laura and
Arnulfo will be back tomorrow afternoon. I already talked to
them."

"You fellas aren't so smart, are you?"

Kique turned his head, but I could hear him snickering. I
wanted to do the same. So did Domingos.

"You're right, Nana. We're not so smart. We can't even
cook." I indicated the remains of the fast food tacos we'd
grabbed from a neighborhood takeaway.

"No, silly. Of course you didn't find any musicians at the
School of Music."

I started to sit up, which was a bit of a challenge. I'd had
at least four beers, but then I'd stopped counting. Actually, I
hadn't started counting, which may have been one of the
problems. I'd called Rachel three times and she hadn't

249

responded, which either meant she had a gig or I was in the doghouse. I was drinking to be safe either way. "What do you mean, Nana?"

"Don't you fellas know anything? It's the second Friday of the month."

"Why is that special?" I asked.

She shook her head. "The three of you don't have enough brains for a poodle. The orchestra has a concert tonight. They would be rehearsing at the theatre."

The poodles sat up straight so abruptly that they practically knocked each other over. As usual, it was Kique who processed the information the fastest. "What time is the concert?"

"*Diós mío*, save me from these *tontos*. Eight o'clock, of course. Like every concert. Every second Friday. For the last seventeen years."

Like a disgruntled elementary school teacher, she turned and left us to our own devices. I grabbed a pitcher of water and poured us tall glasses. We had forty minutes to get ourselves to the concert. No matter what happened, we needed to be ready.

~

"I can't believe I let you guys drag me to an orchestra concert," Kique said. He was kiddingly. Mostly.

Domingos, who was sitting between us, patted Kique's shoulder. "If you're lucky, you might meet a pretty girl."

"Right. One from San Luís Potosí. The last thing I need is a long-distance relationship. Or wait, maybe that's exactly what I need!"

I appreciated Kique's attempts at levity, but I couldn't join in. We'd taken seats in the middle of the theatre, and small chandeliers dangled overhead. I wondered how many bullets it would take to shoot them down. One would probably be enough.

The seats were cushioned, but they were too hard to be comfortable. Instead of relaxing, I squirmed. Something was off, but I couldn't tell what. I looked around for our friends

250

from Mexico City, but no one seemed suspicious.

Kique tapped his watch. "It's ten after eight. Shouldn't this thing start on time?"

"It should but it won't," I said. I pointed at the aisles. People were still trickling in, but they weren't hurrying. These same stragglers probably came late to every concert. I wouldn't have bothered waiting for them.

"I told you we should have gone backstage," Kique said. "If you're such a famous conductor—"

"I'm not famous," Domingos insisted. "Nobody knows me here. I don't have the right to interfere with the concert."

I too had voted for going backstage, but Domingos had insisted on sitting in the audience instead. While we waited, I reviewed the program for the sixth time. There were short blurbs about the various pieces. There was a biography about Maestro Alfredo. There was a smaller biography about the concertmaster, Elizabetta García. She'd started her musical career by studying piano, but once she held a violin in her hands, she never looked back. She believed the key to successful musicianship was hard practice.

Nice and generic. The description probably fit all the violinists in the orchestra.

"How long is this performance supposed to last?" Kique asked.

The woman in front of us turned and frowned.

"It's just a question!" he told the woman. Then he turned to us. "If this concert doesn't start, we'll be here all night."

I indicated the stage. "We're making progress."

The musicians, dressed in concert black, streamed in from the wings and took their places. Aidán was the penultimate cellist. Lalo was the lead trumpet player. David was the second bass player. He looked much more relaxed holding the classical instrument than he had holding a *guitarrón*.

Domingos gripped my arm. "Andy, do you see Horacio?"

I studied the rows of violin players. There were four stands of second violins and five stands of firsts. Even though I kept looking, I didn't see our mariachi player.

"He can't be out on a gig," Kique said. "His other buddies are all here."

"There's an empty chair at the back," I said. "Maybe that's his place."

A stage hand came out and snatched away the chair. "Not anymore," Kique said.

The only empty seat in the orchestra was that of the concertmaster.

"Domingos," I said.

Domingos stared as if he could fill the empty chair via telepathy. "Maybe Horacio had a car accident," he said slowly. "Or a family emergency."

"Domingos," I repeated.

"He could have a sick kid. A dying parent. A flat tire."

"Domingos."

He took a deep breath and closed his eyes.

I wanted to do the same thing so I could block out everything long enough to imagine I was a thousand miles away. It was the kind of moment that required the utmost strength, such as running the last few yards of a race, or getting up in the morning after two hours' sleep. I sucked in my breath and kept my eyes on the stage. As the concertmaster came out, most of the audience clapped. I didn't manage it. Neither did Domingos. It wasn't Liza who nodded to the audience and then asked for the A. It was Horacio.

"Why is Horacio trembling?" Kique asked.

"He should be," I said.

"Why's that?"

"He'll have to play the solos in the Strauss."

Domingos' eyes had opened as wide as a cat's. He was surprised into immobility. So was I. Right when we were the most certain that we would find Liza, she'd evaded us. Again.

Kique snapped his fingers in our faces. "Dudes, she's not coming. We might as well leave."

But none of us got up. The orchestra was still tuning. In a

252

few seconds the conductor would appear.

"Maybe Liza will be—"

"No," Domingos said. "She considers conducting to be below her skill level."

Maestro Alfredo strode out onto the stage and took a deep bow.

"I don't know what to think," Domingos shouted over the applause.

"House," Kique said.

"I know you want to go back to Laura's," Domingos said. "But we ought to hear the concert. At intermission we might talk to some of the musicians."

"Liza's!" Kique said loudly. He stood and started pushing his way past the others in our row.

Of course. Liza's enemies would have made the same assumption we had—that she would be playing the concert. In the meantime she could easily return to her house. Our chance to catch her was right now, and we were probably already too late.

I raced after Domingos and Kique, who were already halfway up the aisle.

The usher scowled as he held open the door. "Where are you going in such a hurry? That's not polite. Not polite at all."

"We left the stove on!" Kique yelled. "The house might be on fire!"

"Go, go!" the usher exclaimed.

He might have saved his breath. We were already running.

Chapter Thirty-One

"Liza!"

On my own I might have been more cautious, but when Domingos rushed into the house, I was right behind him, and Kique was right behind me. Liza was standing in the living room wearing pants and a simple sweater. She had a music folder in her hands, but she dropped it when she saw Domingos.

"Liza!" He ran to her and grabbed her, giving her a full body hug. "You're alive!"

She wiggled away from him. Since she was wearing flat shoes rather than heels, she had more mobility than usual. "What are you doing here?"

"You're all right!"

"Of course." She spoke coarsely, quickly, and without a single shred of gratitude. "What in hell are you doing here? And why did you bring Sancho Panza?"

I'd been called many things. Many of them unflattering. But as far as I remembered, I'd never been referred to as Don Quixote's fat little sidekick.

"You're supposed to be playing a concert," I said.

"I changed plans."

I spread my fingers as if holding a soccer ball, but I imagined wrapping my fingers around Liza's head and shaking her until she squealed. "Horacio is probably having a heart attack right now. How dare you abandon him when you had so many solos?"

Liza shrugged. "His problem. Not mine. Also, I warned him to be prepared."

"You ruined the concert!" I shouted.

"The audience won't know the difference. What do they care anyway? Concerts are free."

I thought about Horacio trembling. I thought about his left hand jumping wildly from note to note and only reaching the desired interval about a fifth of the time. I imagined the concert starting badly and going worse with every measure. I imagined Horacio being scarred for life because he found out he would be playing impossibly difficult passages with ten minutes' notice. Maybe he didn't even get ten.

When I was in charge of music at Noche Azul, I'd played while ill many times. I'd played with a twisted ankle. I'd played on an hour of sleep. In nearly twenty years I'd missed one show the night my moped broke down and left me stranded on the beach without enough cash for a cab. Naturally I'd had a

254

substitute from time to time, usually Joey. But I would have never blown off a performance.

Liza, however, seemed perfectly at ease. Evidently a theatre full of people was a detail. So was Horacio.

"You had a responsibility to play that concert."

"So?"

I didn't know how to deal with such an answer. It lay outside my scope. How could anyone shirk important duties without a second thought? Liza's obligation to her fellow musicians alone was so obvious that I didn't know how to break it down for her. Trying to suggest that something was wrong with her behavior was more hopeless than trying to teach Kique to play a song.

I wanted to say something about the history of the orchestra. I wanted to mention the joy of listening to music, the beauty of delighting an audience with sound. But somehow, I didn't bother.

I resorted to the only argument that I thought Liza might vaguely relate to. "You were getting paid!"

"They pay so little they are lucky I attended rehearsals. But never mind. I need to leave town. You should do the same."

"We're not leaving until you explain what happened in Tucson," said Domingos.

Liza put her hands on her hips and scrunched up her lips, a camel ready to spit. "This is time for stories? Maybe I should bring some picture books?"

Domingos clasped his hands. "I love you! I promised to protect you!"

"But you don't. And so, I protect myself. That's the only way."

I shook my fists like a World Series coach exploding over a blind umpire. "We wasted three weeks looking for you!" We'd wasted hours, literally, chasing a shadow. Arguably I didn't have anything better to do with my time, but Rachel had lost two weeks' worth of private lessons. I'd almost lost my brother. But never mind our wasted time and money. I was embarrassed for Domingos because of his vulnerability. He'd been made a fool by an undeserving woman. Even if he were willing to take the abuse himself, I wasn't willing to stand idly by while it was dished out.

"Quiet, Andy," Domingos said. "The neighbors."

His voice was measured. How did he contain himself? He'd taken more nonsense from Liza in a month than a sane person would stand for in an entire lifetime. "Three weeks of our lives thrown away and you're concerned about the neighbors? You're crazy. Or maybe you're just crazy about her."

I hadn't meant to sound accusatory, but my tongue was quicker than my brain was.

Domingos nodded slightly. "Liza, we did indeed spend time looking for you."

She swung her head back and forth. "Go-Go, when I want something from you, I ask. I told you this before."

Go-Go? I wasn't sure I'd heard right.

Domingos backed off. "Sit. Talk to me. Make me understand."

Liza sat on the edge of the nearest easy chair and crossed her legs as if she were wearing a short skirt we ought to be paying attention to. "What do you want to know?"

I pulled Domingos down on the couch with me while Kique stood like a sentinel. "Quit jerking us around and explain yourself," I said.

"I should tell you what? My bra size?"

I could think of several mean comebacks, including "The size of the bra you wear or the size of a bra that would fit?" but instead I ordered myself to focus. "Let's start with why you fled from the concert in Tucson. You killed a man, and then you ran. Isn't that how it happened?"

Liza tilted her head to the left, which was a natural position for a violinist. "You don't know?" For the first time since we'd entered the house, she didn't sound angry.

256

"We're not smart enough to be inside your head," I said. "Thank God."

"Miguel showed up."

"Miguel! In Tucson?" Domingos asked. "He went to your house?"

"He had no way to find my house. He was at the theatre. Second row. I thought you saw him. Anyway, I had to leave."

"Mid-concert?" Domingos asked gently.

"That was my only chance to escape!"

It was one thing for an angry husband to follow his wife. Another for him to hire a detective. Yet another for him to strangle his woman in their own home. But for a man to sneak into a concert to murder a mistress who happened to be the concertmaster was unimaginable.

"Of course," I said. "Miguel was going to chop off your head in front of hundreds of people. I would have run too."

"¡Idiota! Do you want to hear my story or not?"

Of course I did. I'd been waiting nearly a month for it. The problem was whether or not I would be inspired to believe a word she said. "Go on."

"Miguel said that if he caught me playing in another concert, he would break both my hands."

Ah, two broken hands. The queen of drama had spoken once again. I wondered how many soap operas she'd watched to come up with such nonsense, or maybe she'd been watching too many movies with superheroes.

"Miguel wouldn't be that cruel," said Domingos.

"Go-Go, I don't take that chance."

No. Liza wasn't one to leave things to chance. She demanded control. Without it she became a monster. Suddenly the image of her last concert came to me, the sudden way she left the stage. Liza was cunning and devious, but it shouldn't have taken me so long to catch on.

"Your E-string," I said flatly.

"What are you talking about?" Kique asked.

"The concert in Tucson," I said. "During *Scheherazade*,

Liza created an excuse to leave the stage. Her string didn't break at all."

"Of course not," Liza said. "But you thought it did, no? So did everyone else."

"I've heard enough," Kique said. He headed out the front door. I wanted to follow, which would have been the only sane course of action, but I was glued to the sofa, mesmerized by a lunatic who had managed to dupe all of us.

"You loosened your string and then pretended it broke," I said. "That gave you the chance to run off with your precious instrument. Smart plan."

"I had no plan. The moment came, and I had to act. It's not my fault that F.V. was waiting for me."

"F. J.," I said. "Not that we care. All that trouble for a dress?"

Liza and Domingos stared.

"Not for a dress?" I asked.

"I assume F.J. was working for Miguel," Domingos said sadly. "I should have been more suspicious of his sudden donation to the orchestra. The money came with an agreement that he would become part of the board."

"Of course," Liza said. "So he bothers me all the time. He makes my life hell to make me quit. But his real job is to watch me until Miguel can come."

"What happened to F.J.?" Domingos asked.

"Stupid man! He catches me when I am running down the stairs." She stroked her sides. "He puts his dirty hands all over me!"

"You killed him because he pawed you?" I asked.

"Miguel sees us and he goes crazy. He throws Miguel down and he bounce, bounce bounces down the stairs. When Miguel takes out his knife, I run. You would stay?"

Liza's question was rhetorical. I would have run without thinking twice. I knew of too many lovers who had been killed in the sacred name of jealousy. It wasn't a possibility. It was a probability.

"I would have run too," said Domingos. "But you need to come back to the US and tell your side of the story."

"Ha! Then they accuse me of murder!"

"You couldn't have killed that man. You're not strong enough. That's obvious."

"To you it's obvious. To me. Maybe even to Sancho Panza. That makes a difference?"

"Come back to Tucson so that I can take care of you!"

"You said that last time."

"Miguel needs to go to jail. Otherwise you'll never be free."

"I'm free now, no?"

"I'll get the best lawyers. We'll find witnesses."

"Go-Go, when will you learn? No one cares what you do. It's what people think you do. This becomes the truth, the destiny. I have to leave. I have no choice."

"You could have told me what happened."

"And make trouble for you too? Why?"

Domingos clutched his stomach. "I've been worried ever since you left!"

"I didn't ask for that."

"We went to Delft to find you. And Lyon."

"Ha! I hate both cities. Cold weather. Stupid people. You didn't remember how I felt when I lived there?"

Domingos stood and reached for her. "Liza, come with us."

The woman backed away. "I can take care of myself. I never asked for help."

"The longer you stay away, the worse it looks. Come back to Tucson. I'll prepare everything."

"I can't go back. Not now. Too much has happened."

"I can't concentrate without you."

"You need a new hobby."

"I need you."

"Well, you can't have me."

She went into her bedroom as if she'd tired of us, so now

259

we were free to go. Instead we followed behind.

A suitcase lay on the bed. I couldn't see what was in it because I stayed near the door. "Let's leave, Domingos. She's not worth it."

Liza came straight at me and slapped my right cheek, sending a *thwack!* through the room.

I hadn't been hit by a woman since preschool. My flesh stung, but my pride hurt more. Had I not been so surprised, I might have thought about why Liza felt cornered. I might have been ready to cut her some slack for being stressed and confused. I might have even stopped to consider that Domingos must have some logical reason to suffer such a wildcat.

Instead I didn't think. I slapped her right back.

She reeled backwards but made no sound. I immediately felt ashamed. I hadn't meant to hit her. She'd pushed me to the edge, but that was no excuse. I thought of my mother. She'd slapped me once when I was about ten years old. I'd asked an indiscreet question about the man who came to visit when daddy was away at work. I don't remember how she answered, but afterwards we never had the same relationship.

"Enough!" Domingos stood between us and held out his arms.

It was just as well. My cheek still stung. Liza had an incredibly strong hand.

"Don't blame us, Liza. We have done everything possible to help you," Domingos said.

"Believe me, not everything." She went to her clothes rack, pulled out a blouse, and threw it on top of the suitcase.

"You can't keep running," Domingos said.

"Watch me."

"You have to set things straight. You need to take action."

She straightened and stared at Domingos. "I did." She was on the verge of a smile, but her voice was so cold I shivered. She sounded too calm. Too calculated. Too sure.

Domingos felt it too, a wave of hatred that wafted through the room.

"Oh, God," Domingos said. "Tell me you didn't."

"I didn't have a choice."

"There's always a choice!"

She wiggled her fingers in the air. "Not this time."

"But how—?"

"Twenty sleeping pills. Maybe thirty. I shook them into his beers. He thought I was adding extra salt to go with the limes."

"He didn't notice?" Domingos asked.

She placed both hands under her breasts and pushed up. "He thought of only one thing. Ha! All men are all the same."

"We are not!" I yelled.

Ignoring me, Domingos spoke very softly. "Then what?"

"If you're so smart, figure it out for yourself."

I folded by arms across my chest. At this rate it would take all night to eke out a story from her.

Domingos froze for several seconds. Then he drew his hand over his mouth. When he ran for the kitchen, I followed. The room still stank. I threw open the window, but Domingos didn't notice because he'd become a madman. He yanked one of the pantry doors off its hinges and flung it out of the way with a noisy crash. The pantry floor was cluttered with bags and cleaning equipment, but Domingos sank to his knees and threw items into the kitchen using both hands at once.

I stood behind him ducking the debris, but then I saw a cowboy boot. One that was attached to a leg. Although I was startled, I managed to jump back several feet before Domingos tore off the rags that covered a corpse's face.

"Miguel!"

"So now you know," Liza said as she joined us, suitcase in hand. "Happy?"

Domingos grabbed the case and wrestled it from her.

"Give me the suitcase!" she shouted. *"¡Dáme la mala!"*

La mala. In Spanish it meant "the bad one." It was only in Portuguese that it meant "suitcase."

Kique rattled the bars outside the kitchen window. "Open

261

up!"

I ran to the window and unlatched the safety hinge.

"Crawl out now!" Kique whisper-shouted.

I was closer to Liza than Domingos was, so I ran and put my arms around her. I picked her a few inches off the ground and then carried her to the sink while she kicked and screamed.

"Let go!"

"Out!"

"My suitcase!"

We heard the footsteps of two heavy men running towards the house.

I put my finger to my lips. "Shh! Your friends are here."

Liza's eyes widened. At least she'd understood. She stopped fighting us and reached for the window. Kique helped her out on the other side. I scrambled out of the window myself and pulled Domingos out behind me.

As we crouched down, we heard the men as they entered the living room.

"¿Dónde estás, perra?" "Where are you, bitch?" yelled one.

Kique pushed past Domingos to get closer to the window. *"She's ours!"* Kique yelled.

"Who the hell are you?"

Kique slid his revolver through the window and aimed at the kitchen light. He missed, but then he steadied himself, took aim, and shattered the bulb, leaving the room in darkness.

He turned and gestured for us to run around the side of the house. When Liza stumbled in the dim light, I grabbed her hand and pulled her along. Kique followed behind, caught up, and overtook us. He led us to a neighboring house. He opened the side door and shooed us inside before entering himself. We tumbled over one another as we entered a dark kitchen. Light streaked in between slats of Venetian blinds, but I banged into a table, knocking a metal pot onto the floor.

"Shh," three people told me at once.

"Are they still in the house?" Domingos asked.

262

"I think so," Kique said. "Stay down."

A short distance away, a door opened. *"Cállense,"* yelled a man. "Shut up."

Never mind that a gun had gone off two minutes earlier. We were too noisy. Somewhere a *nana* was trying to sleep.

While the rest of us crouched, Kique stood beside the window. Strips of light illuminated his face. He still had the gun in his hand, and his face showed total concentration. Unlike the rest of us, he wasn't breathing heavily. He was focused and calm.

"What are we going to do?" Domingos asked.

"Shh," Kique said. "Wait."

Someone slammed a door, probably Liza's.

"We could call the police!" I whispered.

"Shh," Kique said calmly. "We will."

I stood, but he motioned for me to stay down. I put my back to the wall and closed my eyes while a man rushed past. Then another.

After that we heard nothing besides the distant hum of TVs.

Liza waited a few more seconds before she stood. Then she headed for the door as if it were a normal evening.

Domingos reached out his hand. "Liza!"

"La mala!" She pushed past us and headed out.

Domingos sank to the floor and covered his face with his hands.

Kique pointed at Domingos. "Is he hurt?"

"Only spiritually."

"In that case he'll get over it."

"My friend, we have a big problem."

Kique showed his eye teeth. "Only one?"

"We've got a dead millionaire in the pantry."

"Of course we do, *menso*. Why do you think it smelled so bad?"

Chapter Thirty-Two

Liza had returned to the bedroom, set her suitcase on the bed, and opened it. She folded a white dress and added it to the clothes she had already packed. Although she moved quickly and efficiently, she didn't seem panicked. She showed no particular expression, as if having a dead man, no, a dead lover, in the next room meant nothing at all. I suppose by then she was used to it.

"Police," I said quietly.

No one took notice.

"Anything else?" Kique asked Liza.

"Music folders."

Kique went to the living room.

"We have to call the police," I said firmly.

Domingos took an aqua-colored dress off its hanger. "You have to take this one." He tossed it in her direction.

Kique returned with the folders. "Which did you want?"

Liza unzipped a side compartment. "Both."

"Kique, we need to call the police," I said.

"There's no hurry." He helped Domingos zip the bag and set it upright.

I stomped on the ground, making a dull thud. "Dead man! In the kitchen!"

"You don't need to say that so loudly, Andy," Kique said. "Not that the neighbors speak great English."

"You have to go home," Domingos told Liza.

She nodded without looking at him.

"That's the only way."

"I know."

Home. *Mala*. Loving someone who was not a lover.

Kique saw me struggling to add two and two all the way up to four. "Let me give you a clue, dude. Her hair is not blond."

No, it wasn't. And now that I looked for it, really looked, Domingos and Liza had the same slender eyes.

Dominos took a credit card from his wallet and handed it to her. "Take this too. You're going to need it."

"Code?"

"The one we used before." He gave her a long embrace.

"I'm calling the police!" I took out my cell phone, but Kique snatched it out of my hand.

"We'll use mine," he said. He turned to Liza. "Have your passport?"

"Yes."

"Money?"

She nodded.

Kique pocketed my cell and made a call on his own. "Help!" he yelled in a fake high voice. "Two men entered my neighbor's house, but I know she's out tonight! That's Calle Parrodi 718. The men look dangerous. They might have drugs!"

For a moment Kique put his hand over the microphone and grinned. Then he returned to his task. "Wait, now they're leaving! They're driving away! No, I can't... wait, it ends in 8301. The license plate is from Mexico City." As Kique abruptly ended the call, he turned to Liza. "Ready?"

She nodded. She dove under the bed for the violin, but Domingos was too fast for her. He dragged it out from the other side and hugged it to his chest. "You can't have it. You know that. You have to let it go."

"Domingos! That violin is my life!"

"Not anymore."

"He can't come after me!"

"He has friends."

"They won't care."

"The hell they won't."

"Give me my violin!"

"No."

A siren pricked the air. Although it was still in the distance, the sound was approaching. And growing.

Kique picked up Liza's suitcase. Then he put his hand

266

behind her shoulder and pushed. "Go."

"She can't just walk out of here!" I said.

"Of course not, Andy. I'm going to drive her." Kique made a V with his index and middle finger and pointed at Domingos and me. "Split up. Walk in opposite directions. Then meet me in the Plaza de Armas in half an hour."

"But—" I began.

While Kique marched Liza out of the room as if she were a delinquent high schooler, Domingos thrust the violin case into my hands. "Andy, take this. It's yours. And help me. I beg you. Please help me."

"She murdered someone, Domingos. She's crazy."

The maestro shook his head as if we were having a mild disagreement about a musical *ritardando*. "Self-defense."

"She fed him sleeping pills. That's premeditated murder."

"Miguel killed F.J. Did you forget that?"

"The killing has to stop somewhere, Domingos!"

"It just did. No more. This is it."

"She can't simply walk away."

Domingos put his hands on my shoulders. He didn't mean to, but he spit in my face as he talked. "I'll give you a 'forever job.' Think of it! Permanent concertmaster."

"You can't bribe me."

"You can choose the whole season's repertoire."

"She killed a man, Domingos."

"Forget about this, and you're hired for life."

"No."

"You don't want to work that hard? I understand. You don't have to play at all. You can be my assistant. Create the fliers. Audition the players. Whatever you want you can have."

I shouted above the sirens. "She's a killer!"

"I can arrange for a job for Rachel. Just help me this one time, Andy. That's all I'm asking."

He honestly expected me to walk away. The idea was ridiculous. There was a stinking dead body in the pantry. A deranged woman on the loose. And soon, there would be a boatload of ruffians searching for us, ready to pop us at their first opportunity.

Domingos took a step closer to the door. "Andy. Please."

By now the volume of the sirens had tripled. Since I didn't have time to think, I reacted on instinct. I flung the violin over my back. Then I started running.

~

There's something strangely peaceful about sitting in a normally busy space when the day is done and the activities wind down. I met up with Domingos near the cathedral and sat silently with him as I stared out into the night. At the moment I had no reason to be on guard. A few cars rumbled by in the distance, but none of the drivers were in a hurry. Behind us were trees, and behind the trees was a sidewalk where a few lingering pedestrians crisscrossed the square. By now parents had taken their children home to bed, so the square belonged to lovers, those hopeful people who imagined growing old with their partners, happy innocents who still held onto dreams.

I would have spoken to Domingos, but I was waiting for him to regain his composure. It was embarrassing to hear another man cry. I didn't want to leave him alone, but I hated being his witness. He was the most successful and most inspiring man I had ever met, and he'd been reduced to a lump. I wouldn't have thought it could happen. I wished it hadn't.

I focused on the details around the square. The smell of roasted meats wafted over from an outdoor, fly-by-night taco stand. The neon lights from a corner store advertised cheap beer. Birds called to one another from safe hideaways in the upper branches of the trees.

I widened my vision. The town's colonial buildings mirrored the ones I'd seen back in Durango. They were a reminder of the richness that had been Mexico, of luxury that had been destroyed by greed. Mexico was a wonderful country full of natural resources and amazing people I was proud to be related to. But something was off with the whole country. I wondered if Kique's sister were right. Meli had joked that my bad luck had to do with *feng shui*, but maybe there was something to it. In a similar way maybe Mexico was out of synch with itself. The Spanish had conquered the indigenous people, but they'd never extinguished the natives' spirit. The people were born with a natural optimism crossed with fierce stubbornness. Even in the twenty-first century, that combination could lead a man like Miguel Sánchez de Avila to dream that he was the one with total control.

Miguel wasn't the first delusional Mexican I'd encountered. He was merely the richest. I wondered if the gods had laughed as they'd taken away his spirit. Death by sleeping pills was hardly a fitting end for a macho tycoon.

I clutched the violin case, slowly brushing away what few dust bunnies hadn't fallen off as I'd run.

"Andy," Domingos said softly. "Whatever you want."

"Never mind about the job."

"Whatever I can give you is yours. Forget about her. Put her out of your mind."

"You couldn't have told me she was your sister?"

"We vowed not to tell anyone a long time ago."

"But why, Domingos? What difference did it make?"

"So that I could hire her, of course. So that people would never say she was merely my sister and not a great violinist."

"Instead they assume she's your lover."

"Yes, Andy. I realize that. But they don't have any proof."

"The lie doesn't help you any."

"It's rather hard to change that now."

"It was a crazy idea from the beginning. Everyone can tell how well she plays."

Again Domingos wiped his eyes with the back of his hands. "Andy, you're new to the classical world. It's cutthroat. It's mean."

"I didn't get that impression in Delft. Or Lyon."

"No, of course not. Those are sweet orchestras where the musicians are content to have the same full-time jobs their whole lives. They're not trying to move up. That's when it gets dirty."

"You could have still hired her. The musicians would have been more tolerant if they'd known who she was."

"Andy, she was the one who insisted."

Of course. Domingos would have been willing to put his reputation on the line. She wouldn't have been. She would have gotten an idea into her head, locked it inside, and thrown away the key. I'd done the same thing myself on more than one occasion, but knowing she was as stubborn as I was didn't make me feel any better about her.

I didn't feel much better about Domingos. "Why didn't you trust me enough to tell me?"

"Well, now you know."

"What other secrets have you kept from me?"

"The one about Liza. That's the only one." He put his hand on my arm as if he were leading me somewhere. He probably felt that he was. "Promise me you won't do anything rash."

"Not me, Domingos. I'm never rash."

"I'm sure you understand why we have to let her go. This is still a macho country. A jury of men wouldn't understand."

"Domingos—"

"They'd lock her up. Or put her to death. She wouldn't get a fair trial. You know she wouldn't."

"Domingos—"

"Think about Joey. He's willing to do anything for you and probably vice versa."

Joey had uprooted his whole family because of me. In a lesser family I might have been disowned. Maybe I should have been. But Joey was there for me the way Domingos was there for Liza, and, presumably, although I wasn't ready to swear to it, the way she would have been there for him.

"You can stop worrying, Domingos. I'm not going to the police. And you don't have to give me a damned job."

I focused my attention on an old-fashioned street lamp. Some kind of avian figure graced the top. Probably an eagle.

270

The Mexican flag depicted such a legendary bird alighting on a prickly pear. Even though the eagle had chosen that very spot, it was a stupid place to land.

Chapter Thirty-Three

We found Nana in the kitchen reading a magazine. She barely looked up. "That was a damned long concert."

"It sure as hell was," said Kique. "Got any tortillas?"

"I might. Did you bring me a beer?"

"I will." He went back outside.

"I've never heard of a four-hour concert before," Nana said. "Maybe on Sunday I'll stay home."

"Afterwards we went out with the other musicians," Domingos said as we joined Nana at the table.

"Now that makes more sense. Good concert?"

"It was all right," I lied.

"What did you think of that woman concertmaster?"

"She couldn't play tonight," Domingos said. "They said she was sick."

"I doubt it."

I pretended to chuckle. "She's superhuman?"

"No. There's fire in her eyes. That kind doesn't get sick. That kind gets even. So how did that other guy do? His name starts with an H."

"Horacio was fine," I said. "He's a little timid is all. It was still a good concert."

"The music doesn't really matter. My hearing isn't that great, but afterwards we go out for drinks."

Kique returned with a six-pack.

"I'll take two of those," Nana said as she slowly stood. "Save you the trouble of bringing me another one." She started down the hall.

"Won't you have dinner with us?" Kique asked.

"I already ate. And I have a *telenovela* coming on in five minutes. There are some frijoles on the stove. You might find something in the refrigerator."

Normally we would have enjoyed a much longer grilling from Nana. It must have been a very entertaining *telenovela*. I wondered how amused she would have been had we recounted the soap opera of our own. I kept thinking about Miguel's body in the pantry, but my companions went about their business as if it were any other evening. Kique turned on the burner and started warming up the pan of refried beans. He found a stack of tortillas and threw several onto the *comal*. Domingos punched away at his phone. I watched them soundlessly, unsure whether to marvel at their resilience or question it.

Domingos held up his phone. "Andy, there's a flight we could take at seven a.m."

"I never said I was going with you."

"We have rehearsal on Monday."

"You can rehearse without me. I think I need a few days off. Maybe more than that."

"It's a comfortable itinerary," Domingos said. "One change in Houston. That's it. Very convenient."

I didn't answer. Instead I focused on Kique, who was whistling. He'd found some cheese to melt on top of the tortillas, and he was carefully monitoring the flame.

"You should come with me," Domingos said softly.

Again I failed to answer. I was thinking about what I would be telling Rachel when I finally returned to Tucson. I didn't want to lie to her. I couldn't lie too much anyway since her own cousin was involved, but Rachel wouldn't want to know that I'd risked my neck for a woman as dangerous as Liza no matter whose sister she was.

Liza. The thought of the woman hung in the room like a musty shower curtain that needed replacing. I wanted to know what she had been thinking. At one point she must have loved Miguel, and at another point her feelings must have started to reverse. I wondered if she could pinpoint the exact moment or if she could have done anything to prevent it. How much hatred had she locked inside her heart, and at what cost to herself? What had she told herself as she slowly fed sleeping pills to her lover? Had he honestly deserved to die? I tried to imagine what I would have done in her shoes, but I couldn't manage it. At any rate I wouldn't have had the stamina to run away. Instead I would have sunk in place, just as I had on the balcony in Lyon. I wouldn't have known to do anything else.

"What about Liza's son?" I asked.

"I don't know," Domingos said. "I haven't worked that out yet."

Kique nodded. "You will. He's with his grandparents, right?"

"Yes. I don't think they know that Liza was in Mexico."

"They didn't need to."

"I want to know where she went," Domingos said quietly.

Kique calmly slid the tortillas onto a plate and brought them to the table.

"You were gone a long time," Domingos continued. "I was beginning to worry about you."

Kique offered us tortillas, but we both shook our heads. "I wanted to make sure she boarded the bus."

"Where did she go?"

"North."

"Is she mad at me?"

"For interfering and saving her life? She'll get over it."

"I'll pay for all your costs," Domingos said. "Let me know the totals. I'll send you money right away. The gas you bought to get to San Luís. Any expenses you incur in Mexico City. Any tickets you buy on Liza's behalf. Anything at all."

Kique smeared frijoles on a tortilla. "My sister Meli is the businesswoman in the family. She'll add things up and let you know."

"I realize I can't repay you for all you've done," Domingos said. "I don't have an appropriate way to thank you."

"Too bad you can't give me an orchestra job," Kique laughed. "But that would get you fired."

Domingos brightened. "You could be the librarian! Ours is quitting at the end of the season. You could scoot right in. No questions asked."

Kique shook his head. "I wouldn't want to live too close

275

to Andy. He's bad luck. If you were smarter, you'd stay away too. But enough about me. Tell us about Liza. Start at the beginning. Back in Brazil."

Domingos stared at the red and white-checkered tablecloth as if he were talking to it. "She fell in love."

"What was the bastard's name?" Kique asked.

"Manuel de Falla."

Kique pounded the table with his fist. "Where does he live? We could meet up for another road trip."

Domingos smiled. "Find a time travel machine and we're on."

Manuel de Falla was a Spanish composer from the early Twentieth Century. He was especially well known for *The Three-Cornered Hat* and other works for the stage, but I preferred his orchestral work *Nights in the Gardens of Spain.* Whenever I heard the piece, I felt transported to a magical world. De Falla's music was like a watercolor with layers of blues and reds dancing in the wind. I'd never performed any of his music, but I'd often heard it. For once I was several steps ahead of Kique. At least I knew the guy was dead.

"So she fell in love with a composer and his music," I said. "Then what?"

"She started obsessing about going to Spain. Spain this, Spain that. For a Brazilian, studying in Europe is a dream for the rich, and we weren't rich. Our mom was a secretary. Our dad drove a cab. We paid the rent, but we didn't get ahead. My parents couldn't send her abroad to study, so she applied for scholarships all over Spain. Nothing."

"So the great Liza wasn't good enough," Kique said.

"Too many qualified applicants."

"Is that why you chose to study conducting?" Kique asked. "Not as much competition? Plus the fact that you get to be the boss."

If Domingos noticed the touch of sarcasm, he ignored it. "I couldn't decide on an instrument. I played cello for two years and loved cello. Then I switched to clarinet and loved clarinet. Then on to the French horn. Another love affair."

"I guess you don't sing," Kique said.

"I studied opera too. But what I liked the most was putting it all together. Making a group of musicians come alive." He held out his palms. "Conducting is a rush. It's like holding the whole world in your hands. I know that sounds melodramatic."

"Get back to Liza," I said. "She couldn't find a scholarship for Spain. What made her think about Mexico?"

"I found out about an opportunity in Guadalajara and urged her to apply. I was finishing my undergraduate degree at the time."

"And she was offered a teaching position," I said.

"A small stipend, as it turned out. But my poor sister. At the time she assumed she would be the top student. Instead she was one of the weakest. Then Nando came along and distracted her. If he had survived, she might have turned into a cheerful housewife and had a regular life. Instead you know the rest. She coped with his death by locking herself into a practice room. Such isolation has a negative effect."

"Wasn't she doing what she wanted to?" asked Kique.

Domingos turned to me. "How would you explain it, Andy?"

I thought about a younger Liza standing in a windowless, soundproof practice room with a music stand and an instrument. She would have spent hours working on individual passages, cursing the composers when the music was too difficult, cursing herself when she couldn't achieve the standards she strove for.

"The situation was different for me," I said. "I had my brother to practice with. I never felt alone. We were fortunate enough to inherit some natural ability."

"Just like me, huh, Andy?" Kique asked.

"He has no ear whatsoever," I told Domingos. "Some people don't. It's probably genetic."

"That's where Andy is fortunate," Domingos said. "He lacks training, but if he can hear it, he can play it."

277

"That sounds like cheating," joked Kique.

"It's dumb luck," Domingos said. "For example I have more of an ear than Liza does. Melodies come to me easily. You might call it a knack."

"Liza doesn't have that?" Kique asked.

"Not to nearly the same extent. Instead she worked like a devil. But the practice sessions shut her away from people."

"That's her excuse for being difficult?" I asked.

"At some point she started resenting the fact that she didn't have time to go to parties or anything else. To be competitive she had to practice, practice, practice."

"Good player, zero personality," Kique said. "I guess it happens all the time."

Domingos nodded. "But to be a star, you need charisma. You have to communicate the music. As it was, after she graduated, she couldn't get a job."

"But you did," I said.

"While I was finishing my degree, I won a competition in Germany. Eventually that led to the orchestra in Delft, which led to the orchestra in Lyon."

"That's how you were able to hire your sister," Kique said. "Sweet."

"No. By then she'd reached a competitive level that allowed me to hire her legitimately. Otherwise people talk."

"Auditions are blind," I said. "Was she better than the other candidates?"

"She was on par with them. Of course I recognized her playing immediately. When I hired her, nobody questioned my reasoning. In Tucson they let me do what I want, so I didn't bother with the audition. Then Miguel came along and ruined everything."

"Things didn't go well for him either," I said.

Domingos threw his hands in the air like someone tossing confetti. "Thirty years of practicing down the drain. Let's see you cope with such a personal disaster."

"To stay hidden she has to quit playing?" Kique asked.

"At the very least she'll have to retrain for a different instrument," said Domingos.

Kique snatched up the last tortilla; he'd eaten all of them himself. "Is retraining hard to do?"

Domingos and I exchanged glances. I knew it was no use. Kique was smarter than I was in almost everything, but there was no way I could explain to him about music.

"It's hard," I said.

"What if she played second violin?" Kique asked. "Nobody notices the second violin players."

"That's just it," Domingos said. "She wants to be noticed."

"I already know what she'll do," I said. "She'll switch to the viola. She'll struggle because it's a bigger instrument. She'll curse and kick and scream. But with hard work, after a couple of years, she could be a lead violist. By then maybe no one will care about Miguel Sánchez de Avila."

Domingos clasped his hands. "That's what we have to hope."

"You claimed that Liza saved your life," I said. "What's the story?"

"I was about three when I almost drowned in a lake."

"You were the little boy."

"Yes, Andy. My parents were busy eating and weren't paying attention. Liza was the one who noticed I was floundering. She jumped in and nearly drowned herself trying to save me." He stood wearily, as if the act of standing took genuine effort.

Kique grinned. "Go-Go, you didn't tell us about your nickname."

For the first time all evening, Domingos had a moment to enjoy a sweet memory. "Once I learned to crawl, I never stayed still. Liza was learning a little English at the time. She's the one who named me."

Go-Go. Maybe that was why Domingos was always on the run. It came naturally to him, and by now such behavior was

279

expected. Maybe we all fell into patterns set for us before we were born. The question was whether Liza could change her path. I wasn't convinced things would work out that way. She seemed to have as much bad luck as I did. Maybe in former lives, we'd both done something really, really wrong.

Domingos stood. "I'd better sleep for a while. You'll take me to the airport?"

Kique nodded. "Sure, Go-Go!"

"Thanks, guys. Thanks so very much." He walked off so slowly he might have been an old man.

Kique waited until the conductor was out of earshot. "What's eating you now, *menso*?"

"Looking the other way at murder is difficult for me. You know that."

"What way did you want to look?"

I shrugged.

"The world won't miss another ruthless businessman no matter his efforts to support the arts. Besides, didn't he murder the guy back in Tucson?"

"That's different. He was in a jealous rage at the time. He misunderstood."

"That makes it okay? What if it had been you, Andy?"

"I'm just saying that in Mexico, you can kill your spouse's lover and get away with it."

"You could in the past. Maybe not anymore. But never mind. Credit Liza for taking control of the situation."

"Miguel wasn't going to kill her for playing a concert in Tucson. He liked threats. They made him feel good."

"First of all, you can't be sure about what he would or wouldn't have done. Second, Liza was Miguel's songbird in a golden cage. What she did was women's lib, Mexican-style."

"She's not Mexican. At the very least Domingos should have told me who she was."

"Would that have helped anything?"

I wasn't sure. Either way I'd been a cog in Domingos' wheel. I might have been anyone else who had the dumb luck

280

to be the perfect person to help him out.

No. Few could have fit such a bill. Joey and I might have been the only ones. The irony was that I didn't regret helping Domingos, not really. But I wasn't at all sure how I felt about helping Liza.

"What else is bothering you?" Kique asked.

"Nothing."

"Andy, you shouldn't lie to me. You're terrible at it."

"I tossed a guy over a balcony in Lyon."

"It was a clear case of self-defense."

"But we don't know who he was or why he was there."

Kique nodded. "He was probably with Miguel."

"Maybe. But now we'll never know."

"A loose end."

"Too loose."

"So we learn more about Miguel," Kique said. "Find out if he's flown to France lately. Then we'll know if you really saw him in Lyon or not."

"How long do you think it will take for the police to identify his body?"

"Let's see. A decomposed body in an ordinary part of town. A wife who wouldn't be suspicious because her husband probably traveled around all the time."

"But what if—"

"It's the weekend, Andy. Nothing will happen before next week."

"What about Miguel's buddies?"

"They didn't get far."

"How do you know?"

"I put nails in three of their tires."

"I wondered why you'd made the call to the police so quickly."

"Now you know. Will you return to Tucson with Domingos?"

"I promised Beto we would go visit. It's the least we can do."

281

"Fine. We spend the weekend with your cousins. Then we go to D.F. to see what we can find out about Miguel."

"Shouldn't you be getting back to your classes instead of going to Mexico City with me?"

Kique smiled. "A couple more days won't matter. Trust me, Andy. I learn more about the law from trying to save your ass than I ever could in school."

~

The international airport serving San Luís Potosí hugged a flat highway less than a half an hour outside town. The control tower was so severe that it should have belonged to a jail instead of an airport. I took that as a reminder of our unfinished business with Liza.

"Change your mind and fly with me," Domingos as when we pulled up alongside the entrance. "There are still some empty seats." He was as chipper as if he'd had a full night's sleep after a restful vacation rather than a couple of hours after finding proof that his sister was a murderer.

We exited the car and walked around to the trunk. Kique pulled out the conductor's suitcase while I reached for the violin.

"Come with me," Domingos repeated.

"I have to take care of some details," I said.

"Do that later. Come back to Tucson with me now." He turned to Kique. "You can come too. I have a big house. There's plenty of room."

As usual his charisma was hard at work. For a moment I was ready to change my mind and follow him the way a puppy follows a little boy, not because I was ordered to, but because no alternative would be as attractive. Who didn't love wild optimism? In his world, everything had already gone back to normal. Liza had done nothing wrong. Miguel was probably still alive. The boot we'd seen in the pantry was attached to a dummy, not a man.

I'd slept less than Domingos had, however. I was able to resist because I was too tired to think. By operating on automatic, I stuck to my plan. "I'm not sure I'm coming back. To tell you the truth, I'm not sure I'm cut out for classical music."

"Of course you are. Next up is the John Williams concert. It's easy."

"Playing well is never easy."

"You're the concertmaster. You're not supposed to miss any rehearsals."

"I never asked to be concertmaster."

"You fell into it. And you're good at it."

"I can fall back out again. Anyway, I promised Beto I would go see him. After all the free lodging at his daughter's house, it's the least I can do."

"You're born to be a musician. You can't lose sight of that."

"Beto has a gig lined up in Paris. He invited me to join him."

"Andy! Remember that Rachel is in Tucson. And you'll love the concert. A little *Star Wars*, a little *Jaws*. A few flashy violin solos. It will be fun."

I felt more tired than ever. "Right. And I'm a regular Indiana Jones."

"Wrong movie, although John Williams wrote that sound track too. Anyway, the first rehearsal is crucial."

"Go-Go has a point," Kique said. I didn't sense he believed what he said. He was angling for the chance to say "Go-Go."

The conductor didn't flinch.

I snapped my fingers. "Go-Go, I'm not like you. You dash from one thing to another like a pinball. No. Like a rocket. You're constantly in hyperspace. I'm not that fast. Maybe you don't remember, but we left a dead guy in the pantry back there. That takes some processing."

"There's nothing to process. There's only something to forget." Domingos checked the time on his cell phone. "If I don't leave now, I'll miss the flight."

"Go. You've got Philip. Let him be concertmaster again."

"Last year he did a terrible job. I prayed during every concert."

"He'll improve over time."

"No, Andy. He'll just get older." Domingos indicated the airport entrance. "Last chance to come with me."

I shook my head. I tried to hand him the violin, but he wouldn't take it.

"It's yours now. You earned it."

"You're loaning it to me."

"I'm giving it to you."

"It's a bribe."

"No, Andy. It's a legacy. A violin needs to be played. It needs to be loved."

"This one is loved by Liza. I don't want anything that's hers. And she would hate me for having it."

"Andy, she may have inhabited it and loved it. But I'm the one who paid for it."

"But—"

"Therefore, it's mine to give away."

"I can't play it in Tucson. The TucAz musicians would recognize it. They would wonder about the connection between us. They would ask questions."

"Andy, don't be so unimaginative. Re-varnish it. Replace the strings."

"Zoran will know. A violinmaker would identify his most prized instrument."

"He won't figure it out right away. When he does, I can deal with him."

Domingos hugged Kique and me as if we might never see him again. As he backed up, he tapped his heart. "Thanks to both of you. For everything." Then he turned and slipped through the automatic doors.

I felt bad for him. I was beginning to understand why he was in a hurry. That was the only way he could leave the past behind. If he ran fast enough he wouldn't have to think about his sister fleeing the continent. He could go on pretending that nothing had changed and that somehow everything would turn out all right.

But that was impossible. Liza was wanted for questioning in the US, and soon Elizabetta Garcia would be wanted for murder in Mexico. I didn't doubt Liza's ability to run. I doubted her ability to hide. The quiet little life wasn't her style. It wasn't even in her vocabulary. At some point Domingos would have to stop covering for her. Maybe he already had.

I crawled back into the car as Kique started up the engine. Things would never be the same for me either. Even if I stayed in the orchestra, I'd never be able to think of Go-Go in the same way. I'd spent too much time with him. I knew too much about him. No matter how much he pretended to be the ultimate musician, in reality he was exactly like me: the ultimate sibling. That was the identity that he would never walk away from. Instead he'd pay the price for it again and again and again.

Kique hit the accelerator and pointed the car towards Aguascalientes. He seemed almost as determined as Domingos. Maybe the conductor was starting to rub off on him.

"And Liza?" I asked.

"What about her?"

Kique was so calm that I knew he'd left nothing to chance.

"You gave Liza your sister's number, didn't you?"

He nodded.

"Is Liza on her way to Durango?"

"Meli already picked her up."

"And then?"

Kique nodded at the road ahead of us. "She keeps going."

Chapter Thirty-Four

I disliked Mexico City. It was crowded, noisy, and dirty. It smelled bad. You had to be on your guard more than in most big cities. On the other hand, you couldn't ignore its crazy energy. The streets were jammed with people going in all directions. Street vendors tried to ply you with every kind of taco, fruit slice, popsicle, or sweet treat. Managers beckoned you to enter their stores. Baskets of sale items tricked you into taking a second glance. If you couldn't find what you wanted in Mexico City, then you didn't want it anyway.

I'd visited the capital city several times, either to visit distant relatives or to help Joey with architecture projects. Once we'd presented plans for a children's facility. Another time Joey had spoken at a conference dedicated to new trends in the field. I could make my way around Mexico City because I sounded Mexican and because I kept my eyes open, but I couldn't feel comfortable.

In contrast Kique seemed as much at home in the capital as anywhere else, but while we walked, his eyes flashed from side to side. He was like a lizard. He knew to pay attention to details. No matter how anonymous you made yourself, there was always a chance that an assailant would pick you randomly. That was the moment you had to watch for.

Miguel Sánchez de Avila had owned a huge office building near the Hidalgo metro stop. His offices were on the sixteenth floor; he rented out all the others. We entered the place right after seven-thirty a.m., which is when the guards unlocked the front door.

As we suspected, not a soul was in sight, but the big glass door separating the corridor from Miguel's office space was accessed via a plastic card rather than a key.

Kique shook his head. "There's no way we can break in."

"You said you knew of a good locksmith."

"Not that good."

"Joey found his house address. We could talk to his wife."

"I doubt that she knew much about him."

"You could sweettalk his secretary."

"Stop being a tightwad. For right now, let's go with Plan B."

"Pretend we're travel agents? It's a bad plan."

"It's brilliant." He raised his voice a notch to sound like a professional with nasal issues. "We regret to inform you that the payment you sent for the ticket to France did not go through. We're sure it's a mistake. Could you please check your records?"

"That's your whole plan?"

"At least we'll have time for breakfast."

"Kique, we don't look like travel agents."

"Trust me. We will."

~

By the time we returned to Miguel's office building, we carried quality second-hand briefcases. We wore modest suits and short-sleeved shirts. I'd even purchased a slim red tie with soccer balls on it. I tried to talk Kique into buying a tie as well, but he assured me that by wearing a collared shirt, he was already incognito. I completely agreed. By the time he combed his hair, I barely recognized him.

We marched into the lobby as if we were trying to catch the last commuter train of the year. Then we stopped short. Behind a tall counter, a thirty-something woman looked up from her computer.

"We need to see Miguel's personal secretary," Kique said. He spoke quickly but not harshly.

The woman turned away from her screen, but she had to squint to see us clearly. Maybe the ceiling lights were in her eyes. "Do you have an appointment?"

"You bet we do," Kique said. He started down the hallway.

"Sir? Sir, you're not allowed to—"

Kique pretended he didn't hear. I followed his lead. As we walked past cubicles, we heard snatches of office chatter.

Monday morning. No one was ready to dig in and work yet.

A woman stuck her head into the hallway. She had such a long neck that she made me think of an ostrich. "May I help you?"

"Miguel's office?" Kique asked.

She waved us on. I was pretty sure no stranger called Miguel Sánchez de Avila by his first name.

Miguel's office commandeered a sizeable back corner. His door was decorated with a big brass sign with his full name on it. In front of the door was an assistant's desk, but no one was sitting at it.

"Think the secretary took the day off?" I asked.

Kique shook his head. He pointed to the desk where a box of coffee pods lay on top of a daily calendar. "Caffeine break."

The desk was cluttered with an old-fashioned calculator on the right side and a tray of scratch paper on the left. The only personal item was a framed portrait of a man. I stooped to take a closer look, but then my throat closed up. I couldn't gasp even though I wanted to. The man was familiar. I'd had a close encounter with him back in Lyon when I'd rolled him over the balcony.

A portly sixty-something woman came towards us carrying a steaming cup of coffee. She wore a plain beige dress that went down past her knees and sturdy shoes that would have served for mountain climbing. At first she scowled, but when I mutely pointed to the picture, she smiled. "My son. Mr. Sánchez found a job for him in Europe. He's been over there several months. Isn't that nice? I don't hear from him often, but I know he's doing well."

A swell little job in Europe. Perfect. Miguel was probably the only person in Mexico who had known about the man's demise. His mother never would.

"How may I help you?" the woman asked patiently.

"We need to see Sánchez," Kique said. He was at once friendly but firm. "Now."

"I'm so sorry. Mr. Sánchez isn't in. Is there something I

can do instead?"

Kique leaned against the desk. "You can help if you have access to Miguel's bank account. He owes us quite a bit of money."

"Oh! Which of you is the hand surgeon?"

Hand surgeon? Visions of splints and plaster casts danced before me. Involuntarily I clenched and unclenched my hands as an imaginary foe punched me so hard in the stomach that he knocked the breath out of me. A hand surgeon! When I was a teenager, I'd played softball for two weeks. Then I strained a finger catching a ball. The fourth finger of my right hand swelled so badly that I couldn't practice the violin for a month without feeling the pain. I'd given up every sport except for swimming and walking. Hand injuries weren't reversible. Instead they reversed careers.

In the three seconds it took Kique to pull up two chairs, he'd assessed the situation and figured out how to react to it. Kique pointed at me. "He's the doctor, and I'm the lawyer. But where is the patient?"

"I, I don't know."

Kique set his elbows on the desk as if they were lead weights. "Do you know what my client here was supposed to do today?"

"He was supposed to perform surgeries on a woman's hands," the secretary said meekly. "She's a friend of Mr. Sánchez's. He was going to pay the bill."

Kique didn't miss a beat. "That is correct. My client was supposed to clear his schedule for the whole day so that he could perform multiple surgeries on two hands. Do you know why?"

"The woman has a terrible generative disease."

"Correct again," Kique lied. "Thus she needed delicate surgeries on both hands. My client prepared accordingly. But guess what happened? The woman didn't show. My client lost a whole day's work."

"I'm sorry, but I don't know where Mr. Sánchez is."

"My client was ready at six a.m. He re-scheduled his other two surgeries. Do you know how much lost revenue that is for a renowned surgeon?"

"I, I don't know."

"His clients arrive from all over the world. Did you know that? People fly here so that he can operate on them. Are you aware of this?"

"I'm sorry, sir, but—"

Kique made a fist and lightly pounded the table. "Where's your boss?"

"I don't know that either! He should have been here at nine this morning, but he hasn't arrived, and he won't answer his cell phone!" The secretary's voice rose and her shoulders tensed. I didn't think she was acting. "I don't have access to his funds."

Kique stood. "This behavior is unacceptable. We'll send a bill. It will arrive at this address tomorrow morning. Thanks for your help." He tapped my thigh. "Come."

Initially I was too numb to move, but when Kique grabbed my arm, I followed him. Silently we retraced our steps to the lobby and out into the hall. Instead of waiting for the elevator, Kique headed for the staircase.

I hurried after him. "You want exercise now?"

Kique checked the ceiling as he entered the stairwell. "The elevator had a security camera." He picked up his pace, and I followed behind.

Miguel had employed his secretary's son to be an assassin overseas. Then he had scheduled surgeries for a lady who would need reconstructions of both hands as soon as she finished her last concert ever. I followed Kique to the subway in the kind of daze I'd felt when my father died. Even though I'd been with him at the hospital, I couldn't believe what I'd seen. I couldn't process the information. My brain couldn't take it in.

"Are you all right, Andy?"

I was so far from all right that I didn't know where to

start.

"Andy?"

"I killed that woman's son." I was breathing so hard I was surprised I was getting any oxygen.

"She'll never know. She'll assume he's having too much fun to contact her."

"Miguel hired a hand surgeon."

"Good thing we didn't introduce ourselves as travel agents. Maybe only doctors wear ties."

"Right."

Kique snapped his fingers under my nose as if waking me from a session with a hypnotist. "You did a good job. You lied just fine."

If I remembered right, I hadn't said anything at all.

Once we sat down in a subway car, I held my hands in front of my face. I was surprised to see so many lines. There were lines that crossed each palm in waves and double sets at most of the joints. I'd never stopped to study my hands, not closely, and I was impressed by their symmetry. My right hand was slightly bigger than my left, but the difference was so small that I'd never noticed it before.

"Andy, you're pale."

"Liza was telling the truth. Miguel was going to break her hands."

"Bones heal, right? That's why he had the surgeon ready. She would play her concert and then—"

As he made the motion of breaking something by twisting it in half, I winced. Simultaneously I groaned so audibly that I garnered a frown from the kid next to us who was wearing headphones.

"What's with you, Andy?"

I held up my hands. "Don't you understand?"

"He wasn't going to kill her. Given the circumstances, that's something she might have been thankful for."

Slowly I caressed one hand with the other. "Breaking her hands would have meant burying her alive."

"Are you auditioning for a soap opera or what?"

Scenes flashed before me. A patient fainting as she entered the surgery room. A patient trying to kill herself. A patient succeeding.

I wiggled my fingers as if I were playing the violin with my left hand and holding the bow with my right. "Kique, you don't understand. No matter how brilliant the surgeon, her hands—and her playing—would have never, ever been the same."

Kique grinned. "She could have become a music teacher."

"No, no, no! She's a performer! She doesn't have the patience to be a teacher. She has passion for the moment of creation, for the synthesis of sounds, for the rapture of the audience!"

He leaned over and whispered in my ear, "So it's okay that Liza killed him?"

I covered my eyes with my hands, hands that had never suffered permanent injuries, hands that allowed me to make a living, hands that were my gateway to the world. "Something like that."

"I better hurry and finish my law degree."

"Why's that?"

"You're going to need me."

Chapter Thirty-Five

Kique booked me a flight for the next morning and made a reservation at one of the airport hotels. That evening he led me around as if I were a zombie. He ordered me tacos but ate most of them himself. He kept telling me to call Rachel, but the most I could do was swim long laps in the hotel pool. The water was too cold to be comfortable, but I liked it that way. I didn't want to be comfortable. I couldn't be. Too much had happened, and my head was spinning too fast.

Kique sat in the pool area on a chaise lounge, mojito in hand. While I swam back and forth, he made one long phone call after another. I caught wisps of his conversations when I came up for air. He spoke to his friends about the classes he'd missed. He chatted with his sister, who had made arrangements for Liza. He left long messages for Rachel, who was at her mariachi restaurant. The last time we'd talked to her, we'd been merry and drunk in Aguascalientes with my cousins. We couldn't have experienced a greater contrast.

After we returned to our room, I took such a long shower that Kique fell asleep before I wished him good night. I turned the TV on mute so that I could channel surf without making any noise, but Kique didn't move. Eventually I used a little volume, but my roommate was sleeping peacefully. Maybe he was dreaming that he was a travel agent somewhere far away.

By choosing the most boring channels, I hoped to fall asleep quickly. Instead I suffered through a cooking show, a political debate, and an exercise program. When I finally fell asleep, I still had the TV control in my hand.

I didn't feel much better the next morning, but I was functional. Over three cups of coffee, I ate several pieces of fruit and a Danish. I nodded as Kique read snips of news from his iPad, but I didn't pay attention to what he said. None of the news pertained to me.

There was no mention of Miguel Sánchez de Avila.

Kique dumped me at the airport a couple of hours early so

that he could start his long trek back to Durango. I had a short flight to Houston with a five-hour layover before my flight to Tucson.

I had to assure Kique twenty times that I would stay alert long enough to make my connection.

~

I hadn't given Rachel my flight number, but thanks to Kique she was waiting for me at Arrivals. She was wearing her mariachi *traje*, so she stood out in the crowd. She wrapped her arms around me, greeting me with a sincere hug and a kiss that made at least three bystanders stop and gawk. Then she took Liza's violin case from my shoulder and led me out to the car.

It was almost seven, which meant it was already dark. The air wasn't cold, but it was crisp. While Rachel arranged my belongings on the back seat, I zipped my jacket and rubbed my hands up and down my arms.

"How are you?" Rachel asked as she hopped in the car.

"Miguel was going to break Liza's hands." I still couldn't fathom it even though I'd thought of little else.

"I know."

"Both of them."

Rachel started the car. "Kique told me. You're lucky Liza killed him before he caught up with you."

I wiggled my fingers. "I would have rather been shot."

"You nearly were."

"I met the sniper's mother. She thinks her son is living it up in Europe."

"There are lots worse fantasies than that." Rachel eased the car out of a tight parking space. Five inches over and she would have rammed into the next car. "It's over now. You don't have to think about it anymore."

As she approached the booth for the parking attendant, I searched through my wallet. "All I have are pesos."

"It's all right, Andy."

When prompted, she handed the lady a dollar and some change.

"I should have called more often, but we were always running around," I said.

"Plus you never remember to carry your phone."

For a moment I felt defensive, but then I realized she was ribbing me.

As she headed down the boulevard, I focused on the scenery. Neon signs popped out at me. So did tall saguaros. Except for the language on the signs, I might have still been in Mexico. I wasn't sure if that would have been better or not.

"I appreciate your coming for me," I said.

"I had time. Barely." She wasn't watching me; she was negotiating the traffic.

"Rachel, I...." I didn't know what to say. I didn't want to talk about Miguel, Liza, or even Domingos.

"I realize you didn't go to Mexico to sit around partying."

"I should have called more often. I know I haven't been responsible."

"Andy, I'll tell you the truth. You're right. You should have called me more often."

"I'm sorry."

"It's okay, Andy. This time."

"From now on—"

She put her foot on the accelerator to make the yellow light at Valencia. "You're better off not making any promises. But don't worry. You're back in one piece. Whatever happened down there, you'll get over it."

"I'm not much of a boyfriend."

"You can be when you put your mind to it. Don't worry. I'll let you make it up to me. In fact I have a big project I need your help with."

Several came to mind. The wooden slats on her porch swing were starting to break. She needed actual furniture rather than a set of bean bags chairs. Her walls begged for a coat of paint.

Rachel slid through another yellow at Irvington. "By the way, your brother called. He said it was urgent, but he couldn't

297

reach you."

"Thanks."

"You might want to call him now."

"It can wait." When Joey said something was urgent, it nearly always was, but my cell phone was dead. I was pretty sure I'd left the power cord back at Beto's.

"They're moving back to the US," Rachel said.

"What?"

"Vegas, probably, but they're not sure. Or Southern California. That would be nice, don't you think? To have them close by. And Christina's brother lives in Vegas."

I stopped listening. At the moment I couldn't think about Joey's situation. I was still wrapping my head around my own. Usually I prided myself on my parallel processing. For example I could perform any number of mariachi songs and hold a surface conversation at the same time. I could go back and forth between Spanish and English from one phrase to the next. But I couldn't shake the thought of a man purposefully taking a hammer to a woman's hands. Or maybe Miguel wouldn't have used a tool at all. He would have used his own brute strength.

"Christina said we could stay with her brother anytime," Rachel continued. "The Arts Council is sponsoring a summer music program in Vegas that I'd like to teach for. If I could save on rent, I'd come out way ahead."

"True."

"Christina's aunt owns a lounge, you know. She might even let me put on a show. Wouldn't that be great?"

"Yes. Terrific."

At the last moment Rachel stopped for the red light at Fourteenth Street. "You're not listening."

"Sure, I'm listening. And you were right. I shouldn't have followed Domingos. I should have let him solve his own problems."

"I know what I said," Rachel said softly. "And I understand why you wanted to help him. By now I even

298

understand why he wanted to help her. You know what they say. You can't pick your family."

"We're both lucky."

"Yes. Excellent siblings."

"I'm also lucky I didn't have to kill myself to become a violinist," I said. "I put in the time, but the experience never changed me. Not the way it changed Liza."

"You practiced more than I did. Maybe I didn't set my sights high enough."

"But you're a good teacher. You enjoy playing. And composing."

"Yes. That's what counts."

"Not for Liza. She had to get ahead. She had to be first. If she had simply concentrated on playing well, she wouldn't have gone ballistic."

Or maybe she would have anyway. Some people had a crazy gene inside them. Maybe that same gene gave them the strength to stay concentrated. Thus they had the capacity to work into a blind passion to achieve a single goal. I never wanted to be that focused. Or that maniacal.

Rachel continued north as Kino turned into Campbell. The airport was an easy twenty minutes from the city center, but in the evening the traffic thinned out and made the journey quicker than usual at the very moment I would have rather it lasted a long time. I didn't want to arrive in Tucson. I wanted to keep in motion as the maestro did. That way I wouldn't have to face anything I didn't want to.

"I never had Liza's dedication," I said. "In her shoes I would have chosen another profession. I would have stopped punishing myself by insisting on a challenge that was too big a sacrifice."

"She got results."

"She never anticipated the price."

"We never do, Andy, do we?"

Rachel was right. We made choices without looking ahead because we never had the right kind of crystal ball. Sometimes we changed directions. Most of the time we plowed ahead the same way we didn't leave town before the hurricane hit. Instead we watched while it came closer and closer and smacked us right in the face.

"Was it really that bad?" Rachel whispered.

When I closed my eyes, I imagined a surgeon deciding which mashed finger to operate on first. He—because Miguel would have chosen a man—wouldn't be able to decide. He would sink into a chair in the operating room because he would have never seen anything as horrible before in his entire life. The enormity of the task would have smacked him worse than any hurricane.

"It still is," I whispered.

"Maybe someday you'll want to tell me the whole story."

But I wouldn't. It was one thing finding a dead man stuffed in a pantry. That in itself was enough to send someone to therapy for the next decade. But it was the scope of Miguel's outlook that threatened my mental well-being. Don't get what you want? If you're rich enough, you can arrange for it. No problem. Then you can cover it up. Liza's actions had been ruthless and reckless, but I finally understood the vastness of the situation she'd been up against.

"That someday might take a while."

"Look, Andy, I realize that things didn't go the way you expected. But who's to say your expectations were the right ones? You helped a woman who really needed your help. You prevented her from a fate worse than death."

"Not me alone."

"You couldn't have done it without Domingos, and he couldn't have done it without you."

"Kique's really the one who saved the day."

"I'm sorry I got mad at you for involving him. You made the right choice after all."

Looking back on it, contacting Kique had been my single best decision. I'd put him in terrible danger, but he would have gladly accepted the risk. He felt satisfied knowing that we'd saved a woman who really needed saving. While Liza had taken care of Miguel on her own, we'd helped deflect his minions. By now Liza was probably halfway to Brazil. Miguel might have had long arms, but they wouldn't extend beyond the grave. Nobody else would share his same warped worldview.

Kique and Domingos and I had gone about things the wrong way. We'd committed about fifteen crimes while doing so. Eventually, though, we would be able to put the story behind us. We would feel strong enough to move on.

Instead of heading to her apartment or to her restaurant, Rachel turned west on Broadway. We traveled in silence for several blocks until we hit Euclid, where she turned north.

"What do you think I should do?" I asked.

"You know."

"I should become Liza?"

"Don't worry. There's no chance of it." She indicated the backseat. "Switch."

Rachel had set Liza's violin case next to mine, which was empty. Awkwardly, given the confines of the car, I removed Liza's prize from its cradle. The wood still smelled of furniture polish, but the violin was brown enough to pass for a different instrument at least for a while. As I set it in the other case, I felt like a thief.

"Maybe I shouldn't go," I said. "It's already after seven. Domingos won't appreciate my being late to his rehearsal."

"You bought yourself license to be late for a lifetime," Rachel said as she rolled through a stop sign. "Although on principle I wouldn't overdo it."

For a silly moment I imagined Domingos yelling at me for playing badly and my yelling back that at least my sister wasn't a murderer. I wouldn't mention not having a sister.

"What will the other musicians think when I waltz in?" I asked.

"Don't worry about the others."

"They'll assume I think I'm too good to take the

301

rehearsals seriously."

"Andy, you were out of town for a few days. Say there was a death in the family. That's almost true."

"They might resent me. I didn't audition to be concertmaster." I rolled down the window a couple of inches as if the cold would magically clear things out. "I didn't go through the proper channels."

"Andy, it's hard to know what's proper."

"Beto is going to Paris to play at a new Mexican restaurant. He invited me to go with him."

Rachel shook her head.

"It might be fun."

"You earned the orchestra job, Andy. The very hardest way."

I considered initial arguments. My cousin was simple-minded and light-hearted, and we would have fun spending quality time together. The one time I'd been in Paris I'd really enjoyed it, so a few months or a year in such a city would be a pleasure. I liked playing for restaurant crowds because they were jolly and enthusiastic, and an international crowd would be much less demanding than an Hispanic one. Best of all, I would be the lead violinist in a small folk group. That was exactly how I wanted things.

I pointed over my shoulder. "I'll feel funny playing Liza's violin."

"It's not hers anymore."

"Nor mine."

"You could call it Domingos' if you want to. After all, he paid for it. Or call it Zoran's. He made it, right? What luthier doesn't feel like the daddy of all his creations?"

"That still doesn't make it mine."

"Idiot," Rachel said under her breath but loudly enough for me to hear. "You wasted a month of your life, and that's the least of it. You took dangerous risks. You might have been shot on five separate occasions. The least you deserve is the fiddle."

She swung into the parking lot of the orchestra's rehearsal

302

hall and stopped beside the entrance. She didn't turn off the motor while she waited for me to get out of the car, but I was halfway to the door when she called me back. "Andy?"

I walked over to the driver's side and bent down to her window. "Thanks for coming to the airport for me. I appreciate it. Really."

"You'll have to ask Domingos to give you a ride home."

"I'm sure he can do that much."

Again I started for the entrance.

"Andy?"

I turned around.

Rachel rolled her window all the way down. "Some of the things you did in Mexico were really stupid."

"I know."

"And you made Kique help you."

"I'm sorry."

"Yeah, well, you should be. And yet I'm proud of you. I want you to know that."

"Right."

"Andy?"

"Yes?"

"If I'd been Liza, I would have done the same damned thing."

I knew exactly what she meant, but I asked anyway. "What do you mean?"

"I would have killed the bastard."

As I lumbered inside, I imagined Rachel crushing sleeping pills into a nightcap. She would be laughing hysterically while she did so.

I continued down the hall but stopped short outside the rehearsal room. The violins were murdering the score from one of the Harry Potter movies. Evidently Domingos hadn't called in the right wizards. Or maybe my cohorts had been too busy practicing to ever enjoy a movie, so they didn't recognize famous theme songs. They were a roomful of Lizas with less talent but only moderate ambition. That meant they might lead

303

normal lives, ones they actually enjoyed.

My intention was to enter the room discreetly, but when Kenny saw me, he stopped playing, and so did his new stand partner. The violinists behind them lost their places and stopped playing as well.

"He's back!" Kenny shouted.

By that time, Philip, who was sitting in the concertmaster's seat, took his nose out of the music long enough to see who had arrived. He got out of the chair so fast that he tripped over the music stand and nearly fell headfirst into the second violin section.

"I told you he'd be back," Domingos said without looking at me.

Kenny started a round of applause. As they clapped, my fellow companions nodded and cheered. I didn't deserve such attention, but then again, people didn't always get what they deserved. In fact, not usually.

Kenny stood and whacked me on the back so hard I nearly choked. "Great to see you!"

"Thank God you're here!" Philip embraced me so enthusiastically that I was surprised he didn't kiss me on both cheeks. Then he sat in the chair next to the concertmaster's, leaving me the number one spot.

I could feel Domingos' eyes on me as I sat and took out my bow, but when I looked up, he was playfully tapping his baton on the score. "How was your 'vacay'?"

"Can hardly wait for the next one, Go-Go."

The conductor didn't flinch. Instead he pointed to the violin. "I see you finally have a better instrument. It's about time."

While all the other musicians waited, I took out my shoulder rest and carefully attached it to the back of my violin. Then I took out my rosin. I slowly drew my bow across the golden lump once, twice, three times.

The bow was fine the way it was, but it was time for me to show off. It was time to act like a real soloist.

Acknowledgements

Thanks to my publisher, Mike Orenduff at Aakenbaaken & Kent for his encouragement and guidance. Many, many thanks to early readers who made comments and useful suggestions, including Elise Moore, Matthew Jackson, Sandra Ransdell, Elise Ransdell, and Kathy McIntosh. Thanks to Peter O'Connor at Bespoke Book Covers for the beautiful artwork. Thanks to Don Maass for his inspiring workshops. And finally, thanks to Maestro Linus Lerner. Thanks to him, I've become a much better musician, a better writer, and a better person.

More books by D. R. Ransdell from Aakenbaaken & Kent:

Mariachi Meddler
An Andy Veracruz Mystery Book 1

Andy Veracruz is the leader of a mariachi band in Southern California, but when his boss goes out of town, the restaurant where Andy performs turns to chaos. Andy tries to avoid the boss's flirtatious wife, but when Yiolanda is accused of murder, Andy isn't sure whether to help her or to run the other way. The more Andy learns, the more trouble he gets himself into. He's a sleuth only by accident!

Island Casualty
An Andy Veracruz Mystery Book 2

When Andy Veracruz flies to a Greek island for a holiday with Rachel, he expects to spend afternoons swimming and nights making love. After his troubles in *Mariachi Meddler*, he deserves a break! But at an outdoor café, he meets a fellow traveler who accidentally leaves behind a package. Before Andy can return it, the man disappears. When Andy substitutes in a bouzouki band, he learns more about the island and its missing man than he intended to.

Dizzy in Durango
An Andy Veracruz Mystery Book 3

Missing women, abandoned children, and a crazy mariachi fan add up to further trouble for Andy Veracruz in *Dizzy in Durango*. The jobless musician travels to Durango, Mexico, to visit Rachel and her relatives, but after a fellow traveler disappears, Andy can't concentrate on vacationing. When he tries to investigate, instead of finding one woman, he loses another! Before he can discover more about the women's connection, he's saddled with two children who aren't his, an angry would-be girlfriend, and a self-appointed younger brother who is more reckless than he is. No wonder he's dizzy! But what will he do when the children start to cry?